DIANE GASTON

———

Lord Grantwell's Christmas Wish

HARLEQUIN®
HISTORICAL™

PLEASE RECYCLE
THIS PRODUCT IS RECYCLABLE

Recycling programs
for this product may
not exist in your area.

ISBN-13: 978-1-335-40739-9

Lord Grantwell's Christmas Wish

This edition published by arrangement with Harlequin Books S.A.

For questions and comments about the quality of this book,
please contact us at CustomerService@Harlequin.com.

Harlequin Enterprises ULC
22 Adelaide St. West, 40th Floor
Toronto, Ontario M5H 4E3, Canada
www.Harlequin.com

Printed in U.S.A.

Diane Gaston's dream job was always to write romance novels. One day she dared to pursue that dream and has never looked back. Her books have won romance's highest honors: the RITA® Award, the National Readers' Choice Award, the HOLT Medallion, the Golden Quill and the Golden Heart® Award. She lives in Virginia with her husband and three very ordinary house cats. Diane loves to hear from readers and friends. Visit her website at dianegaston.com.

Books by Diane Gaston

Harlequin Historical

The Lord's Highland Temptation

Captains of Waterloo

Her Gallant Captain at Waterloo
Lord Grantwell's Christmas Wish

The Governess Swap

A Lady Becomes a Governess
Shipwrecked with the Captain

The Society of Wicked Gentlemen

A Pregnant Courtesan for the Rake

The Scandalous Summerfields

Bound by Duty
Bound by One Scandalous Night
Bound by a Scandalous Secret
Bound by Their Secret Passion

Visit the Author Profile page
at Harlequin.com for more titles.

To Keely Thrall and all the ladies
in the morning writing group.
You are the best!

Chapter One

Yorkshire, December 1817

'*Barren winter, with his wrathful, nipping cold...*'

Where the devil had that dreary quotation come from?

John Grantwell, 'Grant' to his friends, laughed aloud.

He turned away from the window after looking out on the snowfall quickly covering the walkways and gardens of the country house in which he'd grown up. He scanned the shelves of books for an answer.

Shakespeare. Yes!

But what was a captain in the East Essex Regiment doing quoting Shakespeare?

Grant rubbed his face.

He was Viscount Grantwell now, no matter how much he wished he could go back to his army years. He'd been Viscount for more than a year and a half, but he still thought of this room as his father's library and his brother George as the tormenter of his youth. Could he be more doltish? His father had died eight years ago and that meant his brother had spent eight years being Viscount Grantwell.

His poor brother. Killed in a carriage accident, his wife with him, almost two years ago.

Barren winter, indeed.

Grant shook off those less than cheerful thoughts and turned to the desk strewn with papers and ledgers.

Better get on with it.

He opened a ledger and ran his finger down the page of figures.

The hidden servants' door opened a crack—almost every room in the great house had such a door, thanks to his grandfather's abhorrence of even setting eyes on servants. In the crack Grant spied the faces of two children.

His newest responsibilities, an eight-year-old boy and a six-year-old girl. What the deuce were they doing in the servants' passageway?

'You there!' He rose and took a step towards the door.

'Run!' the boy cried.

The door slammed and Grant could hear the pounding of small feet making their escape. By the time he reached the door they'd disappeared. Where was the poor maid into whose care he'd thrust them? Had she lost control of them again?

Grant stared at the expanse of wall that was really the hidden door.

As a boy, escaping from his governess or hiding from his brother, he'd learned every twist and turn of the labyrinth that led to all the rooms. The servants now used the main passages. These unruly scamps had discovered the servants' passageways quickly enough, though.

The children had arrived a week ago—without notice. Before then Grant had not known of their existence. They were the issue from his brother's wife's previous marriage. Another piece of information of which he'd not been informed. Apparently the marriage acquired some scandal attached to it, because the children had been pretty much hidden away at their grandfather's house until he'd died. They'd never lived here with his brother, and none of the servants had ever heard of them.

The executors of their grandfather's estate, in their extraordinary wisdom, decided the best guardian of the children would be Grant, a single man, a former soldier, a new viscount just coming to terms with the complexities of vast estates and responsibilities. Two neglected, unloved, undisciplined children had been sent to a man who hadn't a clue what to do with them.

Was there a Shakespeare quote for that?

He'd inherited an estate riddled with debt, followed by two dismal growing seasons due to this damnable cold weather and the post-war economic hardship, but he'd turned matters around—with help. Although financial solvency *and* a title apparently made him prime prey for every ingenue in the marriage mart.

He must marry eventually, of course, but these marriage-mad mamas thrusting their daughters in his path had just driven him away from a Christmas house party. Or had it been the vivid memories of battle, triggered by the firing of guns in the daily partridge and pheasant hunting?

He'd not lasted a week.

Grant walked back to his desk and closed the ledger. Surely, though, there was something in the pile of papers he'd forgotten to do or had never known to do.

Thompson, who'd been his family's butler since he was a boy, entered the room. 'Beg pardon, m'lord.'

'What is it, Thompson?' Grant's tone turned sarcastic. 'Has the roof collapsed? Did the children break a priceless vase? Has Cook mutinied?'

Thompson seemed to take him seriously. 'Nothing like

that, m'lord.' He sounded incredulous. 'An applicant for the position of governess has arrived.'

'For governess? Already?'

Incredulous, indeed.

Grant had advertised for a governess. Given that the children were apparently running free through the servants' passages, a governess was much needed. But he'd only sent the notice to an agency one week ago. The agency had hardly enough time even to receive his letter. An applicant in person? In a snowstorm?

'Indeed, sir,' Thompson responded. 'On our doorstep. She waits in the hall.'

Grant clapped his hands and stood. 'Well, Thompson! Things are looking up! At least one of my prayers is answered—that is if she does not have two heads or reek of gin or something.'

Thompson shook his head. 'None of those things, m'lord.'

The tables of fate were turning. A governess would be a godsend.

Grant gestured grandly. 'Send her in, Thompson!'

Grant stacked the papers neatly on the desk. Good thing he'd shaved himself that morning. Since giving his valet and most of the servants extra time off for Christmas—that detestable house party was to have lasted until Twelfth Night—he'd been tempted to revert to his days of marching through Spain, when a bearded face had not much mattered.

Thompson reappeared at the door. 'Miss Pearson, m'lord.'

With a ready smile, Grant looked up as the governess walked in and Thompson exited the room.

The blood drained from Grant's face.

'Hello, Grant.'

Standing before him was a woman he'd wished never to see again—the one woman with whom he'd shared an irresistible passion…the woman who'd betrayed him so thoroughly.

God save him, she was as beautiful as ever. Hair dark as night. Eyes like warm chocolate. Nose regal. Lips naturally pursed, as if always ready for a kiss. But she was unusually pale and thin. Her clothes hung on her and he could smell their dampness from the melted snow.

He knew her as Lillian Carris. He'd first seen her feeding the hungry refugees who'd poured into Lisbon over the winter of 1810 when, as a green lieutenant, he'd first arrived in Portugal with his regiment. Later he'd made her acquaintance when attending entertainments with the Portuguese aristocrats who'd remained in Portugal after Prince John and others of the royal family fled to Brazil. She was widowed, she'd told him, and their affair had been as torrid as that winter had been cold.

Until she'd stolen from him and almost succeeded in committing treason on his country and hers.

'Senhora Carris.' His voice was bitter. 'Do not tell me you seek a position as governess.'

She smiled uncertainly. 'I am afraid your butler jumped to that conclusion. I—I am Miss Pearson now. You—you have children, then?'

Did she think he'd had time to procreate? She knew how long the war had lasted.

'They are not mine.' He had no intention of explaining further. 'You deceived my butler?'

'I did not intend to deceive him. He asked me if I was seeking a position as governess, which I am—seeking a position, that is. But I did not know before I came that you needed a governess.'

'Enough.' He held up a hand. 'Why are you here?'

'I—I would not have come—would never have asked
you—' She faltered. 'I need help.'

The timbre of her voice pulled at him. Like a Siren's
song. How could that male part of him still respond to
such allure?

He made himself glare at her. 'Why not ask your husband for help?'

She lowered her gaze. 'My husband is dead.'

Grant gave a bitter laugh. 'Truly this time?' Throughout their affair she'd lied, saying her husband was dead.
Grant despised lies, perhaps above all things.

'He was killed. His family believes I killed him.'

'And you did not?' The woman he'd foolishly let himself love would have been incapable of such a thing. Except she'd been a mere illusion.

'Certainly I did not!' Her eyes flashed. 'But—but they
all believe I am to blame.

By God, this felt familiar. Denying what everyone else
said was true. At any rate, what had this to do with him?

Grant steeled his heart against her. 'If you are hoping
I will vouch for your character, I am afraid I will be no
help to you at all.'

She took a step forward. 'I am desperate, Grant. My
husband's brother is searching for me. To take me back—'

For imprisonment? Hanging? Grant stood stiffly behind his desk.

She faced him from the other side. 'I know I have no
right to ask you. I did not know anyone else—' Her voice
cracked, but she seemed to pull herself together again. 'I
need a place to stay—or money to pay for one—just for
a month or two. By then my old headmistress will have
found me a position and I can disappear.'

'A position?' Was she really looking for employment?

'Governess. Companion. Teacher. Any of them will allow me to disappear.' Her tone was earnest. Panicked.

'You expect me to believe that the wife—pardon me, the *widow*—of a Portuguese baron's son searches for paid employment?'

She gave him a direct look. 'I expect nothing. I ask for your help and I await your answer.'

He turned away from her and glanced out of the window. The snow was now so thick it had turned the shrubbery into mere shadows.

Fate conspiring against him again.

He spoke. 'If you hurry your carriage might still make it to the village. There is an inn there.'

'I have no money for an inn. Or a carriage. I walked from the village.'

He glanced at her shoes, which did appear to be soaked through. As they would be if she'd walked seven miles. In snow.

He turned back to the window. The snowflakes swirled in wayward gusts of wind, as if mocking him. A caustic laugh burst from him. How ironic that she should arrive at this exact moment—he could not send even a dog out in such weather.

She moved forward once more and leaned across his desk. Her voice was filled with emotion. 'I vow to you that I did not have anything to do with my husband's death—'

He swivelled back to her. 'You vowed to me before.'

She did not falter. 'Yes. I did. Because I had nothing to do with the spying—'

'You took those papers from my coat.'

'I did not!' Her voice rose. 'I never knew of such papers. I told you then.'

He'd had papers detailing Wellington's plans for the

winter, documenting areas of weakness along the Lines of Torres Vedras, the fortifications against French attack. He'd stopped to see Lillian, to spend an hour with her—an intimate hour—after which he'd discovered the papers missing from his coat—the coat she'd hung over a chair, out of his sight.

He glared at her. 'Who else had the opportunity?'

He'd left her and immediately sounded the alarm. Fate had been kinder to him in those days, and the papers were intercepted on their way to Marshall André Masséna, commander of the French Army of Portugal. The crisis had been averted.

His anger smouldered with the memory. 'The messenger caught with the papers said you gave them to him.'

She acted surprised. 'But I did not. You must believe me.'

He had once believed in her.

'From what I heard later, you were a known agent of the French.' He'd realised then that she'd involved herself with him purely to gain information. It had been said that her suddenly reappearing husband had begged everyone to forgive her and promised to control her. It had been all too convenient. The husband's absence and subsequent return must have been part of the plan.

She met his gaze. 'I was never an agent of the French.'

He waved her words away. 'Why would I ever believe you again?'

Their gazes held and for a moment Grant heard the Siren's song.

He turned away and gestured to the window. 'Obviously I cannot send you out in a blizzard, tempting though that is.' He was not such a monster. 'You may remain until it is safe to return to the village. But stay out of my way.'

Her voice became very quiet. 'Thank you, Grant.'

Her words struck him like a sabre thrust. As if they were genuine.

He sat at his desk and pretended to look at his papers. 'Return to the hall and ask Thompson to come and see me right away.'

He heard her walk to the door, the tumult inside him threatening to explode.

Lillian's knees were shaking as she crossed the threshold, walked through the anteroom past the ornate staircase with its gilt balusters, and back into the hall.

Her handsome Grant. The mere sight of him had made her errant body come alive with desire. He was every bit as tall and muscular as she remembered, with his dark curly hair and lean face. His expressive brows framed changeable hazel eyes that appeared grey this day, like storm clouds. At least he'd not smiled. His smile, like sunshine on a crisp spring day, would have been impossible to resist. He'd always been smiling during those wonderful days when they were together.

Still, she yearned for that smile.

Deep inside, she hoped he'd realise the truth, that he would welcome her, not despise her after all these years.

His anger hurt like a knife in her breast, adding to the still open wound of his believing she would lie to him, steal from him, betray him.

The butler stepped forward at her appearance. She noticed right away that he—or one of the servants—had wiped up the puddles her clothing had dripped onto the patterned marble floor.

'He wishes to see you,' she managed.

'Very good, miss.'

As soon as Lillian heard the door of the library close,

she hurried to the front door and opened it. A flurry of snow stung her eyes and clung to her skirts. She retrieved the portmanteau that contained everything she now owned from where she'd left it outside the door. When she closed the door again, a pile of snow had blown in, at least an inch deep on the beautiful marble floor. She'd offer to clean it up. What else could she do?

The hall was a wonder. Not even the hall at the Palácio da Anunciada in Lisbon rivalled it. The walls and ceiling were adorned with carved plasterwork, stark white against pastel blue and beige. The circular plasterwork on the ceiling echoed the pattern on the floor. She found the hues and the symmetry calming. And she was in very great need of calm.

The library had been adorned with similar colour and plasterwork, but with Grant glaring at her nothing could have been calming in there.

She glanced back at the snow, now melting into puddles. Where would she find a rag to mop it up? She did not wish to do anything to further displease Grant, if his enmity for her was not already at its upper limit. He had offered her safety, though.

At least for today.

She'd fled from Portugal to her old school in Reading, the only place she'd been able to think of to find help. She had no family to run to—only her mother, who remained in Brazil, where she and her new husband had fled during the French invasion.

Not that her mother would have helped her.

Lillian's former headmistress, though, had welcomed her with open arms. She'd felt safe until Dinis, her husband's brother, the Baron de Coval, had arrived. Looking for her. Vowing to make her pay for her husband's death.

He'd been at her heels ever since. She'd run from

coaching inn to coaching inn, but twice she'd seen him and his servant arrive at the inn just as her coach was pulling out. She'd needed a place where no one would look for her. When the coach she'd hopped on happened to pass through the village near Grant's estate she'd impulsively alighted—no one would dream she'd run to the man who believed her a liar and a traitor. Would they?

All that might be moot now. Grant would likely banish her and she had no money to keep running. Dinis would find her.

But she could not think of that now. Grant had given her time to rest, to think of what to do next.

The wail of a child sounded behind her. She whirled around.

A young boy burst from a doorway. 'She's hurt! She's hurt! She fell down the stairs!'

Lillian followed him through a doorway to what must be the servants' stairs. There on the wood floor rocked an even younger girl, clutching her leg and wailing.

'Help her!' cried the boy, bouncing from foot to foot and pulling Lillian towards the girl. 'Help her!'

She squatted down to the child. 'Where are you hurt, dear one?'

The little girl, her blue eyes red with crying, clambered into Lillian's arms. She was given no choice but to hold her.

'Shh…shh…' She rocked the child gently and patted her blonde curls. 'You will recover. Tell me where it hurts.'

'All over!' the little girl wailed. 'My leg!'

The boy pulled on Lillian's dress. 'Do something!'

She turned her face to him. He had the same fair skin as the girl and the same huge blue eyes, but his hair was as dark as hers was light. Their clothing was too fine for them to be children of servants. These must be the children who needed a governess.

'Let's bring her into the hall, where we can see better,' she said.

The little girl clung to her neck as she carried her to the hall. The boy followed so closely he nearly stepped on her heels.

Grant and his butler appeared from the anteroom.

'What have you done?' Grant accused.

She gaped at him. Did he think she was in the habit of harming small children? 'She fell down the stairs.'

Grant crossed the hall to her. 'How badly is she hurt?' He reached for the child.

The little boy cried. 'Leave her alone!'

Grant stepped back.

Lillian turned to the boy again. 'He was not going to hurt her. He wants to help.'

The boy, looking sceptical, retreated behind her skirts.

At that moment, frantic footsteps on the stairs sounded from the anteroom. A maid, no more than twenty, rushed in, out of breath. 'I have been searching everywhere! I was only gone a moment and they disappeared!' She spied the little girl in Lillian's arms. 'Oh, my goodness! What now?'

'She fell down the stairs,' Lillian responded.

The child still whimpered, her face buried in Lillian's shoulder.

'It was not my fault!' the boy cried, though no one had accused him. 'She just tripped.'

Lillian turned to Grant. 'May I take her somewhere to see if she is injured?'

He looked frazzled. 'Yes. Yes. Up to her room.' He turned to the maid. 'Show her the way, Hannah.'

The maid gestured for Lillian to follow through the anteroom. 'This way, miss.'

Lillian carried the child up the ornate stairs she'd passed before. The stairs turned halfway at a small landing and Lillian could see they led to an arched hallway of the same blue and beige of the hall, but with less elaborate plasterwork.

The maid glanced back at her. 'Are you to be the governess, then? I warn you. They are unruly children. I've never seen the like.'

Not waiting for an answer, the maid led her to a door on the right into a hallway, even more plainly decorated. The nursery hallway, no doubt. The bedroom they entered was spartan. It had two beds.

The maid gestured for Lillian to lay the girl down on the closest one. 'I would not put it past her to have broken a leg.'

That set off a new wail from the child, who clung even closer to Lillian.

Lillian spoke in soothing tones. 'Here, now. I'm sure it is not as bad as all that. Why don't I put you down on your bed and take a look?' She pried the girl from her neck to look her in the face. 'Will that be satisfactory?'

The child nodded, taking ragged breaths.

Lillian placed her gently on the bed. 'Now, show me where it hurts the most.'

'Here.' She pointed to her knee.

'May I take your stockings off?' Lillian asked.

The girl nodded.

The leg looked normal, except for a bruise starting to form on the knee. Lillian gently felt all around it, but nothing seemed broken.

The boy stood next to Lillian, nearly glued to her side. 'Is it bad?'

Lillian shook her head in reply. She crouched down so she could be at the little girl's level. 'I think you had a very big scare and you fell on your knee. You'll have a big bruise there tomorrow, but you'll be right as rain in no time.' She stroked the hair off the child's face.

'Will I be able to walk again?' the girl asked.

Lillian smiled. 'If you want to, you can walk right now.'

She stood, and the child bounded off the bed and carefully tried her hurt leg while the boy watched intently.

As the girl walked back and forth in the room, limping on her hurt leg, Grant appeared in the doorway. Almost immediately the girl began to walk normally.

Lillian looked over at Grant. 'No serious injuries.'

He nodded and backed away.

Before she could think of why he stood there, the little girl skipped over to her. 'I can walk!'

Lillian smiled. 'Of course you can.'

All she knew about children came from her days at school, and her school had not had students so young. It seemed to Lillian that these two were as hungry for attention as she'd been that first day in Reading. What a lifesaver it had been to be embraced by the headmistress and the teachers.

Confirming this impression, when she sat on the bed both children sat next to her, the boy a little farther away than the little girl, who was again plastered against her.

The boy regarded Lillian with a hopeful expression. 'Are you our new governess?'

He so clearly wanted her answer to be yes, and she did not have the heart to disappoint him. 'That would be lovely, would it not?' she responded. 'I am Miss Pearson. May I know your names?'

The little girl responded in a formal, adult-like tone.

'I am Miss Anna Fielding and my brother is Master William Fielding.'

Lillian answered in kind. 'I am very pleased to meet you, Miss Anna, Mr William.' She was dying to know how they were connected to Grant and why they were here needing a governess. 'Is there anything that would make you feel better after your ordeal?'

'Biscuits,' Anna immediately replied.

'Biscuits and milk, perhaps?' Lillian asked. Her stomach rumbled at the mention of food.

Anna nodded. 'Some for William, too.'

'Of course.' Lillian smiled. She turned to the maid, who hovered in a corner. 'I have not introduced myself to you. I am Miss Pearson. And you are…?'

'Hannah, miss,' the woman answered.

'Hannah,' she acknowledged. 'Would it be possible for the children to have biscuits and milk? And—and perhaps some tea for me?'

'It is only an hour or so until their dinner,' the maid responded disapprovingly.

The children frowned.

'I believe we need milk and biscuits now.' Lillian used a more commanding tone, as if she really were the governess—or perhaps the lady of the house, as she used to be.

The maid curtsied. 'Very good, miss.'

Lillian helped Anna put on her stocking and shoe again. 'Where will she bring your milk and biscuits?'

They led her to another room on the hallway, furnished with a table and chairs and cheerful paintings on the walls. Lillian gratefully sat down. Her feet were aching from her wet half-boots and her clothing chafed her skin, but at least she was in a warm, dry place. And at least two little people of this household seemed to welcome her.

She'd rather taken over their care, ordering the maid about. Would Grant be angry at that?

Well, let him be angry. These children needed a bit of fussing over. Besides, she could hardly make him more disapproving of her.

At least with the children she did not feel so alone.

Lillian stayed with the children through their dinner and until they were tucked into bed. When she stepped into the hallway, she had no idea where she was to spend the night.

Luckily the maid, who'd mostly left the children in her care, reappeared. 'Are they sleeping, then, or only pretending to?'

'Sleeping,' Lillian responded. 'Do—do you know what room is to be mine, Hannah?'

'Mr Thompson said to put you in the governess's room.' The maid led her to the first room off the nursery hallway. She lingered while Lillian entered the room. 'Mr Thompson says you are not the governess. You are a guest. So I cannot credit why he's put you here.'

The room had a decent-looking bed and a warm fire, some comfortable chairs to sit upon and her portmanteau. 'It will do very nicely,' Lillian said.

'So are you a guest…if you are not the governess?' Hannah asked.

'A guest of sorts.' She wondered what the servants would be told about her. 'I suppose you could call me a stranded traveller.'

'How unfortunate,' Hannah said. 'I was hoping you'd be the governess. The children are too much for me, I can tell you.'

'If Grant—Lord Grantwell—does not object, I will be most willing to help with their care while I am here.'

It would give her something to do…keep her mind busy until Grant tossed her out and Dinis found her.

'That would suit me.' Hannah blew out a breath. 'Well, if you'll not be needing me, I'm off for my dinner.'

Dinner. The two biscuits Lillian had eaten with the tea had not been enough to keep the hunger pangs away. It had taken all her will power not to stuff into her mouth the scraps of food the children left on their plates at dinner.

Lillian smiled. 'Thank you, Hannah. I will see you tomorrow.'

As soon as the maid left, Lillian took off her half-boots and stockings and rubbed her feet, red from wearing the wet shoes all day. She opened her portmanteau, but all the clothes inside were as damp as the dress she wore. At least her other shoes and one pair of stockings were reasonably dry. She draped her two dresses and her underclothes over the chairs and moved them close to the fire. With luck, her nightdress would dry.

Her stomach growled. She paced around the room a while, trying to will her hunger away, until at last she gathered the courage to go in search of the kitchens. Perhaps the cook would fix her a plate of something. She didn't care what.

She made her way back to that beautiful staircase, now softly illuminated by candlelight. She entered the hall and saw that someone had mopped up the snow she'd caused to be blown in and had forgotten about. Guessing the kitchens would be on the other side of the house from the library, she crossed the hall to another small hallway. She opened a door.

There Grant sat at a small table set for dinner, wine glass in hand.

'I beg your pardon.' She backed away. 'I was looking for the kitchen.'

'Why?' he asked.

'I hoped to get a meal.' She kept her hand on the door latch, ready to leave.

He stopped her. 'You have not eaten?'

She lifted her chin. 'I had biscuits and tea with the children.' A bowl of apples sat in the centre of the table. Would he mind if she dashed in and grabbed one? 'It appears you have not been served yet. I will not trouble you further, if you would be kind enough to direct me to the kitchen.'

'Sit down.' He gestured with his hand. 'Thompson can set another place.'

She hesitated. Was this an invitation from him after he'd ordered her to stay away? What was that about? And did she even wish to share a meal with him when his presence filled her with pain?

On the other hand, she was so hungry she did not care which it was.

Thompson entered the room, carrying a small tureen of soup. He started when seeing her there.

Grant spoke. 'Miss Pearson will join me for dinner, Thompson. Will you set a place for her?'

'Right away, m'lord.'

Thompson placed the tureen on the table and quickly produced another place setting and glasses from a cabinet in the corner. He filled a glass with wine from a decanter on the table, then served her soup first. Lillian was so hungry she would not have cared if she'd been given Grant's portion, but apparently there was enough soup for two, because Grant's bowl was filled as well. It was a simple pea soup, but its aroma made Lillian's stomach growl.

'Anything else, m'lord?' he asked.

'No,' Grant answered. 'I assume Cook has made enough to accommodate Miss Pearson?'

'Indeed, m'lord.' Thompson bowed and left the room.

Lillian fingered her spoon, eager to dip it into her soup but unwilling to eat before Grant.

He took a sip of wine. 'You'll see few servants here. I gave most of them leave for Christmas.'

So that was why no footman stood in the hall attending the door.

'I shall endeavour not to be a burden,' she said.

He finally took a spoonful of soup.

She still held back so as not to appear as eager as she felt. 'If there is any way I might help, please let me know.'

He laughed dryly, dipping his soup spoon into his bowl again. 'They likely need help in the scullery.'

She nodded. 'Very well. I need only to be directed there.'

He lifted the spoon. 'I was not serious.'

'I *was* serious.' She met his eye. 'I am in your debt. I will help in any way you desire.'

He did not respond, but simply attended to his soup.

She took advantage of his silence to attack her soup as well. It tasted heavenly, but only accentuated her hunger. She tried to slow herself down by taking a sip of wine between spoonsful, but too soon the soup disappeared.

It did not escape Grant that she'd emptied her soup bowl before he was half done. Was it nerves or hunger? Or simply for show? Trying to gain his sympathy, no doubt. He must recall how easily she deceived.

She took a sip of wine. Why did he feel she wished to gulp the wine as quickly as the soup?

'Perhaps I could help by attending to the children,'

she said, as if there had not been a long silence since the last time they spoke.

It had shocked Grant how quickly the two children had latched onto her. Or had she latched onto them? The children treated him as if he were some ogre from a fairy tale, but then he had not the foggiest notion how to handle them. He'd given them over to Hannah's care and hardly seen them since, although he'd heard from Thompson that Hannah considered them unruly and difficult to mind. Running through the servants' passageways had certainly confirmed that impression.

When he'd watched them with Lillian after little Anna's fall, though, the children had merely seemed like two lost waifs.

He took another spoonful of soup, aware that he'd not responded to her offer to help with the children. Obstinately, he wanted to refuse her anything she desired.

Thompson entered at that moment, bringing the second course: a roasted chicken, turnips and carrots. Grant carved the chicken and Thompson served slices of it to Lillian, plus some of the turnips and carrots. He poured Lillian another glass of wine. Her gaze was fixed on the food, and Grant felt her eagerness to dig in, but she waited until he was served before she began to eat.

He broke the silence this time. 'How did you know to find me here?'

She put down her fork and directed her gaze to him. 'I simply took a chance. I knew from the London papers—I always read them, even in Lisbon—that you had inherited your brother's title. I confess I did not learn why. Had he been ill?'

'A carriage accident,' Grant responded automatically,

then felt she'd tricked him into talking to her. 'Killed his wife, too.'

'The children are your brother's, then?' she asked.

'No.' It was churlish of him to withhold simple information from her, as if it were as valuable as the papers she'd stolen from him, but he did not care.

She did not press him, though, but merely attended to her food. That irritated him even more.

Grant poured himself more wine. He hated feeling this way. She'd stolen his good humour. The arrival of the children had unsettled him, but she'd taken the rest. He drank half the glass.

'The children are my sister-in-law's from a previous marriage,' he finally said. 'I did not know they existed. They were apparently hidden away with her father until he became ill and died, and then his executors sent them here. They have only been here a week.'

She looked aghast. 'Oh, the poor dears! How awful for them.'

To be sent to him, did she mean? She was probably right.

He finished his wine and poured himself more. 'You may help with them if you wish. Though be certain they understand you will be leaving soon. I'll not have any more surprises thrust on them.'

Her steady gaze captured him. 'Yes, Grant. I understand.'

It seemed his anger ather was reflected back to him in those eyes. What a colossal joke fate had played on him, returning her to him as beautiful as ever, reminding him of how those eyes had once filled with a desire that mirrored his own. He could not gaze at her long without experiencing that once familiar enticement.

Yes. Providence was a consummate prankster, that he

should sit across from her and re-experience his anger at her betrayal at the same time as wanting nothing more than to press his lips against hers and carry her up to bed.

Chapter Two

It was difficult to sit across from Grant—more difficult than keeping herself from gulping down her food and asking for more, hungry as she was. Too many emotions were aroused, none of which she wished to feel.

How distant she felt from those days when his smile and the twinkle in his eye had made her giddy with joy and impatient to feel his hands on her bare skin. That this glowering man across from her could still arouse such thoughts was a shock to her. She wanted only to feel bitter disappointment that he, of all people, would still believe she could betray him and her country.

If only Grant had believed her back then, all the animosity from her husband, his family and everyone around her would have been so much easier to bear.

But this Grant was a complete stranger to her. How little she actually knew about his life. In Portugal, she'd only vaguely known he was a viscount's son. All that had been important to her at the time was that he was a gallant soldier, young and determined to fight for what she believed in, and so generous in his lovemaking with her.

After their traumatic split she'd still thought of him, when reading about those horrible battles to free Portugal and Spain from Napoleon's tyranny. Fuentes de Oñoro. Badajoz. Salamanca...

Her husband and his family—Portuguese patriots, they'd called themselves—had disdained the British soldiers, proclaiming them cowards. Lillian's mother was Portuguese, but Lillian always thought herself English like her father. To her, it had been obvious that Joseph Bonaparte was driven from Spain and Portugal only because the British army had fought to free them. But what could she say when her husband and his family, like Grant, believed she was a traitor?

Lillian managed to leave some bits of food on her plate when the butler came to clear the table before the last course. For some reason she did not understand, she did not want Grant to know she had not consumed more than tea for two days. Excepting those two biscuits with the children.

The butler returned with ginger cake and more wine. She'd had two glasses of wine so far, and in her fatigued and hungry state she could feel its effects. She took a bite of the cake and closed her eyes, savouring the taste. Such a simple dessert, really, like many she'd had when at school. But in her food-deprived state it seemed like ambrosia.

Opening her eyes again, she caught Grant, wine glass in hand, staring at her. She made herself return his gaze before slowly cutting herself another bite of cake.

'You are still in your wet clothes,' he remarked, as if he'd just noticed her for the first time rather than sitting with her in silence for near to a half-hour.

She looked down at herself as if checking it were true. 'I am.'

'Why did you not change?' He sounded accusatory. Did he expect her to have packed a full wardrobe in her small portmanteau? Besides, he had not changed into dinner clothes. Why should she?

'My portmanteau was out in the snow for quite a bit of time,' she explained. 'I fear what I am wearing is drier than my other clothes.'

He frowned. 'You have spent all these hours in wet clothes?'

She lifted her chin. 'As you see.'

He lowered his wine glass and took a bite of cake before speaking again. 'My sister-in-law's apparel remains in her room, I believe. Thompson may show you where it is. Use whatever you need.'

She blinked in surprise. 'Thank you, Grant.'

He shrugged. 'It is of no consequence to me.'

She took another bite of the delicious cake and remembered a happier time eating ginger cake at Mrs Everly's school in Reading. She'd felt so lost and alone there at nine years old, bewildered that her diplomat father had sent her so far from Portugal. Then he died and her mother had been content to leave her at the English school. It made it more convenient for her mother to continue her affair with the Portuguese aristocrat who would soon become her stepfather.

At the school, though, Mrs Everly and the other teachers and girls had made her welcome and had given her a new place to call home.

She glanced up to find Grant gazing quizzically at her. He quickly averted his eyes and stood. 'Please sit as long as you wish. Ask Thompson for anything you need. I'll instruct him to show you to my sister-in-law's room.'

He walked out.

Lillian blinked at this abrupt exit, then finished her cake and guiltily leaned over to take a forkful of the piece

Grant hardly touched. Did she dare take an apple or two from the centrepiece? Best not. It would be noticed.

After a few minutes of stealing more bites from Grant's cake, she heard Thompson come in. 'When you are ready, miss, I will show you to Lady Grantwell's bedchamber.'

Miss? So Grant had not told the butler she was not a 'miss' at all but the widow of Estevo Carris, a fugitive pursued by his brother, who'd vowed vengeance on her. What *had* Grant told him, though?

Lillian smiled at the servant and stood. 'I am ready now, if it is convenient for you.'

He picked up a branch of candles and led her past a back staircase—one used by the servants, she supposed. Was she not to be considered a servant, then? They crossed the hall to the main staircase and he led her to a large bedchamber facing the front of the house.

The bedchamber was adorned with the same plasterwork that made the ground floor so impressive, but the room seemed more personal. Lady Grantwell's dressing table still held its scent bottles and pots. Small trinkets and mementos remained on the mantel and the tables. A book lay next to the bed. The room did not look precisely as if a woman had just left it, but it certainly looked as if it were awaiting her return.

Thompson placed the candles on a table and opened the door to an adjoining dressing room. 'Some of Lady Grantwell's gowns are stored here. Not her ball gowns, of course.'

'Of course,' agreed Lillian who could not have felt more like a trespasser.

He gestured to a wardrobe. 'You will find other items of clothing in here.'

She nodded.

He edged towards the door. 'Would you like me to summon a maid to assist you?'

'That will not be necessary.' She did not want to make more work for the servants, especially if they were short-staffed. 'I only need a few things.'

He bowed. 'Then I will leave you. Goodnight, miss.'

'Goodnight, Thompson. And thank you.'

He left the room.

Lillian stood in the centre of the room, reluctant to intrude. On one wall was a large portrait of a beautiful lady, painted in the style of Thomas Lawrence. Lady Grantwell, she presumed. In the portrait her chin was lifted, so that it appeared she was looking down on everyone and everything. Her expression was smug. Disapproving.

'Lady Grantwell,' Lillian whispered. 'Forgive me. I wish only to borrow a few things and I will see them returned.'

The windows rattled and Lillian jumped. But it was merely the wind and not the portrait admonishing her.

Lillian walked over to look outside, where a light snow continued to fall. The snow, covering everything, illuminated the otherwise inky-black night. The road she'd walked upon to reach the main entrance was now indistinguishable from the lawn on either side of it. The gate she'd crossed through looked like a distant ship in a sea of white.

Lillian shuddered. She might have been caught in the blizzard that created that sea of white had Grant not allowed her to stay. Or felt forced to allow her to stay. At least her pursuers would be hampered by the same storm. They could not traverse the roads any better than she could. She was safe for the moment.

She turned and walked over to the wardrobe and found a nightdress and robe, which she thought was all she would need. Knowing the hallways to be lit, she blew out the candles the butler had carried.

In the sudden darkness of the room she imagined the portrait's eyes still upon her. She hurried out through the door.

Grant stood at the library window, glass of brandy in hand. Only that morning the view from this window had been comfortingly familiar—the same view of walkways, shrubbery and lawn that had been there since his boyhood. Now all that was familiar was obscured in a thick blanket of white, as if a spell had been cast on the land.

Grant once felt as if love had cast a spell on him, when he'd first found Lillian. Even with the constant threat of attack by the French he'd felt happier with her, lighter, as if he could soar into the heavens like the birds.

But it was all illusion. She'd taken advantage of his manly desire, his inability to resist her bed. He'd come crashing to earth again when the spell was broken and he'd discovered who and what she really was.

Now, just when he'd begun to accept his new role as Viscount, she arrived at his door. Had she conjured up the storm that now made every path and road impassable? That trapped her here with him? Well, he would not—*could* not—allow himself to be bewitched by her again, even though he'd found it nearly impossible not to stare at her at dinner. Good God, even to glimpse her bringing the soup spoon to her mouth had been a torture.

She'd been extremely hungry. He was pretty certain of that. That much could not have been feigned—not when it had been clear to him she was holding back from gulping her food and licking the plate. He would admire such self-control if he did not think it part of the reason she'd fooled him all those years ago. At least her hunger suggested some part of her story must be true, the part about having no money. The rest of it? What could he believe? That her husband was dead again? That she was being pursued? That she needed his money?

That last part. Yes. He could believe she needed his money.

He turned away from the window and picked up the decanter of brandy. Why sit here, in this room where she'd appeared to him again, when he could simply retire to his bedchamber, strip off his jacket and neckcloth, and comfortably finish off the brandy?

He strode over to the door and, juggling his glass and the decanter, opened it to make his way to the stairs. It had taken him almost a year to move from his childhood bedchamber to the one meant for the viscount. He'd done so thinking it might help him assume the role.

It had yet to accomplish that aim. At the moment, he continued to feel as if he'd invaded his father's room. He still thought of his father as Viscount Grantwell. He'd never really known his brother George in the role, except in those very early days.

Shortly after his father died Grant purchased his commission in the army and left for war. It had seemed the best thing to do to avoid being dictated to by his brother, who'd always made it his business to lord it over him.

Grant had never even met his brother's wife, the mother of the children now dropped into his care, but he gathered from the servants that she had been haughty and disagreeable.

The perfect partner for his brother, then.

Moving the glass and decanter to one hand, Grant reached for the door latch.

The door to the Viscountess's room next to it opened. Lillian stepped into the hallway and took a step back in surprise when she saw him. Grant nearly dropped his brandy. How rotten could his timing be? Or was fate playing its tricks on him again?

'I borrowed a few things, as you offered.' She acted as if he were about to accuse her of stealing—again.

A nightdress and robe were draped over her arm and an image sprang to his mind of her dressed in night clothes, her rich dark hair tumbling over her shoulders.

He averted his eyes. 'Use whatever you wish. I have no attachment to any of those things.' Indeed, he had no idea what to do with them.

'I thank you again, Grant.' She hesitated a moment.

He could not resist another glimpse of her, however, but needed something to say to justify it. 'You may ask the servants for whatever you need.' He spoke sharply, but he certainly had not intended she go hungry all day, as if he'd refused her food.

'Thank you. I have no intention of unnecessarily burdening them.' She almost smiled. 'I have learned to be remarkably self-sufficient.'

What did that mean? What had happened to her since the incident with the stolen papers? After her husband suddenly reappeared? Grant heard that her husband protected her from being punished for working for the French—out of a need to protect the family's pride, he'd heard—but that was all he knew.

Stop, he told himself. He refused to be curious about her.

He nodded to her—in dismissal, he hoped.

She must have understood. She walked quickly towards the children's wing, her gait graceful and regal.

He opened the door and entered the bedchamber he had yet to feel was his own.

* * *

Grant woke early. When the clock struck four and he could not get back to sleep, his mind filled with Lillian. Dash it all. After seven years he'd finally managed to avoid thinking of her and now she was in his house and back in his head. Even if he contrived to avoid her over the next few days, the knowledge that she walked these hallways and slept within these walls consumed him.

He rose and padded over to the window to view the now bright sea of white. Something else to add to his worries. The snow had ended, but clearly it was deep. At least two feet, if he guessed correctly. True, there was not much to be done on the estate over the next couple of weeks, which was why he'd allowed so many of his workers to take leave, but what would this uncalled-for weather do to his livestock and, even more, the people here who depended upon him? Would they all have enough food?

He'd seen enough starving people in Spain; he'd be damned if he'd allow it on his estate. But how would he discover who was in need? Could he really trudge miles through two feet of snow to find out? Could he ask that of anyone else? It would be days before the roads cleared enough for travel. Would those he'd given leave have difficulty returning? Or, even worse, would they take risks to come back?

Grant swore that war had seemed much less complicated than this.

He washed, shaved and dressed himself. His valet was one of the servants who took leave, but the army had made Grant used to caring for himself. He dressed warmly and pulled on his oldest pair of top boots.

He could make it to the stables, he surmised. He could at least check on how the stablemen were faring. And the horses. Besides, one of the older fellows there might tell him what should be done.

And if he were out of the house, he would not encounter Lillian.

Grant left the room and made his way down to the kitchen wing where Cook, with only two helpers, was already awake. The scent of baking bread tempted him to stop and beg for a sample right then and there, but he resisted.

He encountered Thompson, coming out of his room, and walked with him towards the kitchen. 'I'm off to the stables to check on the men. Is there anything I might do for you first, though?'

Thompson looked pained, as he always did when Grant acted in any way that was not viscount-like, such as offering to help. When Grant had been a boy, though, Thompson had had no such constraints and had been much more apt to act *in loco parentis*.

Before Thompson could speak, Cook, apparently having heard Grant's voice, called from the kitchen. 'If you are going to the stables you can take the men their breakfast. No sense them coming here and dragging in their wet boots and coats.'

Grant turned around and entered the kitchen. 'Good morning, Mrs Bell.' He smiled at the older woman who'd run the kitchens for as long as he could remember. 'You have an errand for me?'

She used to send him on 'errands' quite often when he was a boy—to get him out of the kitchen. 'That I do, Master John—m'lord, I mean.'

He gave her a quick hug and a peck on the cheek. 'Come now. I'll always be Master John to you, will I not?'

She pulled away, laughing. 'Stop your nonsense.'

He pretended to be sober. 'What is my errand?'

'Take a basket of food for the stables, if you are bound there anyway. No sense everyone dragging in dirt.'

'As you command.' He grabbed a sausage she'd just put on a plate and popped it in his mouth.

She slapped his hand.

Grant sat on a stool, likely the same one he'd sat on as a boy when angling for anything sweet coming out of the oven. He gazed around the kitchen. 'Are you faring well enough, Mrs Bell? This is not too much work for you, Mary and Sally, is it?'

She busily packed a huge basket full of bread, cheese and sausages. 'We are managing, m'lord.'

'I do not expect any extra fuss just because I decided to return early from the house party,' he assured her.

'Well, the children deserve a little fuss, do they not?' she countered. 'But we do not mind.'

And there was their unexpected guest, as well.

She finished packing the basket and Grant took it in his hand.

When he walked out of the kitchen Thompson was wringing his hands in the hallway. 'Smith was expected back today, but I doubt he will make it.'

Smith, who'd been Grant's batman during the war, was one of his footmen. He'd only gone as far as the village.

'I hope he does not attempt it,' Grant responded. 'We'll manage, though—will we not, Thompson?'

The butler looked less than certain. 'Yes, m'lord.'

Grant carried the basket to the boot room, where he donned a heavy overcoat, a warm hat, scarf and gloves. He left by the boot room door and stepped into fresh, untouched snow, sinking almost to his knees.

The walk to the stables was a slog and was made more awkward by carrying the basket. Grant was winded by the time he reached the door. He walked in and stamped his feet to remove as much snow as possible. His toes begged for a fire to warm them.

The horses snorted and shuffled in their stalls, and some poked their heads out to see who had arrived in their domain. One horse whinnied a greeting. Excalibur, the horse that had seen him through every battle from Sabugal to Waterloo, bobbed his head.

Grant called over to the stallion. 'I'll visit you in a minute, old friend.' He walked towards the stairs leading to the rooms above the stables, where the men lived. 'Halloo, men! I bring breakfast.'

The door to their communal room opened and one of the stablemen met him at its entrance, taking the basket from his hands. 'M'lord! Did not expect you.' He turned to the four others, who promptly stood up from where they'd been seated around a table drinking tea. 'We were about to draw straws to see who'd fetch the food. No sense us all going to the big house.'

'Cook did not want you, believe me,' Grant replied. 'I came not only to feed you, but to seek your advice. I have not a clue what needs to be done in a storm like this.'

'What do you need to know?' his old coachman asked.

Grant edged closer to the fireplace and gestured to the food. 'Nothing that cannot wait until you eat. Please do not stand on ceremony. Sit and enjoy your meal while it is hot.'

'We cannot sit while you stand, m'lord.' His old coachman moved away from his chair at the head of the table.

Grant removed his hat and gloves and shrugged out of his coat before accepting the seat.

'Have you eaten, m'lord?' his coachman asked.

Had the man noticed him eyeing the still-warm bread, cheese and sausage? 'Only one pilfered sausage. And after that journey from the house, I am famished.'

They had not yet finished passing around the food when Grant's estate manager appeared at the door.

'What the devil are you doing here?' Grant asked.

'Should I not be asking you that question?' his manager responded. 'It is my job to be here.'

Grant's estate manager was his close army friend Rhys Landon. The two of them had met in Portugal, shortly after the debacle with Lillian. They both were new lieutenants then, with newly purchased commissions and a great desire to succeed. They'd endured every battle together, becoming closer than brothers. What was more, Rhys had been through something of his own with a woman. He and Grant never talked about it, of course, but that special misery they shared had further bonded them.

At least Rhys managed to come out of it well now married to that woman he'd loved. Grant was happy for them both, and very grateful Rhys had accepted his plea to become his estate manager. There was no one he trusted more.

Rhys and his family lived in the finest cottage on the estate. It was even farther a walk than Grant had managed from the great house. He gestured for Rhys to sit, and the stablemen made a place for him.

'I came seeking advice from the men about what needs to be done.'

Rhys was given a chair near him. 'Excellent idea.' He tossed an amused look at his friend. 'Except that this is precisely what you hired *me* to do.'

Grant suppressed a smile. 'Well, I expected you to have the sense to stay in your house with your wife and your son.'

The men stared at them both, forks raised. Were they waiting for Grant to give them permission to eat?

'Pour yourself some tea,' he said to Rhys. He took a

bite of his sausage and the men, looking relieved, dug into their food.

Grant supposed he would eventually have to tell Rhys something about his unwanted house guest. He also supposed Rhys would see through him, just as Grant had seen through Rhys's excuses when Rhys's love had shown up in Brussels just before Waterloo.

Unless Grant could figure out a way to avoid mentioning Lillian altogether.

'Miss? Miss?'

The voice roused Lillian from a deep sleep—the best she'd had since fleeing Lisbon. She opened her eyes, momentarily unsure of where she was. Oh, yes. Safely at Grant's country house, with a maid looking down at her, arms akimbo.

She sat up. 'Hannah?'

'Mr Thompson says you are to take care of the children so I can be doing other things. They will be waking up soon.' Her voice sounded disapproving.

'Yes.' Lillian climbed out of bed. 'I did offer. If this will be a trouble to you, though—?'

'Oh, no.' The maid interrupted her. 'I'll be glad not to have the charge of them. They are two rascals, they are. Mr Thompson has charged me to find out just how much you intend to do, so he knows what chores to put me on.'

Lillian had not thought this through. What part of caring for them would be difficult for her to do? She scanned the room in thought and saw her clothes draped over every available surface. 'Um… Could you see to their clothes? And perhaps to their food, as well?' Then she would not then have to work out the laundry or the kitchen.

The maid brightened. 'I can do that, miss. I was used

to helping care for m'lady's clothes when she was alive. Bless her poor soul.' She gestured to Lillian. 'I see you are wearing m'lady's nightdress.'

Lillian looked down at herself. 'I am. Lord Grantwell gave me permission to borrow her clothes.' She pointed to the clothes scattered everywhere. 'Mine were wet from the snow.'

Hannah nodded. 'I can see that.' She walked over and touched some of them. Surely they'll be dry by now? 'Mrs Ward—she's the housekeeper, y'know—was going to train me to be a lady's maid someday.' She sobered again. 'I guess that won't happen now. Unless his lordship marries. But they say he must not be interested, or he would have stayed at that house party he was invited to.'

Grant? Not interested in marrying? Lillian forgot about clothes. 'Lord Grantwell was invited to a Christmas house party?' she asked.

'Yes, miss,' Hannah went on. 'He was to have stayed through to Twelfth Night. That's why so many of the servants were allowed to visit their families and hardly anybody is here. But he came back after staying less than a week there. And it is a good thing he did, because the children arrived and we would not have known what to do with them.'

'I see.' Although Lillian did not see at all, but she feared asking too many questions. 'Well, perhaps you can assist me, like a lady's maid would? That is, only when I really need it.' She put on her borrowed robe.

Hannah's face lit up again. 'Could I?'

A servant who was pleased to serve her? The servants in her husband's house, made to believe she was a traitor, had served her grudgingly. 'I would greatly appreciate it.'

Hannah's hand swept over the drying clothes. 'I will see your things are laundered, then, and your dresses cleaned. They look in great need of it, if you do not mind me saying.'

'I have been travelling for many days,' she explained. 'But I need one of those dresses. I only brought the two.'

Hannah started gathering the clothes into her arms. 'Never you mind that. I'll bring you one of m'lady's dresses—if you are allowed to borrow one.'

Clean clothes? That sounded like heaven. 'I was given permission to borrow whatever I needed.'

'I'll be back in a moment, then.' Hannah grinned.

Chapter Three

Hannah's choice of dress was perfect—one made of light wool, designed to be more practical than fashionable. Perfect for a governess, which was what Lillian would be for these next few days, and gladly so.

When she neared the children's bedchamber, she could hear their voices, but after she knocked and opened the door, they were both under their covers, pretending to sleep.

'Good morning,' she said, in her most cheerful voice. 'I know you are awake. I heard you talking.'

Little Anna seemed to spring from the bed and threw her arms around Lillian. 'You came back! I did not think you would come back!'

Lillian hugged her back. 'Of course I came back! I am only a visitor, though, and I must leave when the snow clears, but until then I am going to take care of you.'

'Like a governess?' Anna asked brightly.

Lillian laughed. 'Exactly like a governess.'

'Grandfather sent our governess away,' William piped up. 'And then we had to go away to school.'

'You went away to school?' she asked. They seemed far too young. 'How old are you?'

Anna piped up, 'I am six years old. William is eight.'

Much too young to be sent away to school, Lillian thought.

'And then Grandfather died,' Anna added. 'And then a man came and brought us here.'

'Our mother lived here,' William said. 'She's dead, too.'

Lillian carried Anna over to William's bed and gathered them both in her arms. 'You poor things! That is a lot to endure!'

She wanted to say that they had a home here now, and that Grant would take care of them, but she did not know for certain if it were true, even though Grant told her they should have no more surprises.

'Let us get you dressed and get breakfast, shall we?'

After breakfast the children showed Lillian the schoolroom, which looked as if it had been swept and dusted and polished, but little else. There were a few books. Two slates and pieces of chalk. A worn deck of cards. Where were the toys?

'Goodness! There is not much here.' Lillian stated the obvious. 'What have you been doing since you came here?'

'Hannah made us help her clean the room,' William said with some resentment in his voice.

'And practise our letters,' Anna added, copying his tone.

The room was quite large. The one long table—at a child's height, with chairs to match—was dwarfed by the space. Surely there were toys that would fill the empty spaces. Cupboards filled one whole wall.

'Have you looked in the cupboards?' she asked.

Both children, with guilty looks on their faces, averted their gazes. Apparently the answer was yes.

'Let's explore them again!' Lillian said.

The cupboards contained many more slates, more books, but also some toys. A set of spillikins. A box of wooden blocks. A cup and ball. A stack of composition books.

'Now, this looks more promising.' Lillian lifted them off the shelves.

Anna frowned. 'Hannah told us we'd better not play with them.'

'Nonsense!' Lillian winked at William. 'These must be for the children in the nursery to play with and you are the children in the nursery. Is that not so, William?'

The boy lifted his chin as if this was an act of defiance. 'Indeed, Miss Pearson.'

The children set up a game of spillikins, carefully picking up each stick so as not to move the others and squealing loudly when they did not succeed. Lillian sorted through the books.

Some were above their level, and others looked deadly boring, but there were some that could be read by a child of six and others were suitable for an eight-year-old. Still others Lillian could read to them, including one that seemed timely—a book entitled *Christmas Traditions: A Compilation of Manners and Ways of the Past.*

Before too long William tired of the game and instead leaned his elbows and chin on the windowsill, looking out on the expanse of white.

Lillian knelt down next to him and Anna immediately sought her lap. 'The snow is lovely, is it not?' she asked.

'I wish we could play in it,' William said testily, as if such a request had already been forbidden.

Lillian wondered how Hannah occupied the children when they were under her care. It seemed as if toys were forbidden. Were they also prevented from playing outside?

'Did Hannah take you outside before the snow?' Lillian asked.

'No,' William snapped.

'We mustn't get our clothes dirty,' Anna added.

The clothing the children wore did not seem anything special to Lillian, and nothing that could not be laundered. She'd wash them herself, if laundering was the problem.

'What would you do out in the snow?' Lillian asked.

'We made a snowman with Miss Young once!' Anna said.

'Miss Young was your governess?'

Both children nodded, their sad expressions mirroring each other.

Lillian eased Anna off her lap and stood. 'Well! Let us look through your trunks and see if we can find some warm coats and proper shoes for playing outside!'

Grant trudged back from the outer buildings with a greatly improved mood. He, Rhys and some of the men had made a plan to begin tamping down the snow on the estate roads and pathways so his people could at least move about freely and get food and other supplies to their cottages and their animals. Before the end of the day someone would have checked on every cottage family and seen to any of their needs.

Tracing his own footsteps back to the house made the going a bit easier. And as he approached, he heard the shouts and squeals of the children and the unmistakable laugh of the woman with whom he had once shared a passionate bed.

He could avoid them. Walk around to the front of the house.

But then he would drag himself through the snow, and where it was crusted onto his topcoat would melt onto the marble floor. More work for Thompson and the maids.

He plodded forward.

The children were making snowballs as quickly as they could and lobbing them at Lillian who scooped up snow and made a show of fighting back from behind two clumsily made snowmen. Snow was flying as if they'd created their own little storm. Chances were he could pass them unnoticed.

Thwack! Grant's cheek stung as one particularly well-thrown snowball shattered against his skin. Icy pieces slid down his neck and covered his shoulder.

When he managed to open his eyes, three figures stood as stiffly as soldiers at attention, one with a terrified look on his face. Even the enemy French soldiers had never looked so frightened of him. It made his heart ache.

'Who threw that snowball?' he growled.

The boy—damned if Grant could remember his name... William? Yes, William lifted his chin bravely. 'I did.'

'Well.' Grant leaned down and took a scoop of snow in his hands and formed it loosely into a ball. 'That was the best snowball that has ever hit me in the face.'

With a smile, Grant threw the snowball towards William, deliberately missing him. He scooped up more snow. The children were slow to react—still frightened of him—but Lillian caught on right away.

'Do you think *that* was a good snowball? Take this!'

She threw a snowball that managed to hit him in the chest.

He threw one back that shattered on her skirts. Anna laughed and tossed a snowball that came nowhere near him.

'You too?' Grant cried, throwing one to land right in front of her.

Both Lillian and Anna began to pelt him with one snowball after another.

'Two against one!' Grant cried. 'Unfair!' He turned to the boy. 'William, I need your help.'

'No!' Lillian called back. 'Stay on our team!'

William hesitated, but then joined the other two in pelting him, quite effectively, with snowballs. Grant's coat was hit so many times it was even more caked with snow than before, but he made certain his ammunition never hit hard.

He pretended they drove him to his knees. 'Enough! Enough!' He held up his hands. 'I surrender.'

Little Anna threw one more snowball at him and then laughed joyously. William was almost smiling. Lillian's eyes sparkled and her skin was brightened by the cold. But it was her smile that reached some hungry space inside him.

Good God. He needed to get away.

She extended her hand to help him up, but he ignored it and rose on his own. Her smile disappeared.

'We were a good army,' William said proudly.

'Indeed you were,' Grant responded, forcing himself to smile at the boy. No reason why the children's happy mood should be spoiled. 'I am now retreating to the house to change into something warm.'

Lillian turned to the children. 'We should go in as well. You both have very red noses and cheeks.'

As did she, Grant could not help but notice.

The children ran ahead through the path they'd made from the house. Grant followed behind Lillian.

She turned to him as they reached the door. 'Thank you, Grant.' Her expression sobered and her voice lost the lightness with which she'd addressed the children. 'They needed some fun, I think.'

'I think they needed to hit somebody,' he said.

Who was it? he wondered. Their grandfather? His executors? The men who'd brought them here? Or himself?

They removed their wet coats, hats, gloves and boots in the boot room.

'Go to the kitchen and have Cook give the children something warm to drink,' Grant said. 'She used to make my brother and me hot milk and honey.'

He did not look back as he walked down the hallway to the staircase.

When Grant left the boot room, Lillian glanced up from where she'd bent down to pick up Anna's wet coat. What just happened with Grant was more mysterious and surprising than his reaction to her sudden appearance the day before. It must have been for the children. Had he perceived William's fear? It certainly seemed so. He'd made a joke of it. How like him. In the short time she and Grant had been together, he'd always been kind.

Until he'd assumed she was a thief.

She stood and hung up Anna's coat. 'Let us put on our dry stockings and shoes.' She'd had the foresight to bring those with them. 'Then perhaps we will visit the kitchen? Warm milk and honey sounds nice, does it not?'

'I want milk and honey!' Anna cried happily.

William nodded.

When first showing them to the boot room, Thompson

had pointed out the other rooms in this wing of the house. The kitchen, the housekeeper's room, his own room, the servants' hall, and all the rooms associated with preparing food and washing and storing dishes. He'd not introduced them to the cook, but of course the cook must know who they were.

She and the children stopped in the kitchen doorway. The kitchen was a bustle of activity, although there were only three women working there. Lillian supposed the oldest of them was the cook.

'Excuse me,' she called from the doorway.

The cook looked up. 'What 'ave we 'ere?' Her smile transformed her plain face into one that gave them a warm welcome.

Lillian smiled back, grateful for the friendly response. 'Lord Grantwell said these two very cold children might be able to have some warm milk and honey. If it is not too much trouble?'

The cook wiped her hands on her apron and walked towards them. 'Warm milk and honey? We can do that.' She gestured with her arm. 'But come in. Sit down and get warm while we heat the milk.'

One of the kitchenmaids poured some milk into a pan and put it on the stove.

Anna bounced in. William entered more warily, but both were soon seated at a long wooden table. Already the warmth of the kitchen from the stove and the ovens had wrapped around Lillian like a comforting blanket.

'This is Anna and William,' Lillian said to the cook and her helpers. 'This is their first visit to the kitchen, I believe.'

'Indeed!' The cook patted Anna on the head. 'I expect we'll see more of you, though.' She walked over to a shelf and lifted the lid from a ceramic jar. A moment later each child had a plate and two biscuits set before them. 'Now, you may call me Cook, like Master John does, although my name is Mrs Bell.' She pointed to the maids helping her. 'And this is Mary. And Sally.'

They both nodded a greeting.

'How nice to meet you,' Lillian said. 'I am Miss Pearson.'

The three women gave her curious assessing looks.

The cook's welcoming smile quickly returned. 'Yes. Have a seat, miss. We don't stand on ceremony here—at least not with the lord. You are the guest, are you not?'

'A stranded traveller,' Lillian corrected. 'I volunteered to care for the children.'

Mrs Bell bustled by but leaned closer to Lillian as she passed. 'Which is a good thing. Hannah was not up to the task, if you ask me.'

Her helpers tittered in agreement.

Cook walked over to the kettle. 'And you would like a cup of tea, I expect?'

'Very much. Thank you,' Lillian responded.

Mrs Bell poured water into a teapot and spooned honey into the milk on the stove. She grated some ginger into the mixture and heated it some more before pouring it into two cups.

She set the cups in front of the children. 'Take care. It's hot.'

When Mrs Bell poured Lillian's tea, she poured a cup for herself and joined them at the table, asking the children about what they did outside to get themselves so cold and wet.

'We had a snowball fight with Lord Grantwell!' Anna told her. 'And we beat him.'

'Did you, now?' Cook shook her head. 'Imagine that.

He was no match for you, eh? And him being a soldier and all.'

William looked up from his warmed milk. 'He was a soldier?'

Cook nodded. 'Indeed. A captain at the end. He fought battles in Spain and was even at Waterloo. A proper hero, he is, by my reckoning.'

William's eyes grew huge with interest, but he asked no questions.

Lillian smiled to herself. At least in this kitchen these forlorn children would receive the warmth they so desperately needed.

Grant had dressed himself in dry clothes and shoes, but had not completely dispelled the chill inside him from his long time out in the cold. Nothing warm milk and honey wouldn't remedy. If he rang for Thompson, some could be sent up to him, but he'd not seen Thompson since he'd entered the house. The poor man was probably attempting to do three tasks at once elsewhere.

The plan had been for Thompson to have one of the footmen to help him while the others took their leave, but then Smith had presumably been stranded in the village by the snow. That left two housemaids and Hannah. Those numbers would have been sufficient if Grant had stayed at the house party, if the children had not arrived—and if Lillian had not come to his door.

As Grant saw it, those extra burdens were his responsibility.

Buck up and stop your complaining, he told himself. *Wellington accepted responsibility for the fate of all of Europe. What is one man's country estate to all that?*

What Grant needed was a good military campaign and the hardships of a long march. Had a year of soft living turned him into a man who could not make his own way to the kitchen?

Grant rubbed his still-cold hands and opened his door. No need to bother Thompson.

Cook's laughter reached his ears as he neared the kitchen. From the threshold, he could see her seated at the long wooden table with the children.

And with Lillian.

He almost turned away but Cook saw him. 'Master John!'

Lillian and the children glanced his way, surprised expressions on their faces. Of course who would have expected 'Master John' to be Lord Grantwell? Lillian quickly averted her gaze.

No chance to retreat now.

He entered the room and nodded to the children. 'I see you took up my suggestion for milk and honey. Am I too late for some?'

Cook stood. 'We're heating another batch.' She turned to her helper. 'Mary, add more milk for his lordship.' She gestured for him to sit, next to Anna and across from Lillian and William. They were still in their damp clothes, so must have come directly to the kitchen.

Anna turned her curly head and smiled up at him.

What did one say to a little girl? 'Do you like the milk and honey?' he finally managed.

She nodded vigorously and took a bite of the biscuit in her hand, still staring at him.

He averted his gaze, but that meant facing Lillian. 'Should you not have changed out of wet clothes first?' Curse him. His words conjured up an image of Lillian in tantalising states of undress. Her smile now had a sharp edge to it. 'Warm milk and honey was too tempting to resist.' She glanced around. 'As well as the warmth of this lovely kitchen. Besides, we did put on dry shoes and stockings.'

William gave her a worried look. 'Did we do something wrong, miss?'

Grant kicked himself. He did not want to worry the boy. 'Nothing wrong.' He tried to explain. 'I meant I thought you'd go directly to the nursery, not here.'

William's young brow furrowed. 'Should we not be in the kitchen?'

Grant tried again. 'Of course you may be in the kitchen. Unless Cook needs to scoot you out, but that is up to her. I spent many a fine hour in this kitchen when I was your age, but I warn you, Cook might put you to work.'

'Work?' Anna fidgeted excitedly in her seat. 'What sort of work?'

'Peeling potatoes,' he answered. 'Slicing carrots. But you are too young for all that.'

Anna straightened in her chair as best she could with her legs dangling a foot from the floor. 'I would like to slice carrots.'

'It would not be safe,' William interjected. 'You would cut yourself with the knife.'

'I would not!' protested Anna.

Grant pointed to the boy. '*You* could be trained to use a knife, though,' he told him.

William stared at him, as if trying to figure out what sort of creature was before him. Lillian looked at him as if she already knew and did not approve.

He turned to the friendlier face. 'I am certain Cook could find many things for you to do that would not require a knife.'

Little Anna beamed up at him.

Cook appeared placing a cup before him and pouring milk and honey from the pan. 'Mary and Sally are all the help I need today, Master John.' She refilled the children's cups.

Grant held the cup in both hands, warming them, and took a sip, savouring the hot, sweet liquid. He glanced over at William, who was still staring at him.

Grant gave him a wink. 'As good as when I was your age.'

William glanced away.

These two children did not seem to be troublesome in the least, and yet his sister-in-law had left them behind when she married his brother? It made no sense. The executors' explanation had been equally unsatisfying. They said only that the children were from her earlier ill-fated marriage, one that was best forgotten. Apparently her husband had had the good graces to die so she'd been free to marry George. Even if some scandal had accompanied her earlier marriage, what would be scandal enough that she'd not keep her children with her? Or was it that his brother had forbidden her to bring the children here? It would have been just like him.

Good God. Grant had been much more troublesome at those ages which Cook happily corroborated. She started to regale the children with all the myriad ways he'd caused mischief as a boy.

'And when His Lordship was about your age, Master William,' Cook went on in a very dramatic tone, 'he once escaped from his governess and disappeared. It was a cold winter day, much like today. He was gone for hours and no one knew where he was.'

'Where was he?' Anna asked, wide-eyed.

Grant remembered all too well. 'I took a walk in the woods,' he said. 'I found some fox footprints in the snow and followed them all the way to the fox's lair. I felt very clever having found him, too, I must say.'

'Well, your governess was certain you'd fallen in the pond,' Cook said. 'The whole house was in an uproar, and by the time you came back, your father, the old lord, was raving mad at the disruption.'

Yes. Grant remembered having no concept of time. He'd escaped the house all in a lather after his brother had been taunting and teasing him. As soon as he'd trudged through the snow to the woods it had seemed as if he'd entered a magical place, a place he was as much a part of as the fox. He'd felt at one with the world and at peace.

'What happened then?' Anna asked Cook.

Cook gave him a quick glance. 'Oh, well, he was punished for worrying everyone.'

Which meant his father had given him one of the worst floggings of his boyhood while his brother had smirked nearby.

William stared at him then, his expression serious.

Lillian kept her gaze averted, but he knew she'd been listening.

Grant felt a great need to create some levity.

He smiled at Cook. 'Tell them how the month after, at random moments and in various places, my father, brother and governess found dead mice among their things.'

'That was you?' Cook laughed and regarded the children again. 'I told you he was full of mischief!'

The boy still stared at him, though, as if seeing some creature from a storybook come to life.

Lillian glanced up at him, but only for a fleeting moment.

Grant took another sip of his milk and honey.

When the children had finished theirs, Lillian stood.

'I think we should change into dry clothes now we are sufficiently warmed up.'

The children obeyed without hesitation—which was so unlike Hannah's report of them. Was that Lillian's doing?

He watched them leave, his eyes following Lillian all the way out the door. He'd deliberately not acknowledged her—that was what he'd insisted upon, was it not? That she should not show her face to him while she was here?

Impossible, he now realised.

It was not like him to ignore a person's presence, whether it be friend, foe or servant. But he felt justified in ignoring Lillian after what she'd done to him.

With the children gone, Cook turned to stir something in a big pot. Mary and Sally continued with their tasks and Grant finished his milk and honey alone.

Chapter Four

Lillian soon had the children dressed in warm, dry clothes. Hannah had provided her with another of Lady Grantwell's day dresses, so soon they were all comfortable again in the nursery. She supposed she ought to teach lessons or engage the children in drills, but she did not have the heart for it. These children needed play. They needed fun more than writing letters or adding numbers. The time spend out of doors, particularly the snowball fight with Grant, had convinced her of that.

She'd needed play as well. For a few moments in the snowball fight she'd forgotten she was being pursued. She'd actually felt light-hearted.

She put the choice to the children, quite certain of their reply. 'Shall we do lessons or have some play?'

'Play!' cried Anna.

William said nothing.

'Very well,' Lillian responded. 'We found some toys and games this morning. Choose something you would like.'

Anna opened a cupboard Lillian had not yet explored and took out a box of dominoes. 'Play with me, William?'

William nodded and the two divided the tiles, made of

bone with black pips, and began to take turns connecting them through matching pips.

Lillian continued her exploration of the cupboards, starting with the one that held the dominoes. She found other games there. A chess set. A wooden draughts board with matching wooden pieces. A Fox and Geese set. Apparently some children in this nursery used to play many games. Had it been Grant? His brother?

In Portugal, Grant had talked of winning the war, of besting the French. She understood the drive to win. When she was a child, she and her father had played such games as this nursery possessed. At school she'd always been a ready partner for a game and always relished the exhilaration when she'd won.

Then word came that her father had died. All joy in everything had disappeared for a long time.

The pain of losing her father flashed through her again, the pain and the loneliness. Her mother did not sent for her to come home so she could be comforted. Even her mother's letters came infrequently, although Lillian had written to her often. Much too soon after her father's death a letter from her mother announced her marriage to a Portuguese aristocrat.

Yes, Lillian knew what it felt like to be abandoned by a mother. She knew the pain these children carried inside them.

She glanced at William and Anna. Anna with her open countenance showing every emotion in her dear little face; William—one could not tell what he was feeling. There seemed to be much emotion in him, though, hidden from view. Her heart ached for them.

Lillian shrugged off the wave of grief—her own and the children's. She continued her search. The top shelf held a paint box and several pots of pigment powder.

Best to keep that out of view for the moment lest Hannah have a fit trying to wash paint out of clothes. Below that shelf was a wooden board that looked like a game at first, but it had seven rows of slots in it. She took down the box next to it and opened it to find tiles with numbers on them and the names of the months.

'Here is something,' she said.

The children looked up.

She held it up for them to see. 'We can make a calendar.'

'A calendar?' Anna said.

'A calendar to show what month it is. So we can see how many days until Christmas.' And to help her not lose what day it was in her own mind. 'I'll set it up for us.'

'Your turn,' William said impatiently, turning back to the dominoes, their length growing longer and more complicated.

'I want to see the calendar!' Anna protested.

'You were the one who wanted to play dominoes,' William countered.

'No need to fuss,' Lillian said. 'The calendar can wait until the game is over.'

William's brow furrowed at the word *fuss*. Why would he worry about such a mild rebuke?

The dominoes game ended quickly with Anna the excited victor. William's choice of tiles had become quite careless at the end. He'd let Anna win, Lillian realised.

'Put the dominoes back in the box and we will make the calendar.' Goodness. Lillian was sounding like one of the teachers at her school.

Perhaps being a governess would suit her. It would be a good place to hide, at least. If her brother-in-law did not find her first.

She glanced out of the window. The snow made her safe for the moment. She could relax.

The dominoes were swiftly stowed away and Lillian poured out the tiles from the calendar box.

'Who knows what month it is?' she asked.

'Is it still December?' Anna asked.

'Of course it is,' William said. 'Miss Pearson told us we'll be counting the days until Christmas.'

'What will happen at Christmas?' Anna's face pinched in worry.

Lillian's heart ached for her again. 'Well, we will celebrate. Let us see how many days we have to prepare.' She turned back to the tiles. 'Do you know the rhyme that tells us how many days December has? *"Thirty days hath September..."*?'

'"April, June and November,"' William went on in a bored voice. *'"All the rest have thirty-one..."'*

They picked out the numbered tiles and placed them in the slots, from one to thirty-one.

When done, they set the calendar on a table by the window.

'Look.' Lillian pointed to the day. 'This is today. December the twenty-first—oh, dear, it is Sunday. But there was no chance for us to attend Church services, was there?'

The children gave her blank stares. Perhaps they were too young for attendance at Church. She swept her finger along the tiles marking the days. 'It is only four days until Christmas! We shall have to prepare.'

She was acting as if Grant was not going to toss her out. What if the roads were passable before Christmas? What was she to do then? She had no money. No friends. How was she to hide from Dinis? How was she to live until it was safe to contact her headmistress again?

It was no use to dwell on all that. She pushed the worry aside. She'd simply pretend she would stay with the children through Christmas. She'd help them prepare for a festive holiday. Try to bring them some enjoyment, at least.

'How do you celebrate Christmas?' she asked them.

'Miss Young used to give us gifts,' Anna said. 'And we ate Christmas pudding.'

Miss Young, their governess, had given them gifts, not their grandfather?

'And then we had to stay quiet upstairs and not bother Grandfather's guests,' added William.

How sad that sounded.

'When I was a child I mostly celebrated Christmas at school,' she told them, to distract from their unhappy memories. Her mother declared it too far for Lillian to travel back to Portugal for the school holidays, so she'd spent Christmas with the headmistress, the teachers and the few other girls who had nowhere else to go. 'We decorated with evergreens, sang songs, played games and we gave gifts, too.'

William rolled his eyes. 'Who would we give gifts to?'

Another pang to Lillian's heart. He did not feel attached to anyone—except his sister. Everyone familiar to him was gone.

'To each other, of course,' she answered him. 'And would it not be nice to make gifts for the servants who are here? Those who could not go to their families?'

'And we could make gifts for Lord Grantwell,' Anna added.

'Yes. Lord Grantwell, too. Of course.'

Would he even choose to celebrate Christmas? He had, after all, sent his servants away and fled a Christmas house party. Was it Christmas festivities he wished to avoid?

She could not think of him. Not without upsetting herself all over again. Of all people Grant should have known she would never have stolen from him and would never have betrayed England or Portugal. They'd been so intensely close. How could he not have believed in her?

She must not dwell on that, though.

Lillian stood up and walked over to pull a book from the shelf. 'I found a book. *Christmas Traditions: A Compilation of Manners and Ways of the Past*. Let us look through it and make plans for how we will celebrate Christmas.'

They spent the rest of the day learning about Christmas traditions, like decorating the house with evergreens on Christmas Eve and mummers plays and wassailing. And gift-giving.

'How will we make gifts, Miss Pearson?' Anna asked.

How, indeed? At school they'd purchased gifts at the village shop, or bought cloth, ribbons, coloured paper and other bits with which to make presents for the teachers and the other children who'd remained over Christmas. But if Lillian could make it to the village shop, then Dinis could catch up with her and all would be lost.

What was she thinking? She had no money for either gifts or escape. They must make do with what they could find in this house. Surely somewhere here in this vast house there would be scraps they could use...

'We will use whatever we can find. I'll ask Hannah. She will know what we will be permitted to use.'

Grant paced around the library, at a loss as to how to occupy himself. He spent far too much time staring out of the window at the snow, which only reminded him of

Lillian gleefully throwing snowballs at him and the children's laughter ringing in his ears. Her face had glowed with the exertion and her eyes had sparkled with delight. He'd once had glimpses of such playfulness with her in bed, but her sparkling eyes soon darkened with passion and they'd shared other delights.

He'd believed her emotions to be genuine back then. But it had all been playacting. Was she playacting now? If so, how could she sustain it, especially with the children? Her enjoyment of their snowball fight had seemed genuine even before they'd spotted him.

The children.

Their grandfather's executors could not have found a more unsuitable place for them. With him, unmarried and unused to children. He was more comfortable amongst his soldiers in the midst of battle than with children. They were unwanted by everyone, apparently. Certainly unwanted by their grandfather. Their mother. And presumably Grant's brother—it would have been just like him to want them out of sight, out of mind.

Grant knew a little about feeling unwanted. His parents could not be bothered with him. He was the spare, useful only if their first-born son should meet with death before producing his own heir, which, of course, was exactly what happened.

Good God, Grant was challenged every day with meeting the needs of his estates and people—how could anyone expect him to be the guardian of children too? He must find them a good governess, even though he had no idea what a good governess would look like.

A vision of Lillian flashed through his mind. She seemed so much at ease with the children and they with her. And yet he wished her gone as soon as possible. Another loss for the children.

Grant shook his head. See? He was not up for this task. He would cause these children another loss, merely because he'd given her permission to assume their care. Why had he not anticipated this?

Fate was certainly teasing him to plunge into gloom. Well, he would have none of that. There was nothing he could do to change his decisions of the past. He'd make the best of it as best he could. Muddle through somehow.

He turned away from the window and crossed the room to the door. He needed a distraction. Perhaps he would venture outside again, see how the men fared. See if Rhys was still about.

He entered the anteroom just as someone descended the stairs.

Grant looked up.

It was Lillian, dressed in a plain but lovely dress that flattered her figure and swirled around her legs as she moved. A paisley shawl was wrapped around her shoulders.

She stopped when she saw him and started to turn back.

Her retreat should not surprise him. He had ordered her to stay out of his sight, after all. As if her being out of his sight helped him not think of her four times every hour.

'What are you doing?' he demanded. She was supposed to stay with the children, not wander around the house.

She turned back. 'I am in search of Thompson.'

'Thompson? Whatever for?'

She lifted her chin. 'I wish to ask him something.' Her words were clipped.

Why should she speak as if he were the one who'd wronged her?

He held her gaze. 'Ask me instead.'

'But you said not—' she began, but stopped herself. She took a breath. 'Hannah suggested I seek out Thompson. The children and I wish to prepare for Christmas… to make things for the day. Gifts for the servants who remain here—'

'I assure you I plan to well reward my people on St Stephen's Day. Or whenever they can safely return.' At least he planned to do it now. He'd forgotten all about Christmas, but had not Rhys mentioned it even before his brief trip to the house party?

She tensed. 'I was not implying that you were not giving Christmas boxes. I merely desire permission to use whatever scraps of paper or cloth or other frippery we can find that would be of no use to anyone else, and to have Hannah help us find such things.' Her graceful hand gripped the banister. 'If I do not have your permission, I need not seek out Thompson.'

'You have my permission. If it gives the children pleasure.' Not because *she* was asking, although he remembered when she could have asked him anything and he would have said yes. 'You need not bother Thompson. Tell Hannah you have my approval.'

He gave a dismissive nod. He needed to remove himself from her presence as soon as possible. God help him. He felt her allure almost as strongly as his anger surged in her presence.

Her expression softened. 'Thank you, Grant.'

He turned to walk away, then turned back. Why was it so hard to leave her? 'I confess I do not know where you might look for such items. The attic, perhaps. Have Hannah take you up in the attic. Use whatever you like there. If it is in the attic, it cannot matter. Use whatever makes the children happy.'

She nodded. 'The attic. I'll tell Hannah.'

'Do that,' he said curtly.

Her company turned him into a man he disliked—an angry, disgruntled, suspicious version of himself. He detested his emotions getting the better of him, especially the ones that reacted to her beauty and the memories of moments when he'd savoured every inch of her. He wanted only to remember her betrayal.

He could feign good humour with everybody else, why not her? Long ago, when he was younger than William even, he'd learned that if he acted light-hearted, he soon felt it.

He bowed to her and forced himself to walk away. Only then did he wonder if the roads would be passable by Christmas. It would be odd if they were not. And if the roads were passable before Christmas, he'd be sending her away.

Problem solved.

A little while later Hannah showed Lillian the way to the attic, where a trunk containing remnants of fabric, ribbons and trims was stored, as well as spools of thread, needles and pins, everything necessary for sewing. There were also boxes of decorative paper, foils, wallpaper and tissue paper.

She took the children up with her to select what they might use.

'Now, you must not disturb the other things up here,' Lillian warned them. 'We will just look in the boxes and trunks that Hannah told me about.'

Anna, a little afraid of the attic's dark corners with their mysterious, shadowy shapes, stayed close by, but William, more daring, was a bit harder to contain.

Lillian riffled through the trunk of fabric and trim.

'What do you think of this idea, children? For Cook and the maids we could make up packets of fabric, lace and ribbons that they might wish to use to trim a dress or a bonnet.'

Anna clapped. 'That is a good idea!'

William looked over from some trunks he'd been exploring nearby. 'I do not want to make up packets of lace.'

Lillian could not blame him. 'Then we must find something more manly for you to do. For Thompson.'

William dragged over a wooden crate. 'Look at this.'

The crate held bits of wood of all sizes, a small saw, and a leather pouch Lillian supposed contained woodworking tools.

'I could make Thompson a box to hold his important things,' William said. 'Rogers taught me how. He was one of the footmen at Grandfather's. I can show you the box he helped me make. He taught me to whittle, too.' His expression turned sad. 'I suppose we'll never see Rogers again either.'

Lillian's heart lurched for the boy. Yet another loss for him.

She looked into the box. Was it wise for a boy his age to use such tools? On the other hand, except for the snowball fight, the woodworking box was the first activity that had seemed to capture William's interest.

Lillian would simply have to watch him carefully. 'Well, that is an excellent idea. Anna and I will make the gifts for the women and you can make one for Thompson.'

They filled the basket she'd brought with them full of fabric and trim, and also managed to carry down the box of woodworking pieces. Bringing it all to the nursery, they started work.

As William set to measuring and sawing, Lillian and Anna sorted through the fabric and lace.

After they'd put together two packets, and tied them up with ribbon, Anna rested her elbows on the table and put her chin in her hands. 'Will you be with us for Christmas, Miss Pearson?'

The child had not forgotten, then, that Lillian would be leaving them, like everyone else.

William paused in his work, as if waiting for her answer.

She wrapped her arms over her chest. 'I will have to leave sometime. Perhaps not before Christmas.' Unless the snow cleared and she'd be tossed out to fend for herself.

'Why do you have to leave?' Anna asked, a catch in her voice.

Lillian's heart cracked. 'I—I am only here because I was stranded in the snow.' Otherwise she would have been banished already. 'I do not belong here.'

'Where *do* you belong?' Anna asked.

Nowhere, Lillian wanted to say. 'Not here. I was travelling to another place.'

'Where?' Anna persisted.

William returned to his work, but Lillian was certain he was listening to her every word. She searched for some answer. Any answer.

'Scotland,' she replied. 'I was bound for Scotland.'

Anna sat back in her chair and folded her arms around herself like Lillian had. 'I want you to stay. I want you to be our governess. Ask Lord Grantwell if you can be our governess.'

Lillian felt her throat tighten with emotion. She already felt attached to this boy and girl in a way she could not imagine being attached to others, and she could not bear to be the cause of more hurt for them. But what could she say?

'It would be lovely to stay with you,' she said, avoiding a direct answer. She rose and walked over to Anna and scooped her up in her arms, holding her close. 'I would like nothing better. Perhaps I can stay through Christmas. That would be something.'

Grant's dinner was a solitary affair. When he'd walked into the small sitting room near the kitchen, where he preferred to take his meals—it was preferable to being seated in the cavernous dining room, with its bright yellow walls, dining table for twenty, and paintings of his ancestors overseeing every bite he took—there was only one place setting at the table.

Thompson informed him that Miss Pearson had dined with the children. Good. A relief, in all actuality.

After another excellent meal Cook provided, and plenty of good wine from his brother's cellar, Grant wandered into the library. He settled into a deep, comfortable chair near the fireplace and sipped his brandy. The only sounds were the crackling of the fire, the ticking of the mantel clock and the whistle of the wind that had picked up outside. The solitude seemed oppressive now, although it had been precisely what he'd relished most after fleeing the compulsory social obligations of the country house party.

What he really missed was the camaraderie of a military campaign, though many a night had been spent in great discomfort, either too cold or too hot, or too wet or too dry. Or too wrenched with the memories of a day's battle and the inescapable smell of death.

He shook his head. What an odd creature he was. So restless and unsatisfied. Think of how privileged a life he led. He was alive, for one thing, in one piece, and not yet in the poorhouse—as long as next year's crops flourished and no other disasters ensued.

He finished his brandy and poured another and let the warmth of the fire, the ticking of the clock and the wind's whistle lull him. He must have dozed for a moment when the door opened and the room brightened a little with lamplight.

He twisted around in his chair. 'Thompson?' he asked.

The figure carrying the lamp stopped. 'No. It is I.'

Lillian.

She was the last person he wished to see in this dark room, him all mellow with brandy.

He stood. Had she come looking for him? Had Thompson told her she might find him here? He ought to instruct the servants that she was not to disturb him.

'Do you have a reason to be here?' He'd not meant his words to come out in such an accusing tone. Or had he?

'I came to see if I might find a book,' she responded.

Did she now? Could he believe this? Or had she come looking for him?

'I did not know you would be here.' The lamp illuminated her face, which certainly did not look pleased to see him. 'I assumed I could borrow a book as long as I put it back—which I would.'

The light on her face also reminded him of candlelit nights, when he could not get enough of gazing at her.

She straightened her spine. 'Do you wish me to leave?'

He shook himself out of his reverie. 'No. No. You have come to the right place if you are indeed looking for a book.' She made no move towards the bookshelves. 'I must tell you, though, there are few novels on these shelves.'

'I do not seek a novel,' she retorted.

'What, then?' he asked.

'A book about Scotland.'

Grant almost laughed. 'Scotland? Whatever for?'

The glow of the lamp showed her lifting her chin. 'I must hide somewhere. I mean to learn if Scotland will do.'

He had forgotten she was on the run—if that story was true. 'Oh, yes. Someone is pursuing you…'

'My brother-in-law,' she said.

He lifted his brows. 'Your brother-in-law, you say? Out to avenge your husband's murder.'

She glared at him. 'I did not kill my husband.'

'Your brother-in-law is seeking revenge in the wrong place, then?' he went on.

'Yes,' she shot back.

'Well, you betrayed your country; why should they not believe you would kill your husband?' Did he believe her? Was she capable of murder? Not the woman he'd thought she was.

Her eyes flashed. 'I did not betray my country. Not Britain. Not Portugal. I did not steal. Or spy. Or commit murder.'

'Then why did you run?'

'Because no one would believe me!' Her voice trembled with emotion. 'And I do not wish to hang for something I did not do.'

Could he bear to think of her being hanged? He could not—no matter how she'd betrayed him.

'I simply want to disappear,' she went on. 'I need to find a place to disappear. Like Scotland.'

Scotland probably would be a good place to disappear. 'Hence the book on Scotland,' he said rhetorically. 'I do not know what books on Scotland might be on these shelves. Let us look.'

Her body relaxed. She blinked rapidly as if batting away tears.

'Let us look at the section with histories and geographies.' Someone his father hired years ago had once organised the library into topics. Grant had no idea if it still was so.

She followed him over to the shelves next to the arched doorway into the next room. She handed him the lamp and he climbed the library ladder and held it close to the shelves.

'Ah, this might do.' He pulled down one book and handed it to her. *'The Beauties of Scotland, Volume I,'* he said. 'There are five volumes. Shall I pull them all down for you?'

'The first will do for now.' Her voice had softened.

As he stepped off the ladder, the hand that was holding the lamp moved towards the doorway for a moment.

Lillian gasped, as if in fright, and jumped into his arms.

'What?' He held her with his free arm as the lamp illuminated the next room—the sculpture gallery.

She pulled away from him and gave an embarrassed laugh. 'Oh! They are statues! I thought I glimpsed a real person!'

He was unprepared for her instinctive leap towards him as if wanting him to protect her. He stepped through the archway and gave the room more light. 'My grandfather's statues. He—he amassed quite a collection of Roman sculpture during his Italian tour.' He hoped he didn't show how much her touch had shaken him. 'Come. Have a look.'

The statues did take on an eerie appearance in the dim light. It was like walking into an ancient Roman temple in the middle of the night and having the statues all turn their eyes upon you. In interest? Or judgement?

'Oh, my!' Her face lit with awe. 'They look as if they might start moving at any moment!'

'Indeed.' He still felt her hands upon him, smelled the scent of her hair. So familiar. 'Startling if you do not know they are here.'

For a brief moment they were as they'd been in Portugal, marvelling together at something they'd shared.

He wrested that sensation away and led her back into the library. 'You are free to look at them in daytime, if you wish.'

'Yes. Thank you.' She glanced down at the book in her hands. 'Well, I have what I came for. I need not trouble you more.'

She, too, must have felt it. That sense of being one, of having no barriers between them. Surely an illusion. The walls between them were as solid as the marble of the statues.

He handed her the lamp and watched her walk to the anteroom door. Before he knew what he was about, he spoke. 'You ate dinner with the children, Thompson said.'

She turned and the lamplight glowed on her face again. 'Yes. I did.'

'Were you served enough food?' Good God. Was he trying to keep her with him a few minutes longer?

She looked as puzzled by his speaking as he was himself. 'I thank you. I had a nice dinner. Perfectly adequate.'

It was on the tip of his tongue to ask her to dine with him the next day. What was happening to him? Was her allure enticing him again? He'd not have it.

She stared at him a long time, as if she knew he was wrestling with himself. Finally she said, 'Thank you for the book, Grant. Goodnight to you.'

Chapter Five

The next day Grant rose early to venture out on the estate and see how everyone was faring. He met up with Rhys and they discussed priorities, seeing the people and animals had food, working on the roads so they could move about freely. He asked about Christmas boxes. Rhys and his wife were already working on them, one for each of the tenant families, one for each worker and servant.

When he walked back, he saw Lillian. Why must he encounter her at every turn? It was like ripping the scab off a wound, over and over, flooding him with erotic memories and the enormity of her betrayal.

Lillian was helping Anna build another snowman—a snow *woman*, he realised. They were shaping the snow into a long dress. William worked on a snowman of his own, one impressively tall, taller than the boy. They made an appealing picture, one he had no intention of disturbing.

Grant started to walk by as William tried to lift an oddly shaped snow head onto his snowman. The head looked to have been made by stacking two large balls of snow, one on top of the other. The top one, though, had more of a cylindrical shape. William held the head as far above him as his arms could reach, but he needed a few more inches.

Lillian could have helped, but she was busy with Anna's creation and did not notice.

William tried again to place the head on the torso, to no avail.

Grant paused a moment before striding forwards. 'Do you need a little help, William?'

William dropped the snow head and stood stiffly, staring at Grant in alarm. The boy was still frightened of him? Even after yesterday? Grant was simply not good with children. Why would he be?

Lillian and Anna stopped their work, as well, and turned to him in surprise. Grant had intruded, obviously. How familiar that felt to him. How many times had he walked in on his father and brother, heads together in some joint project? How well he remembered the expressions on their faces. His presence was not welcome.

This intrusion did not feel precisely like that, though. Certainly his father and George were never wary of him.

Grant walked over to William and squatted down to examine the oddly shaped head. 'It is still in one piece. Would it help if I lifted it and put it where you tell me it should go?'

William, eyes still wide, nodded.

Grant lifted the head and deliberately placed it askew.

'No,' William said. 'Put it in the middle.'

Grant, very aware that Lillian was watching him, did as he was told, looking back at William for the boy's approval.

William nodded.

Grant stepped back and surveyed the snowman. 'Impressive height.'

'He is a soldier,' William said.

Grant gave an approving laugh. 'Of course. I see it now. He is wearing a shako.' The cylindrical shape on the head was very like a soldier's hat. William had even fashioned a brim. 'Well done.'

William almost smiled.

Grant turned to the figure Anna and Lillian were making. 'And yours is a lady—is that right, Anna?'

Anna beamed. 'Like the painting of the lady on your stairway.'

On the stairway? There were paintings of generations of ladies throughout the house. Had the children even seen all the rooms of the house? Except for their trek to the outside door, their visit to the kitchen and their foray two days ago into the servants' passages, had the children been much out of the nursery?

He turned his gaze from Anna to William. 'I would say your snow people are not like paintings, but like sculpture.' He glanced at Lillian. Was she also remembering their near embrace in the archway of the sculpture room? She gave no sign of it. 'My grandfather would approve. Sculpture was his favourite sort of art. He made a whole room to display them.'

'The stone people?' Anna piped up.

'Anna!' William cried.

Grant nodded. 'So you have done more exploring than I gave you credit for. I daresay you should have a proper tour of the whole house. Since this is to be your home—' What other choice of a home did they have, the poor waifs? '—you should at least know it.'

Like Grant knew every nook and cranny of the house—he'd explored as a child as well.

He turned to Lillian. 'Would it suit you to come to

the hall after the children are dressed in dry clothes?' he asked stiffly.

Her face was as stone-like as the statues. 'If you wish it.'

He glanced back at the children and smiled. 'After they have had their milk and honey, of course.' They would want a warm drink after playing in the snow again. 'I will see that Thompson gives you all a proper tour of the house.'

Anna looked awestruck. 'The whole house?'

Why was this such a novelty? Had they not been allowed through their grandfather's house?

'Well, as much as Thompson has time to show you. It is a very big house.' Eighty rooms, in fact. Grant turned to William. 'Keep up the good work. You are sculpting a fine soldier.'

He nodded his farewell and made his way towards the house. At the door, he glimpsed the melting icicles hanging from the canopy. Perhaps in a day or two the road to the village would be passable again and he could send Lillian away.

A pang of guilt struck him. But what of the children? Could he tolerate Lillian a few days longer for their sakes?

It would be torment.

Lillian did not have to hurry Anna through her warm milk and honey and a change of clothes, and even William did not tarry. Was a tour of the house so inviting? Or was calling Grantwell House their *home* the attraction? It did warm her heart when Grant told them that.

Even when she wanted to rail at him for his mistrust of her, he'd do something like this—something so very kind, so very *like* him.

It felt much safer to be angry at him. To rediscover his kindness only reminded her of what she'd lost after he so abruptly ended their affair.

But what did it matter? When her husband miraculously reappeared, not dead at all, more like a resurrected Portuguese hero, she'd have lost Grant anyway.

But at least she would have known he loved her.

She had to admit she was curious to see the whole house. The rooms she'd glimpsed so far were incredibly beautiful—with the exception of the nursery wing, of course. Would the rest of the house reveal even more delights?

How lovely to have such a beautiful home. How lovely to have a home at all. When she'd been small, she and her mother and father had lived in a comfortable home—not nearly as grand as this, though. Then she'd been sent to school and her father died and by the time she returned to Portugal it had been to her stepfather's house, not her home. Even the houses she'd shared with her husband never felt like places she belonged, merely places she must live.

If she secured a position as a governess or a companion that was what it would be like—merely a place to live.

She would be lucky to have even that. And it would be much better than Dinis catching up to her and taking her back to Portugal to hang.

After the children had finished their milk and honey, they lost no time in dressing in clean, dry clothes and setting off for their tour of the house. Their excitement had them barrelling down the stairs.

'Do not run!' Lillian shouted.

They did not heed her. The children charged into the hall. Lillian followed them, and again was struck by the beauty of the room that had so amazed and impressed her on that first day—a mere two days ago? It seemed impossible.

She had become so attached to these children in two short days. They were kindred spirits. They, like she, had no one else.

Except Grant. They did have Grant—who would at least provide a home for them. And would be kind.

The children halted in front of the huge pastoral painting that filled one whole wall of the hall. They tilted their little heads back, transfixed by the bucolic scene of cows and goats and a dog.

Grant appeared. 'There you are! Ready for your tour?'

Lillian's heart pounded at his unexpected entrance. 'Yes,' she managed. 'We are waiting for Thompson.'

The smile he had for the children turned stiff when he looked at her. 'Thompson will not be coming. He has *many things to do*, to quote him. And, because I am entirely at liberty, I shall be your guide.'

'Do not worry, Lord Grantwell,' Anna assured him. 'We will not complain if you show us your house.'

Grant looked down at the little girl. 'It is your house now, too, Anna. Yours and William's.'

The children gaped at him. There it was again. Grant being kind, recognising that the children longed for a home, for a place to belong and someone to belong to. Surely he would not turn on them as he had on her and make this home and the people in it merely something more for them to lose.

No. She was the only person he wished to banish.

Anna reached for his hand and his long, strong fingers curled around hers. William held back a little.

For Lillian, any pleasure at viewing the house had disappeared. She could not help but remember what it once felt like to be near him, to have those fingers curl around *her* hand. And she could not forget how he so quickly changed when he decided she was a thief and a traitor. And how now, if it were not for the snow, he would turn her away, penniless, to a fate that most likely meant death.

Grant led them to the anteroom, with its lovely staircase and gold balustrades that echoed the design in the hall.

He pointed to two large portraits that hung on the wall as they ascended the staircase. 'The lady is my great-grandmother and the model for your snow woman, Anna.' She giggled and nodded energetically.

He pointed to the other portrait. 'And that is my great-grandfather, who willed my grandfather a fortune with the stipulation that he rebuild the house and make it into a showcase.'

He turned back to his audience and went on to describe how his grandfather had travelled throughout the Continent, learning about architecture and paintings and statues—and spent lavishly.

Grant seemed proud of his heritage, of the grandfather who'd created this amazing house. She and the children might now belong to no one and nothing, but Grant's place in this house had been secured for generations.

He took them into the library next. 'This time you will get a proper look.' He gave both William and Anna a wink. 'Not a mere peek from the servants' door.'

Lillian did not know what that meant, but she, too, might get a proper look at the room. Her first sight of it had been blurred by her desperation and Grant's rejection. The dim light of the night before had made the room seem intimate, especially when Grant had stood close to her. And when she flew into his arms.

A scan of the bookshelves in the light of day revealed an impressive and valuable library of beautiful leather-bound and gold-embossed volumes. Atlases, the works of Shakespeare, books on classical architecture, biographies of famous names and names that once might have been famous.

Grant had known the library well enough to find her a book on Scotland with little hesitation, but instead of pointing out to the children all the priceless books upon the shelves, Grant showed them small items. An inkwell made from a horse's hoof, a much-beloved horse that had once belonged to his great-grandfather. An automaton clock with a bird in a cage that twirled and chirped on the hour. A small wooden carving of a dog.

Anna's interest was obvious. William held back, but when Grant put down the dog carving to go on to the next thing, William picked it up and examined it more closely.

Grant turned and noticed. 'That is a very small sculpture, made from wood, not stone. Or snow. Do you like it?'

William put it down, as if he'd been scolded for touching it.

'Well!' Grant said, with a tone of grand fanfare. 'Would you like to see the stone people?'

He stepped into the sculpture gallery—the site of their momentary embrace. This time the room's windows filled the space with light, dispelling the eerie shadows of the night before. Even so, the space still felt like the sanctuary of a church. Even the children approached the room with reverence.

Each of the full statues had an alcove to itself, like a reduced apse. Marble busts were displayed on pedestals between the alcoves.

Anna stopped in front of a statue of a Roman youth whose private parts were at her eye level, then walked over to gaze up at a naked statue of Venus. 'Where are their clothes?'

Grant hesitated a moment. 'Perhaps Miss Pearson can explain.'

Was he being mean-spirited, putting her on the spot like this, or was it his idea of fun? Lillian could not tell.

But she repeated what her headmistress had said when she and a group of fellow tittering schoolgirls viewed an exhibition of Roman statues at a country house near Reading.

'The Greeks and the Romans thought the human body was beautiful to behold, so modesty was not important to them.'

She glanced at the statue of Hercules, but was only reminded of Grant, magnificent in his nakedness, muscles firm and rippling, his male parts...a thrill. If Hercules was meant to depict perfection, the Romans had never seen the likes of Grant seven years ago.

She glanced over at him and imagined that his masculine beauty had not faded.

He caught her staring at him and his smile fled until he turned back to the children.

'I will tell you the statues' names,' he said.

'They have names?' Anna responded.

'Most of them do.'

He named Hercules and Venus, Galatea and Athena, and others, and explained to Anna who the Romans were and how they believed in many gods, not just one. He told them there were books in the library about the gods, if the children wished to learn more.

'I learned a little of it at school,' William said. The boy stood in front of one of the busts that Grant had not named. 'He is a soldier, is he not?'

Grant walked over to stand next to him. 'He is indeed. How did you know?'

'His helmet,' William answered. 'It is much like the helmet of a French carabinier.'

The helmet of the Roman soldier was engraved ornately, with a swooping top piece that must represent some sort of plume.

'Indeed.' Grant sounded genuinely impressed. 'It is very much like the helmet of a carabinier. I believe the French copied the helmet, like they copied the eagle symbols they carried into battle.'

'They copied the eagles from the Romans?' William asked.

'They did,' Grant replied.

'What is a cara—cara—carabinier?' Anna asked.

'A French horse soldier,' William told her, as if everyone should know such a thing.

'Where did you learn about carabiniers?' Grant asked.

'From a book at school. It showed pictures of the uniforms of all the armies,' William responded.

'We shall have to purchase such a book for our library, shall we not?' Grant said, a throwaway comment that made William gaze at him wide-eyed.

Grant again had spoken as if his home was the children's home. Did he realise what an impact that must have on the children? It certainly touched Lillian.

Grant directed Anna to the statue of Athena. 'Athena was a soldier of sorts. She was the Greek goddess of war and a daughter of Zeus, the most important god. She was a brave and fierce warrior.'

'A woman?' William asked sceptically.

'Well, a goddess.' Grant laughed.

They left the sculpture gallery and visited the other rooms on the ground floor. A magnificent drawing room, decorated with tapestries and an Axminster carpet that complemented the design on the ceiling. A formal dining room painted yellow, with more family portraits but without the ornate plasterwork of the other grand rooms. A smaller, less formal sitting room, and the study where Lillian had dined with Grant.

They walked up the stairs to the first floor, with the hallway leading to the nursery rooms, and other hallways leading to other bedchambers.

Grant took them first into the room used by Lady Grantwell. 'This was your mother's bedchamber.'

The children stopped just inside the doorway and did not venture further. Before them was the large, full-length portrait of their mother. Her expression was no more welcoming now than when Lillian had first seen it.

Anna pulled on her brother's sleeve. 'Is that our mother?'

How old had they been when their mother left them? If Anna did not remember her, Anna must have been little more than a baby.

'Did she look like that?' Anna asked.

William nodded.

Neither took their eyes off the portrait.

Anna's voice grew very quiet. 'She never liked us, did she, William?'

'No,' he answered, barely audible.

Lillian's heart was breaking for them. She shared a glance with Grant, and fancied he felt the pain as well.

He broke the sudden silence. 'Shall we look in my bedchamber next?' he asked. 'I can show you my army uniform.'

William nodded, and followed Grant obediently.

That night Lillian could not settle. She tried reading by lamplight, but the book about Scotland merely reminded her of being with Grant the night before. Though ready for bed in Lady Grantwell's luxuriously soft nightdress, she could not sleep.

She rose from the bed and donned a robe and stood at the window.

A light snow fell outside, like a fresh layer of icing on a cake. Perhaps enough snow would fall to keep her here a few more days? She could hope.

Would it have been better, though, if she had never come here? She'd seen how greatly affected the children had been by the portrait of their mother. She'd heard them speak of their governess and a few servants to whom they'd been attached. They'd lost them all. Would she merely be one more person for them to lose?

What other choice had she? Her brother-in-law was on her heels and she had no money left. She'd been desperate. She'd be even more desperate after Grant tossed her out. What was she to do?

She'd so believed Grant would help her. She'd believed his fundamental kindness would be extended towards her if he knew her plight. His empathy towards the children did not include empathy for her, though.

After the disastrous visit to their mother's room, Grant had tried to distract the children, especially William, by showing them his army uniform and mementos. The sight of his uniform, its gold epaulets, the red fabric of its jacket, had disturbed Lillian just as the portrait disturbed the children.

It brought back to her that first sight of him, with his officer's sash and tall black shako. She'd been distributing food to the poor in Lisbon. The French had been driven back by the Portuguese, but food was in short supply. She'd caught Grant watching her and boldly told him he'd be more useful if he helped her.

She remembered how her senses had sparked to life as he'd stood next to her, handing out bags of flour and boxes of potatoes and carrots. Her husband had never made the colours around her brighter, the sounds crisper, the scents more intoxicating as Grant had done merely by standing near her. And she thought her husband no longer mattered. He'd been killed by the French, she'd been told.

But before she could learn the name of this British soldier she'd been called away and feared she'd never see him again.

Until three days later when he was one of the officers attending a ball she'd been required to attend. Ignoring the disapproving clucks of her in-laws, she'd shown Grant how to dance the fandango. And then—

She turned away from the window. What use was it to think of those wonderful days with Grant? They could never return. And he was not about to lend her money or allow her to stay until her headmistress could find her a suitable position, a place for her to hide for ever and be safe from Dinis. In the meantime, she must not allow the children to become attached to her—as she was becoming attached to them—because, no matter what, she must leave them.

She walked back to the bed, kicked off the slippers she'd borrowed from Lady Grantwell and untied the ribbons of her robe. She should rest, even if sleep failed her.

'No!' came a distant cry, followed by a crash.

Anna's voice.

'Stop it! Stop it!'

Lillian dashed out of her room and ran to the children's room, farther down the hallway. She flung open the door.

William was pulling the linens off his bed. A candlestick lay on the floor, and a table and chair were turned over.

Anna was tugging at his nightshirt. 'Stop it, William!'

He turned and pushed her away. She fell against her bed.

Lillian grabbed William, who fought against her with swinging arms and legs.

'He had a bad dream,' Anna cried. 'He woke up and—'

William broke from Lillian's grasp and ran out through the door. Lillian lost her footing and almost fell on Anna, who bounced to her feet and tried to help Lillian up.

'What is wrong with him, miss?' Anna sobbed. 'What is *wrong* with him?'

'Are you hurt?' Lillian asked her.

Anna shook her head.

'Then I must go after him.' Lillian ran from the room.

Grant was at the bottom of the staircase when he heard the commotion. He took the stairs two at a time, just passing the first landing as William sped by and reached for the latch to his mother's bedchamber.

'William!' Grant bellowed, but his commanding voice had no effect.

By the time Grant reached the bedchamber, William had climbed atop some furniture and was tugging at the huge portrait of his mother.

'No, William!' Grant commanded.

He snatched the boy away and held him.

'I hate her! I hate her! I hate her!' William flailed wildly.

Grant managed to sit them both on the carpet and wrapped his arms around the boy. 'Shh… Shh, now,' he murmured. 'Calm yourself.'

Lillian and Anna appeared in the doorway. Grant shook his head in warning for them to stay back. Lillian lifted a distraught Anna into her arms.

'I hate her.' William's voice lowered into a sob. 'She left. She left and I dreamed it. She left. I dream it all the time.'

Grant turned the boy to face him and held him tightly against his chest. 'There, now. That was bad of her, was it not? Damned bad of her to leave you and Anna at your grandfather's. You needed her.'

The boy clung to him. 'She did not want us!'

Grant ran his fingers through the boy's hair. 'That may be. Or perhaps she planned to send for you. We will never know, because she and my brother died. But this you need to know now. You are home. This is your home.'

He let the boy cry until his young body relaxed and his breathing eased. Then Grant glanced at Lillian and saw tears streaming down her cheeks and down the cheeks of little Anna in her arms.

'What should we do with this portrait of her, eh, William?' Grant asked. 'I think we should take it down—what say you?'

William buried his face in Grants chest. 'I want to cut it with a knife!'

'No,' Grant answered calmly. 'We don't cut portraits with a knife, but I think it might be crated up and stored in a far corner of the attic. What do you say I have that done tomorrow? Then we won't ever have to see it again unless we want to.'

'I never want to see her again!' William cried.

'Very well. It will be done tomorrow.' Grant stood, still holding the boy in his arms. 'But now it is time for sleeping, is it not?'

Lillian, still in the doorway, spoke. 'I'll go ahead of you and make the bed.' She hurried away, carrying Anna.

William paid no attention to her or to his sister. He

gave a scathing glance at the portrait. 'I don't want to dream of her!'

'Then I shall teach you a trick so you won't dream of her,' Grant told him.

He carried William out of the room to the nursery wing. At the doorway to the children's bedchamber, he saw a room in shambles. Furniture upturned. Items scattered on the floor. Lillian had the boy's bed linens in her arms. Anna was seated on her own bed.

Anna patted the space next to her. 'William can sit with me until his bed is made.'

Grant put William down next to his sister, who immediately put her little arm around him. While Lillian made the bed Grant put the furniture back in order and picked up everything off the floor.

'Your bed is ready, William,' Lillian said.

The boy dutifully hopped off his sister's bed and climbed into his own. She covered him with the blankets, but he sat up again and leaned towards Grant. 'You said you would teach me a trick so I won't dream of her.'

Lillian moved away, so Grant could crouch next to the boy's bed. 'Well, first tell me what is your favourite thing? What do you like to think about?'

'Soldiers,' the boy said without hesitation. 'A boy at school had some fine toy soldiers. My grandfather had some, too, but they were very old and I was not to touch them.'

Was there nothing these children could remember that did not show them unloved?

'Well, here is the trick,' Grant told him. 'Make yourself think of those favourite things before you fall asleep. Think of them very hard and chances are you will dream of them and nothing else.'

William lay down again, and this time Grant tucked him in. 'I can do that,' the boy said.

Grant then turned to Anna, straightened her covers and brushed a hand through her hair. He watched Lillian lean down and kiss William on the forehead as he moved towards the door.

He waited for her out in the hallway, some distance from the children's room.

She closed the bedroom door quietly behind her and gazed over at him, her face filled with emotion, emotion that mirrored his own. Or mimicked his own.

The boy's angry desolation propelled Grant back to every instance his own parents brushed him aside while fussing over his brother. He shook inside with the memory. If there had been a portrait handy of his mother and father and brother, he might have felt that same impulse. To shred it with a knife. In fact, he was sorry he'd not allowed William to do that very thing.

Lillian walked towards him. 'Those poor children.'

She joined him against the wall, as if they both needed something to hold them up. 'I was a little older, but I remember how I yearned for my mother to send for me to come back home from school, to be with her after my father died. But she never did, not even for school holidays. Not until I was too old to stay at the school any more. How angry I was at her, but how desperately I wanted her to care about me.'

They'd never spoken of such matters in their brief passionate time together. He'd known that her mother, with her second husband, had joined the elite in fleeing to Brazil when the war came, but that was all.

Grant turned to gaze at her.

She faced him but did not meet his eyes. 'It is not the same as poor William, I know. I was older than he must have been when his mother left, and I had great stability at the school. It is what his pain made me think of, that is all.'

So she knew that pain as well. Of a mother who did not much care.

He noticed then that she was dressed in night clothes, a filmy nightdress and robe. Her hair was down, her curls caressing her shoulders and forming a lovely halo around her face. He wanted to hold her. Wanted her to hold him. Wanted to dispel the emotions aroused by a poor boy who'd suddenly been overcome by the pain of being unloved and abandoned.

He pulled her into his arms.

Chapter Six

H er body was soft and warm pressed against his, only the barrier of her night clothes between him and the skin he remembered being soft and smooth. He ached for her, and he ground against her in need.

She responded in kind, pulling his head down to hers, seeking his lips. Her kiss seemed as full of need as his, and his body flared with arousal. Somewhere deep within him he knew they were both merely reacting to what William's pain aroused in them, but his body did not care. He wanted her and it was clear she wanted him.

'Which room is yours?' His voice was suddenly thick.

She pointed to an open door, further down the hall-way. He lifted her into his arms and she wrapped her legs around his waist, her arms around his neck, as they continued to kiss on the way to her room.

He kicked the door closed behind him and carried her to the bed, shedding his shoes as he went. He placed her on the bed and her fingers immediately worked to un-button his jacket and waistcoat. He pulled them off and stepped away long enough to remove his pantaloons, stockings and drawers.

He pulled his shirt over his head and time slowed to

a crawl as she peeled off her robe, first one sleeve, then the other. Those same fingers that worked magic on his buttons grasped the soft fabric of her nightdress and, like revealing a hidden treasure, slowly lifted the garment over her head.

The crackle of the fire, the ticking of the clock, the sounds of their frenzied breathing—all seemed to cease as he gazed upon her naked beauty.

God, he had missed her. Missed this. No other woman had ever come near to her. Making love to her transported him to a better place. Made him a better man in a better world.

Over the years since her betrayal he'd convinced himself all that had been an illusion. Well, what did he care? At this moment he needed that illusion, like he needed food. Water. Air.

He climbed on the bed above her and her hands wrapped around him and caressed his bare skin. She arched her back and pressed him down to her. With an inward sigh of relief that he would finally be whole again, he entered her.

Lillian gasped at the force of his entry, but she wanted this joining with him so desperately that she met him eagerly. How had she ever felt complete without him? How had she ever survived without this?

Theirs was a frenzied, wild coupling, filled with a raw emotion she rarely allowed herself to feel. How acutely she'd missed him. How painful his rejection had been, but now, did it matter? Now he was back. Joined with her once more.

She felt the sensation build until thought escaped her and her release came with his in a shattering of pleasure both familiar and new.

He collapsed atop her and then slid to her side. They both were panting from the effort, even while her body felt like warm butter.

She turned to him, cupping her hand on his cheek. 'Grant,' she whispered. There were no words for how she felt at this moment.

She remembered how much she'd wished their love-making would have produced a child, a part of him she could keep with her for ever. It would have meant terrible scandal, a humiliation of the husband who so unexpectedly returned from the dead, a further ostracising from his family and friends. Still, she'd often lain awake, wishing it would have happened. Even as she'd lie grateful that she'd never borne her husband's child.

That had been another reason her husband and his family despised her. She'd never borne him children. She'd never yearned for her husband's child, but the wish for Grant's had been strong.

She could feel that yearning once more. If only. If only. If only his seed could grow inside her.

He stared back at her, his eyes searching her face. 'What is it?'

She tossed the thought away. 'Nothing.' *Everything.* 'I have missed this.'

Without speaking, he touched her again, swept his strong hands down her languid body. He rubbed his palm against her nipple and sensation built in her again. A divine torture as her body craved him once more.

'We could always do this, could we not?' he said, his voice rough but his tone unclear.

Did he feel the pleasure of being together again as she did? The rightness of their bodies joining as one? Did it feel to him, as it did to her, that the need to be loved was for once met, its bowl overflowing, in fact?

She touched him as well, and felt his member harden. Need grew in them both, but this time their lovemaking was intense in a different way, more intent, more focussed.

She moaned with the pleasure of each stroke inside her and tried to move in such a way to give him as much pleasure as she received from him. She would not care if it took days to reach the apex this time; the journey together was exquisite.

Do not let it stop! she cried to herself. All at once she feared something terrible would be on the other side. Separating them. Separating would be terrible. How odd that the pleasure of joining peaked right before its loss. Of course they would become separate again.

She tried to prolong this togetherness, but her body defied her, as did his. His strokes came faster, harder and her body happily matched his pace until, again, they reached the release together, that explosion of joy. Again it led to their bodies parting.

This loss would be tolerable, she thought, as long as he lay next to her and she could touch him, as long as she was no longer alone.

But his gaze changed from sated with pleasure to something akin to panic, then to a steely hardness. He moved away and left the bed. 'This was a mistake,' he said. He donned his shirt and drawers and gathered the rest of his clothing in his arms. 'My fault. My weakness.' He cast a quick glimpse at her. 'Nothing is changed. This never happened.'

She sat up in bed, the linens clasped around her naked body, wanting to protest.

He fled through the door and was gone.

Good God, what was he about? Grant strode down the hallway, his bare feet cold on the wood floor. He emerged from the nursery wing and hurried to his bedchamber. At least the scarcity of servants meant there was no one to encounter him in his state of undress.

No one to know where he'd been. What he'd done.

He wished he could lay the blame on Lillian. Tell himself she'd enticed him. Played on that carnal attraction that they'd so obviously experienced in Portugal. But he knew that was not true. She was dressed as she was because it was night-time and she'd run to the children heedless of the clothes she wore. She'd not known she would encounter him. She'd not planned to seduce him into her bed.

No. No. It was his fault. *His* fault. It was he who'd taken advantage of her. She'd revealed that pain he knew so well. That pain of being unimportant. Unloved. He felt it, too, all over again. The desolation of realising that he—and William—and Anna—and Lillian—mattered to no one. No, Grant had been desperate in that moment for the illusion he and Lillian so effectively created in Portugal. That what they shared in bed was love.

She might have been manipulating him in Portugal, but one thing he was now assured of. Her passion for lovemaking was real, and this night it was he who'd exploited it. Exploited *her*. She who had shelter and food and safety merely at his pleasure.

Grant entered his bedchamber and threw his clothes into a heap on the floor. He opened the cabinet where he'd asked Thompson to place a decanter of brandy and make certain it was full each night. Grant poured himself a glass and flung himself into a nearby chair. He downed the glass in one gulp and poured another.

It was bad of him. Bad of him to bed Lillian. To allow his emotions to so drive his behaviour. He prided himself on hiding those dark feelings deep within him, leaving only his good humour and his sense of fun and absurdity to have free rein. It was the world that was out of control, not him. He was free merely to observe it. Make fun of it. Keep pain at bay.

He downed his brandy and poured a third.

The room was lit only by the glow of the fireplace and one candle. In its shadows he fancied he could see his father's and brother's spirits, regarding him with disapproving eyes.

Grant laughed aloud. Now, that was absurd! Since when had his father or brother cared enough about him to even notice? If they bothered to think of him at all, they would probably be annoyed at his good humour. His father would accuse him of being flippant. Say he'd never amount to anything so he might as well have a commission in the army. When they were very young, his brother had used to enjoy making him cry. Once Grant had figured that out, he'd tormented his brother by being happy.

In any event those two would never have considered the bedding of a woman, willing or otherwise, to be much of an issue. His mother might have fretted about possible damage to the family's reputation, but only because it might affect his brother.

Grant took another sip of brandy and placed the glass on the table beside him. He rose to pace the room, still clad only in his shirt and drawers. What was he to do now? Apologise to her? Certainly. Assure her it would never happen again? As long as she remained here, could he even promise that? How did he know he would not again experience another moment of weakness and again carry her to bed?

He must simply try to stay away.

* * *

His plan to stay away lasted until morning.

Grant was seated at his breakfast table when Thompson announced Lillian. He girded himself. Surely she would confront him about the night before.

Thompson left the room and Lillian entered.

Grant stood.

'Forgive me for interrupting your breakfast, Grant.' Her voice was stiff.

He gestured to a chair. 'You may join me if you wish.'

She shook her head. 'I've eaten with the children.'

He raised his brows and waited. Like waiting for a punch in the stomach.

'It is two days to Christmas—'

What had *that* to do with anything?

'I came to ask you two things.'

To ask him things? Not accuse him of misusing her?

'Go ahead.' He crossed his arms over his chest.

'First I ask that you allow me to stay until after Christmas. For the children's sake. I want them to have a little holiday celebration. To distract them. To give them something enjoyable to think about.'

After taking such advantage of her the night before, he could not precisely throw her out into the snow now, could he? Even though her staying brought more temptation... He'd keep his distance, he vowed.

'You may stay until after Christmas.' He almost added *for the children's sake*, because his anger at her rekindled.

Why did she not speak of last night? Did it mean so little to her? The pain of Portugal came back to him, of when she'd used him.

'What is the second request?' he asked, his voice stiff.

She took a breath as if steadying herself. 'I wish to ask if there is any worker who might be spared today who could take the children and me to some woods to cut evergreens to decorate the nursery for Christmas.'

Decorate. With evergreens.

A memory of climbing trees and cutting branches flew into his mind. The brisk winter air stinging his face. The thrill of being so high. The sharp scent of pine and the softer scent of fir. How long had it been since he'd cut evergreens for Christmas? Before the war, certainly.

He could not even remember last Christmas. He'd stayed in London, he recalled, straightening out his brother's tangled financial affairs. He could not recall Christmas Day.

He could recall a Christmas day in Portugal. It had been just before he'd first glimpsed Lillian…

Who now stood before him, waiting for an answer.

He uncrossed his arms. 'Of course.'

'How might I arrange it?' she asked.

He'd not thought this through. Could he spare anyone? Was the sleigh even ready? Would it make it through the snow to the woods?

'I will arrange it,' he said, brushing away all the ways he could not. 'I'll have word sent to you about what time to be ready.'

'Thank you, Grant,' she said simply.

Their gazes held for a moment, a moment that should have been filled with the confrontation he'd expected from her. But she merely nodded, turned and walked out through the door.

Grant collapsed in his chair. What did it mean that she'd said nothing?

Lillian's heart pounded as she left Grant to his breakfast. She could not decide if she was glad or gravely affronted that he had failed to say a word about the night before.

But then neither had she.

She reached the staircase and leaned against the banister. It was not only her heart that reacted to his presence. Her whole body throbbed with the memory. Of his touch. Of the exquisite pleasure he'd created.

All this and she was still reeling with the tumult of emotions created by William's fervid outburst. It had been that brief moment of vulnerability in Grant and in herself that had sparked the passion, so unabated, so unaffected by the harsh words and actions between them.

How good it might feel to tell herself he'd forced himself on her, that she'd had no choice, but the truth was she'd wanted him every bit as intensely as he'd wanted her. To make love with him again had been so glorious, so settling—as if she'd mattered to someone at last.

It was a mistake, he'd said. He considered her a *mistake*? Certainly that was what it was. A mistake to succumb to those carnal urges between them.

Before she'd finally fallen asleep last night she'd resolved to avoid him completely.

Her resolve had been fleeting, had it not? In the morning she'd steered the children away from the tumult of the night before and distracted them with Christmas plans. They'd promptly asked to cut evergreens with which to decorate.

It should have posed no problem. She'd simply ask Thompson to help her arrange such a thing, but Thompson deferred to Grant. Lillian had had no other choice than to seek out the one person she needed most to avoid.

Luckily there had been enough distance between them that the wanton lure of him could be managed—almost. From him, though, there was no indication he'd even given it a thought. Had it meant so little to him? A mere mistake? Made and then forgotten?

She hoped she had not shown any signs of how affected she she'd been. Let him think it was of no consequence to her as well.

She returned to the children, who were busy making Christmas gifts.

The day before Lillian and Anna had created more pretty packages of cloth, lace and ribbons, for Hannah, Cook, the two kitchenmaids and the two housemaids they'd barely glimpsed. Then Anna had begged Lillian to teach her how to make a handkerchief, so she could make one for Lord Grantwell. They'd cut a piece of white cotton cloth and Lillian showed Anna how to sew a hem around it. Perhaps, if there was time, she'd teach her some simple embroidery to decorate it with. William had worked the whole day on a box for Thompson and it had turned out rather fine.

Lillian entered the nursery to find Anna carefully pushing a needle and thread in and out of the cloth. The girl looked up at her entrance. 'William is using knives, Miss Pearson.'

Lillian glanced over at William who was, indeed, scraping at a tall block of wood with a small knife.

'I am making something,' William immediately retorted.

His tone had been sharp with both her and Anna this morning. After his traumatic night, Lillian was loath to scold him for it.

'I know how,' he insisted. 'Rogers taught me to carve wood, too.'

Oh, yes. William's grandfather's footman—perhaps the closest thing William had had to a father-like person. Of course Rogers was another person he'd lost from his life…

'Did he?' Lillian responded.

'I'll show you.' William jumped off his chair and ran out of the room. He returned a minute later and thrust his open palm out to Lillian.

In it was a little figure of a dog, clumsily carved out of wood, but unmistakable in its shape and charm. Now she understood his interest in the carved dog in Grant's library.

'William!' Lillian exclaimed. 'You made this?'

'Yes,' Anna piped up. 'But Rogers was there to help him.'

'I learned how to use the tools. I don't need Rogers now,' William snapped.

Lillian took it in her hands and examined it closely. 'This is very well done, William! And it is the first you'd ever done?'

The boy seemed to swell with some pride. 'Yes, Miss Pearson.'

She handed it back to him. 'Well, be careful with the knives,' she said. 'It would not do for you to cut yourself.'

'I won't,' William declared.

Anna piped up again. 'Will we be able to cut down evergreens?'

Lillian nodded. 'Lord Grantwell said he will arrange it. He will send word to us, so we must be prepared to get ready quickly.'

'We will!' Anna grinned.

Grant checked at the stable only to find the men busy with the care of the livestock and horses, as well as continuing to make the roads as passable as possible so that necessary supplies—food and fuel—could be transported to the families on the estate.

He trudged over to Rhys's office and was lucky enough to find his friend in.

Rhys greeted him warmly. 'Come in, Grant. I've just made tea. Have a cup with me.'

'Gladly.' He'd only been outside for a few minutes but was chilled enough to welcome a hot beverage.

After taking the tea and asking about Rhys's family— his wife, who was pregnant with their second child, and their son, now a year old, Grant got to the point. 'Can you spare another man or two? The children want evergreens to decorate with, so I need someone to take the sleigh to the woods and cut some.'

Rhys knew all about the children. He knew nothing about Lillian being there and very little about Grant's affair with her. It had happened before Rhys arrived in Portugal. Rhys knew only that Grant had experienced a disastrous love affair. That was all. Grant felt it a testament to their friendship that Rhys had never pried nor asked for details.

Rhys frowned. 'You'd need Dawson, as well.' Dawson was Grant's woodsman, in charge of tending to the wooded areas of his estate. 'I assume he could come, but he's too old to be climbing trees. I've sent everyone else to other tasks.' He shrugged and smiled. 'I suppose I could be spared. You and I could do the task, could we not?'

Grant almost laughed at the paradox. He and Rhys were the last two people he wanted on this expedition. He, because he needed to stay away from Lillian. Rhys, because he wanted to avoid explaining her to his friend. So naturally they were the only ones at liberty to undertake it.

Grant shook his head with a rueful smile. 'There is more to it.' He wished he did not have to explain.

Rhys's brows rose in interest.

'I have a house guest—an unwanted one—who came to the door when the snowstorm was at its worst. She has been stranded here and has taken on the care of the children until she can leave. Apparently she has promised the children they can come along to gather the evergreens, so the expedition will include her and the children.'

'Not a problem.' Rhys continued to gaze at him expectantly.

Grant rose from his chair and paced the room for a moment. He kept his head turned away from Rhys. 'I believe you know I had a brief affair in Portugal.' he began.

Rhys responded in an ironic tone. 'I believe you told me a little about it. A very little.'

Grant forced himself to keep a smile on his face. Better to focus on the absurdity of his situation rather than the more disturbing emotions Lillian aroused in him.

'Well, perhaps I did not tell you that the affair ended because she stole some papers I carried and they almost found their way into French hands. By sheer luck the courier was intercepted.' He continued to pace. 'In any event, you can imagine how I wished never to see this woman again.'

'Indeed.' Rhys's tone was unchanged.

'It was she who appeared at my door in the storm.' He made himself laugh.

Rhys's expression was puzzled. 'She is the house guest? What is she doing in England?'

Grant blew out an exasperated breath. 'That is a whole other story.' And one he was not sure he wanted to share. Why? Was he loath to have Rhys think her a murderer?

Rhys waited for him to continue, and when he didn't his friend asked, 'Why come to you?'

'Why, indeed?' Grant responded. 'She claims to be desperate.'

Rhys shook his head. 'This is not making sense. She came all this way to ask you, of all people, for help? It is not as though your estate is on the beaten path.'

Grant drew a breath. When he released it, he told Rhys the whole story. How her husband had been murdered and she was accused of it. How she was being pursued by her brother-in-law who wanted to return her to Portugal to hang. How she planned to flee to Scotland, become a governess and hide for ever.

'She arrived at the perfect time,' Grant concluded. 'I could not send her away in the storm, and she agreed to help with the children who've been running Hannah in circles. The children have taken to her—which I am certain she intended—so I'll let her stay through Christmas, at least. God knows we need the help until the rest of the servants return. And the children have had enough upheaval...' He glanced at Rhys and made himself smile again. 'So once again I have stumbled into a bramble bush and need to get myself untangled.'

Rhys nodded. 'I look forward to meeting this villainous lady.'

'Oh, she protests being a villain, I assure you.' Was he defending her?

'But you do not believe her?' Rhys asked.

Grant frowned. 'I do not believe she killed her husband.' He could not believe he had been that poor a judge of her character. 'But at the time the papers were stolen she and I were the only ones present.'

He went through it again in his mind. He'd lain in the bed, sated and content, and she'd excused herself, walking just out of his sight to where their clothes had been discarded on the floor. That had to be when she'd stolen the papers.

Rhys's brows knitted. 'I confess, this makes little sense. It makes more sense she would avoid you. Do you believe she is desperate, as she says?'

Grant shrugged. 'She does seem to be completely without funds, I will admit.' And she had been very hungry that first day.

'I am even more intrigued.' Rhys put down his teacup and stood. 'I'll attend to the sleigh and stop at Dawson's cottage. See if he can meet us with a wagon. There is a small one on runners. If he cannot, I'll send word, but I can probably have everything ready in an hour. Would that do?'

Best to get it over with. 'That will do nicely.'

Chapter Seven

When word came to the nursery that they should be in the hall in a half-hour, to meet the sleigh, the children did not tarry. Boots, coat, hats, scarves and gloves were donned with the greatest speed and the children had to wait for Lillian, who was last to be ready.

They clamoured down the stairway ahead of her and ran into the hall. Lillian entered, expecting to see Thompson or a stableman. Or anyone except… Grant.

He greeted the children with smiles. 'Are you all set? Prepare yourselves, because gathering evergreens for Christmas decoration means a great deal of work.'

'We are ready!' Anna cried, bouncing with delight.

Lillian felt William's excitement, too, though the boy remained quiet and still. She also noted that Grant only glanced at her once and glanced away.

From outside they heard the soft plodding of horses' hooves on the packed snow of the driveway in front of the house and the jingle of bells on the horse's harnesses.

Grant opened the door. 'Let us go!'

The children ran outside and Lillian followed, very aware of sweeping by Grant, who held open the door. Waiting for them were two horses harnessed to a sleigh, its black leather seats piled with blankets and a winged design on its side painted in bright yellow. It had a large front seat and a smaller rear seat. A man whose coat was too fine to be a stableman stood at the horses' heads, holding them.

'William... Anna,' Grant said. 'This is Mr Landon, my estate manager. He will take us to the woods.'

Mr Landon greeted the children with a grin. 'Are you ready?'

'We are ready!' cried Anna.

Grant moved closer to his friend. 'You may drive the horses. William and I will sit in the back to give the sleigh ballast.'

Grant lifted the children into the sleigh before turning to Lillian and then back to his friend. 'Rhys, may I present Miss Pearson?' It was as if she was a mere afterthought. 'Our house guest.' He glanced briefly at Lillian. 'Mr Rhys Landon.'

It seemed to Lillian that Mr Landon regarded her with special interest. Had Grant spoken of her?

'Miss Pearson,' he said, tipping his hat.

As she nodded a greeting, Grant came near and put his hands at her waist to help her into the sleigh. Though he was gloved, and she wore several layers of clothing, his touch sent sparks through her body. She busied herself wrapping Anna and herself in blankets while he climbed in after her. She peered back to see him tuck a blanket around William and place another one over his lap. Mr Landon climbed into the driver's seat, next to Lillian and Anna, took hold of the reins and they were off, gliding over the packed snow.

'Look at me!' Anna wriggled in her seat between Mr Landon and Lillian. 'I am at the front!'

From behind her, Grant spoke to William. 'If you like, you may sit in the front seat on the way back.'

'I do not need to,' William replied in his serious tone. 'I will help you with the ballast.'

As they left the tree-lined drive that led to the house, a snow-dusted landscape of fields and hills emerged like the unwrapping of a gift.

'Oh, my!' exclaimed Lillian at the sight. Stone fences crisscrossed the fields, dotted with copses of trees and bushes here and there. A flock of sheep ran across one field. 'How lovely it is!'

'Like a fairyland!' Anna cried.

Lillian hugged her. 'Exactly like a fairyland!'

Grant's voice came from behind her. 'Rhys, the sheep are out.'

Mr Landon turned his head. 'Simmons said they needed exercise and air. He will call them in before too long.'

Did Grant not see the beauty of his land? Lillian wondered.

Mr Landon turned the sleigh onto the road. Apparently some vehicles were getting through because the snow was more packed, making the road clearly evident. Would Grant notice this as well? Would he send her away straight after Christmas? Had the night before ensured that he'd send her away as soon as possible? Even after their impassioned night? Or because of their impassioned night?

She trembled. If the roads were improving, did it mean Dinis was closing in on her?

With Grant, with the children, she could almost forget the danger that stalked her. She could almost feel she belonged with them, instead of being a stranded traveller her host was eager to be rid of.

Although he had wanted her in bed the night before. As she'd wanted him.

But he'd said it was a *mistake*.

As they glided on the icy surface Lillian heard Grant talking to William, pointing out various things along the way. His kindness towards the boy melted her heart just when she wished she could coat it with ice. This was the Grant she'd shared passionate days and nights with in Portugal, not the Grant who had turned against her and refused to believe she would never steal papers for the French. She'd die first.

'Have you not been to Yorkshire before, Miss Pearson?' Mr Landon's voice broke through her reverie.

'Never. I grew up mostly in Berkshire. In Reading. We were rarely in the country, though,' she responded.

'In Reading?' He sounded surprised. There was a distinct pause before he spoke again. 'I would guess Yorkshire has a more untamed sort of beauty than Berkshire.' He smiled then.

Mr Landon was a handsome man, Lillian observed. Especially when he smiled. But somehow his smile did not make her heart sing like Grant's smile had always done. She sensed an ease between the two men that did not seem like employer and employee. Perhaps they had grown up together.

'Are you from Yorkshire, then, Mr Landon?' she asked.

'Not at all. My wife and I hail from Cheshire,' he responded. 'I came when Grant asked me to manage his estate.'

Grant? Not Lord Grantwell? She must be right about their relationship being more than employer and employee, but how if they did not grow up together?

Anna, seated between them and wrapped in a blanket, fidgeted. 'How long before we get there?'

Mr Landon grinned down at the little girl. 'Oh, we have a way to go yet. We want to get to the best woods, do we not?'

'Yes!' Anna answered with enthusiasm. 'The *best* woods.'

More than a quarter of an hour later they pulled up to a thick wooded area where a man as grizzled and weather-beaten as only an old farm worker could be awaited them. He stood next to what looked like a wagon on runners. A big farm horse grazed in a pasture nearby, where patches of grass poked through the snow which had been blown into drifts here and there.

'M'lord.' The man, dressed every bit as warmly as the rest of them but in humbler clothes, tipped his hat to Grant.

Grant jumped out of the sleigh and shook the man's hand. 'How do you do, Dawson?'

'Getting by, m'lord,' he replied.

'Family well?' Grant asked.

'Very well, thank you, m'lord.'

William jumped out of the sleigh as Grant had done. Mr Landon also climbed down, reaching back to lift an eager Anna.

Lillian was last. She rose to climb down herself, but Grant appeared in front of her. He grasped her by the waist again to assist her from the sleigh and excitement flared through her once more. A glance passed between them before he released her.

The heightened sensation of the brief encounter lingered.

Grant turned to the man with the wagon and then

back to the others. 'William, Anna, Miss Pearson, this is Dawson, my woodsman.'

Mr Landon unharnessed the horses and led them to the pasture. He, Grant and Dawson pulled saws, clippers and a hatchet out of the wagon.

Dawson led them into the woods. 'I've scouted some trees and branches that might be cut.'

The ground, canopied by the thick trees, had not enough snow on it to make walking difficult, but it still frosted the earth and the branches. The wind blew down gentle flakes, which only added to Anna's description of a fairyland.

Grant took William in hand, showing him how to saw off low branches of pine and fir. Mr Landon let Anna help him cut strings of ivy and sprigs of holly. Dawson showed them what they could and could not cut down. It was a woodsman's job to keep the wooded areas of the estate healthy enough to produce the wood that supplied the estate's needs. Lillian stacked the greenery, ready to be carried back to the wagon. She had plenty of time to watch the others.

Mr Landon was patient with Anna, keeping her eagerness to help within safe boundaries. And Dawson, who'd scouted the area ahead of time, made the tasks so efficient they would not be out in the cold for too long. It was Grant, though, whose manner most warmed Lillian's heart. He was so good with William, letting him do most of the cutting, and praising his efforts. William did not display much of a reaction—the boy rarely said a word and his expression remained bland—but Lillian could feel him soaking up this manly attention like a dry sponge might soak up a puddle of water. What a good man Grant was.

Good to all but her.

* * *

Grant glanced at William, so intently focussed on the branch of spruce he was sawing off. Something in the boy pulled at him, as if he were watching himself at that age, so eager to do a man's work, so hungry for a man to tell him it was a job well done. The boy was so morose, though. Grant wished he could tell William he'd make it through so much easier if he pretended to be happy.

The branch broke free and William turned to look at Grant.

'Well done!' Grant told him. 'That one is filled with green needles. It will do very nicely.'

From a little way ahead, Dawson called, 'Found something, m'lord!'

Grant clapped William on the shoulder. 'Should we go see?'

Lillian stepped forwards. 'I'll take your cuttings.'

William handed them to her and she carried them away. Grant was trying not to pay attention to her, but, in truth, he was aware of wherever she stood, whatever she said. Her complexion looked exceptionally brightened by the cold air and physical activity. He imagined her lips, if kissed, would feel cold to the touch.

But he must not think of such things.

'Come, William,' he said.

The two strode towards Dawson. Anna and Rhys were already there.

Dawson stood next to a fallen tree. 'Looks like it came down a while ago. Are you wanting a yule log? We could cut a fine yule log from this one.'

Grant turned to the children. 'What do you say, Anna and William? Do we want a yule log?'

'Yes!' cried Anna brightly. She hesitated a moment before adding, 'What *is* a yule log?'

He walked over to her and picked her up. 'A yule log is a big log that we burn in the fireplace on Christmas Eve, and then we save a coal from it to use lighting next year's yule log. Do you want us to have one?'

Anna's eyes grew huge and her expression sobered. 'Will William and I be here for next year's yule log?'

That pierced his heart. 'Of course you will,' he responded, his voice raspy with emotion. 'This is your home now.'

He glanced over at Lillian, needing to share this emotion with the one person who would understand.

He saw it in her eyes.

By the time they finished, the wagon was loaded with fragrant greenery and a huge yule log. Lillian was cold, weary, and her muscles ached from carrying bundles of cuttings and branches, but on the whole the outing had been a lovely adventure. Little Anna, though, was completely fagged, and had to be carried back to the wagon in Grant's arms.

Every moment of the outing increased Lillian's admiration of Grant. The respectful way he treated his employees. His own willingness to do the work. His patience and attention towards William. And now his tender kindness to Anna.

Not towards her, though. Besides helping her in and out of the sleigh, he acted as if she were not even present. What clearer indication could there be that he wanted her gone? That their lovemaking had only been to slake his desire, as he might with any woman as willing as she had been?

Mr Landon climbed into the driver's seat and took the ribbons. 'One more stop,' he said cheerfully.

She wanted to protest that they'd gathered enough to

decorate the whole house, let alone the nursery, and that
the children were cold and tired, but they seemed to be
heading back the way they'd come, so she said nothing.

. Dawson in the wagon led them to another part of the
estate. The house was in view, but still some distance
away, and they stopped near a row of trees that lined both
sides of the path on which they were travelling. These
trees, however, were bare of leaves.

Dawson pointed upwards at one tree. 'There, m'lord.'

High in the otherwise bare tree were three balls of
green. 'What is it?' she asked.

'Mistletoe.' Landon climbed off the sleigh.

'What is mistletoe?' asked Anna.

Another old custom of Christmas time.

Before Lillian could answer, William spoke. 'You
hang it above a doorway, and whoever stands under it
must be kissed.'

Anna laughed.

Dawson, Grant and Mr Landon all stood under the
tree, necks craned to look up at the mistletoe tree, their
arms akimbo.

Mr Landon shook his head. 'Those branches will not
hold one of us.'

Grant turned to William. 'William, are you game for
climbing this tree?'

William scrambled out of the sleigh.

'Is William going to climb the tree?' Anna asked Lillian in a worried voice.

'I expect so,' Lillian responded, although she wanted
to scold them all for even thinking of such a perilous
thing. The tree might be slippery. A branch might break
under his feet.

They armed William with a knife and Grant hoisted

him up to the lowest branch. The men shouted instructions to him as he climbed higher. And higher.

'You are doing well,' Grant called to him.

'Has William done much tree climbing?' Lillian asked Anna, trying to sound unconcerned.

'Oh, yes,' Anna replied a little too cheerfully. 'Some...' she added, her voice dipping.

William must have been almost twenty feet off the ground when he reached the mistletoe. He had to balance himself on the branch with his legs while cutting away the clump of greenery.

'Just let it fall to the ground,' Grant told him.

Dawson caught it and William started back down.

Halfway, his foot slipped, and Grant immediately moved to stand right underneath him. Lillian held her breath until William reached the lowest branch.

'Just let go,' Grant said. 'I'll catch you.'

William hesitated only a moment before dropping into Grant's arms. His face beamed when the men each patted him on the back and regaled him with cries of, 'Well done!'

Lillian's heart finally slowed to a normal beat and she could breathe again.

When William sat in his seat next to Grant, in the back of the sleigh, she turned around to him. 'That was very brave, William.'

'Was a trifle,' he mumbled, but he blossomed under the praise.

When they arrived at the house Dawson drove the wagon to the back, but Mr Landon stopped the sleigh at the front door.

Grant jumped down. 'We'll let you off here, but Rhys and I will be helping Dawson unload the greenery.'

'May I help, too?' asked William.

Grant gave him an approving nod. 'You certainly may.'

Lillian turned to Anna. 'Do you wish to help?'

The little girl, who'd said hardly a word on the drive back, shook her head. She looked dead on her feet.

'Then we'll see you up in the nursery, William, for some dry clothes and a warm drink.'

'Milk and honey?' managed Anna.

Grant smiled at her. 'I'll tell Cook.'

'Good day, Mr Landon,' Lillian said as she and Anna started for the door.

He tipped his hat, again looking at her with an indecipherable expression. 'Good day, Miss Pearson.'

After the activity of the day, the children spent a very quiet afternoon. Anna sat on Lillian's lap, turning the pages of *The History of Little Goody Two-Shoes* and gazing at its woodcuts. Lillian had already read the book to her twice. William returned to his whittling. And Lillian, weary herself, savoured the rare repose. She felt calm and peaceful and safe—for the moment.

Anna closed the book and climbed off Lillian. She sat across from William, her elbows on the table and her chin resting on her hands. 'What are you making?' she asked.

Lillian had wondered the same thing. Whatever it was, it was not a dog—unless a dog stood tall and thin like a post.

'A soldier,' replied William. 'An infantryman.' He carefully surveyed his work and found a spot that needed some more whittling. 'Lord Grantwell and Mr Landon were officers in the infantry,' he told his sister. 'Did you know that?'

Was that how the two men knew each other? Lillian wondered.

'What is the infantry?' Anna asked.

'Foot soldiers,' William explained. 'Lord Grantwell and Mr Landon were captains. They fought in Spain and at Waterloo.'

Spain? Had Mr Landon known Grant in Portugal as well? It would explain his curious looks if he knew about her. How much did he know? He seemed too cordial to believe her to be a spy for the French—as Grant believed. Or to think she was being pursued for murder.

Where was her brother-in-law? she suddenly thought. Could he trace her here? She hoped Dinis would never believe she'd seek help from a man who so despised her, but if Dinis managed to reach the village and heard Grant's name, what would he conclude?

That she had gone to Grant for help.

Her heart pounded in anxiety. She'd been foolish to come here. But she'd felt so alone and frightened, and the next coach leaving from the inn where she'd stopped had been travelling through this village. She'd impulsively disembarked there. She should have gone on. But how could she have when she had no money?

She didn't know she'd be snowed in, or that Grant would feel forced to help her. She didn't know she would find two children to love and witness Grant at his kindest—towards them.

Not her.

Anna hopped off the chair and took her book to a corner of the room where she'd placed the cloth doll Lillian had fashioned for her out of leftover fabric scraps. It was no more than rolled-up fabric in the shape of a doll, but the little girl had immediately taken the rags under her care.

These poor children. If she had any money and could have reached a toy shop she most certainly would have purchased a proper doll for Anna. And a proper set of toy soldiers for William. Here these children willingly busied themselves making gifts for the servants, but there would be no gifts for them.

She stood. 'I am going to leave you alone for a little bit,' she told the children. 'You are playing so well. I'll return in a moment.'

The children barely looked up.

Lillian made her way to the attic. With more fabric, she could at least make a better rag doll for Anna. Perhaps she would discover something she could also make for William.

The attic door was open and sounds came from within. She stood in the doorway.

Grant and Thompson were moving something into a far corner of the attic. As her eyes became accustomed to the dim light Lillian saw that they were moving the huge portrait of the children's mother.

Just as Grant had promised William he would do.

Chapter Eight

While Thompson covered the portrait with a dust cloth, Grant took a step back. 'I'm glad that's done. I would hate for the boy to see it again.'

It had fallen to Grant and his old butler to move the painting and he felt sorry for the man, who was weary from doing the work of a half-dozen footmen.

'The poor lad,' remarked Thompson, suddenly less formal and more like the Thompson Grant had grown up with.

Grant inclined his head towards the portrait. 'What was the lady like?' How could she leave her children behind? he meant.

Thompson surveyed the covered painting as if he were seeing the lady's image. 'I'd not have guessed she had children before marrying your brother,' he responded. 'I do not recall them ever being mentioned. I'd say she was not unhappy being Lady Grantwell, though. She rather enjoyed ordering the servants about.'

Grant gazed at the covered portrait himself. 'She looks disagreeable to me. Did she love my brother, do you think?'

Thompson paused as if in thought. 'As much as one could.'

Grant laughed, although he was certain the butler did not mean to be funny. 'Well, that is something, I suppose.' What part had his brother played in her abandonment of her children? Grant would never know, he supposed. He brushed the dust off his hands. 'Thank you for helping, Thompson.'

'Anything else, m'lord?' the butler asked.

'Not a thing.' Grant grinned at him. 'Unless you have not yet refilled my decanters of brandy?'

'Already done, sir.' The older man's mouth twitched.

'Excellent,' Grant responded, and then, in an exaggerated tone, 'I am in great need.'

He turned towards the doorway and his good mood faded.

'Lil— Miss Pearson.' What the devil was she doing here? Searching for him?

Thompson hesitated and looked uncertainly from him to Lillian.

'You may go, Thompson,' Grant said.

Lillian stepped inside the attic so Thompson could pass by her.

'I—I came to search for more fabric,' she explained after the butler left.

Grant tried to gather his wits. He'd not been prepared to encounter her here. In a darkened space, no less. The dim light from his lamp and hers made the cavernous space seem intimate.

'To make a doll for Anna,' she continued, sounding as unsettled as he felt. 'As a gift for Christmas. There are no gifts for the children for Christmas and no way to buy them.'

No gifts. He'd not given gifts a thought, not having

given or received any for many years. The poor children. How unfortunate for them to have wound up in the care of a man who could not even guess their needs.

He stepped around boxes and trunks to make his way to the doorway. Past her. 'Well, then. Of course you may use whatever you find.'

He ought to have thought of Christmas gifts for the children even before the snow. He and his brother had always received toys for Christmas. Well, his brother received lavish toys from their parents, and Grant always received at least one good one from his Uncle Alstrom. Uncle Alstrom sent him the best of his toys.

Lillian walked over to a trunk and opened it. 'I wish I could think of something to do for William, though.'

The poor lad.

At least it seemed that Lillian's regard for the children was genuine. He could believe that much of her character. How ironic. She was the one person in the household who anticipated the children's needs and he'd be sending her away.

'I wish I could find him something to play with,' she went on. 'He so needs to play.'

Something for William to play with...'Wait. I have an idea.' Grant pulled his thoughts away from his own turmoil and walked through the maze of boxes and trunks. Years ago the housekeeper, in one ambitious impulse, had imposed some organisation upon the attic, grouping like items together. Grant, only a boy then, had helped the footmen move the boxes. Certainly organisation had fallen by the wayside in later years, but vestiges of the effort could still be seen.

He found the area set aside to store items from the nursery. There was the old rocking horse that had once been his father's. A mahogany cradle.

He opened a large trunk and rooted around in it. 'Ah! Here!'

He looked up to find Lillian close by. The effect of her interested gaze jolted him a little, but he turned his attention to the box in his hand. 'I do not know if William will like them. They are rather old and out of date—'

'What are they?' she asked.

'My old set of toy soldiers.'

'Let me see.' She walked over to him.

He opened the box.

'Oh!' She sounded awed. 'Oh, Grant! He will love them. I believe he is mad for soldiers.'

Grant had seen finer, newer sets on display in London's shop windows, toy soldiers from the war, formed and painted in accurate detail, miniatures of the men he served with and those he fought. These were more crudely made of tin, painted in single colours, and old enough that the soldiers wore tricorn hats.

He gazed up at her again. 'Do you think so?'

'Oh, yes!' Her smile filled him with warmth. 'Especially because they were yours.'

He did not know what to make of that.

She glanced down at the fabric in her hand. 'Poor Anna. I'm afraid my rag doll will not compare.'

Grant suddenly felt a renewed enthusiasm, much as he'd felt that morning, gathering evergreens. 'Let us keep looking. There should be generations of toys packed away up here. We'll find something for Anna.'

Together they opened boxes and trunks, selecting anything they thought the children might enjoy. Spinning tops. A game of ninepins. A kaleidoscope. Another ball and cup. Another whole set of blocks.

They searched together, side by side, remarking on their finds, discussing whether to leave the items where they were or to select them for the children. For the first time since she showed up on his doorstep, Grant felt at ease with her. Not enflamed with desire nor livid with anger. Comfortable.

On the heels of that realisation came a wave of sadness. It would not last. How could it?

Lillian felt cocooned with Grant in the lamplight of the attic, and it seemed as if the very air had changed, taking them back to when she'd first seen him in Lisbon and he'd helped her distribute food to the poor. The air between them had been anything but companionable that day when they'd worked together on a common task. Since then it had been either passion or anger bristling between them.

At this moment, though, she loved how at ease she felt. It warmed her heart that he'd become intent on finding gifts for the children. That he'd made her a partner in the search seemed very natural, yet certainly this must be some accidental aberration. If so, she'd savour it while it lasted.

They'd found several items that would make fine gifts for the children, but only such toys as could be enjoyed by either of them. There was nothing special for Anna— nothing akin to the tin soldiers for her brother.

Grant dragged yet another trunk into their small circle of light. 'This is an old one. Before my childhood or my father's, I'd guess.'

He opened the trunk, which appeared to contain girl's clothing, each item carefully wrapped in tissue.

Lillian held up one of the pieces—a silk brocade dress of a style she'd seen only in portraits painted nearly one hundred years ago. 'Look at this! How beautiful.' The dress looked as if it would fit a child a couple of years older than Anna.

'I have not a clue who it belonged to,' Grant said. 'A sister or a cousin of my grandfather? I don't recall knowing of one.'

Lillian stroked the fine fabric, its colours as vibrant as the day they were woven. 'Someone took care to preserve all this.'

Children's clothing was typically passed down to younger siblings or taken apart to be used to make another garment. Or the clothing was given away, often to the poor of the parish.

'Here is a book.' Grant unwrapped a small leather-bound book. 'A catechism for children.' He opened it. 'It is inscribed simply "To Mary". No other name.' He glanced up at her. 'Perhaps I can discover who she was.'

Was this a beloved child who had died? That seemed the best explanation, but Lillian did not speak her thoughts aloud. She did not need to. She sensed Grant had surmised the same.

He set the catechism aside and reached into the trunk again. This time he lifted out a different sort of package, not clothing, not a book.

His eyes lit up and he handed it to Lillian. 'I think I know what this is.'

She felt it, too, when she took it in her hands. She smiled at him before unwrapping it. 'Oh!' she exclaimed.

It was a doll. And such a doll! Carved of wood, painted white, with jointed arms and legs. She was beautifully detailed, even down to carved fingers and fingernails. Her cheeks and lips were tinted pink and a fine line for eyebrows was drawn above almond-shaped glass eyes. Her dress was of as fine a silk as any of the clothing they'd discovered in the trunk. It was in the style of an earlier generation, with a tightly cinched waist and a wide full skirt, but that was the only clue that this doll was made nearly a century ago. She could have been made yesterday. She even had hair, fashioned from sheep's wool probably and covered with a lace cap.

Their gazes caught, sharing the pleasure of the find. Even in the joy of the moment Lillian sensed it was ephemeral. She vowed to remember and treasure it.

'She is perfect!' Lillian finally exclaimed. 'Quite as good a gift as the tin soldiers. I will make some other clothes for her, I think. Something more modern.' She smiled at him again. 'This will make a fine Christmas for them. Thank you, Grant.'

He glanced away. 'I'd not have given any of this a thought if not for you.'

Her heart beat faster at his words even if they had been tossed off as if inconsequential. If only this feeling could last, this peace between them. But it would be fleeting, she knew. It was merely because of the children.

Because of Christmas.

They carefully repacked the trunk and closed it again. While Grant pulled out a crate to hold the toys they'd found, Lillian selected more fabric and lace to make dresses for the doll. They packed up all the toys except the doll into the crate.

'I'll take these,' Grant said. 'So the children do not find them. Thompson can find me some paper and string for wrapping, I'm sure. Perhaps you can come after dinner tomorrow and we can wrap them?' He paused as if another thought came to him. 'It will be Christmas Eve. Perhaps you and the children should dine with me and we can wrap the gifts after they go to sleep?'

Again her heart raced. 'If you wish it.'

'I do.' He smiled.

Her voice turned breathless. 'Very well, then.'

He did not speak to her again, but simply parted from her, carrying their load of treasures.

Lillian hid the doll in her room and hurried to the nursery. When she opened the door both children jumped and quickly hid what they were doing.

'Miss Pearson!' Anna exclaimed.

William stood and raised his chin as he faced her. 'Miss, will you go away again? Anna and I wish—wish to do something in private—with you not here.'

Their faces held determined expressions, not guilty ones.

'It has to do with Christmas,' William added.

Lillian smiled inwardly. 'Shall I ask Hannah to look in on you?'

Their stiff shoulders relaxed. 'Hannah can come in,' William said.

She felt tears stinging her eyes. They were making her gifts; she was sure of it. At least she would have something to remember them by.

'I will be in my room, then,' she said. 'Knock on the door if you need me.'

She found Hannah and asked her to look in on them from time to time, then went to her room to make doll clothes and to think of how lovely it had been to feel at peace with Grant. She'd cherish that moment because soon she would never see him again. Or the children.

Then she would be alone and penniless. And pursued.

Chapter Nine

The next morning Lillian and the children dawdled over their breakfast. The night before, the children had begged Lillian for a later bedtime and she suspected they were still at work on their gifts. They'd been slow to wake up and dress, but then so had she. She'd sewn by lamplight until her eyes burned with the strain, but she now had a small set of modern-day clothing for the hundred-year-old doll.

Hannah appeared at the door. 'Lord Grantwell wishes you all to appear in the hall as soon as you may.' She corrected herself. 'He commands you to appear.'

'In the hall?' They were *commanded* to appear?

Lillian's anxiety flared. As did the children's.

Anna looked frightened.

William cried, 'Did we do something wrong?'

It was exactly the question on Lillian's lips.

'Very well, Hannah.' She stood. 'We must wash first.' And tidy the children's hair and clothes. 'We will be there within a quarter-hour.'

Hannah's lips pursed, but she nodded and hurriedly turned away.

'Come, children,' Lillian tried to sound calm. 'We must be presentable.'

They washed faces and hands, and Lillian tied Anna's hair with a ribbon while William tried to comb his into some semblance of neatness.

'Is he angry with us?' Anna asked.

'Not with you and William,' Lillian assured them. But she was not so certain about herself.

Anna held her hand as they walked down the stairs much less joyously than they had done the morning before.

When they walked through the threshold between the anteroom and the hall Grant was there, along with Thompson. Hannah and the two housemaids held baskets of evergreens, filling the room with the scent of outdoors. On a side table were balls of string, a basket of ribbons, and vases of various sizes.

Grant turned with a smile on his face. 'There are our three slugabeds!'

He was dressed much as the day before, as if he were one of the labourers and not the viscount, nor the handsome soldier who had first caught her eye. Still, her heart leapt at the sight of him.

Only because she anticipated his anger, she told herself.

The children were less able to read his mood and hid behind her skirts.

'What is this, Gr—m'lord?' she asked.

'What you wished for,' he responded with a sweep of his arm. 'You requested evergreens for decoration and today is the day to decorate. We are at the ready.'

'But I meant only the children's rooms. I did not presume—'

He cut her off. 'Come, now. It will be Christmas in all the rooms, will it not?'

William peeped out from behind Lillian. 'Do you mean we must put evergreens in *all* the rooms?'

He'd told them Grantwell House had eighty rooms, though they'd seen maybe a quarter of them.

Grant walked over to him and clapped a friendly hand to the boy's shoulder. 'Not all of them. What do you think?' He drew the boy to his side. 'This hall, certainly. The drawing room. Your rooms, of course—'

Anna skipped over to him. 'May we decorate the stone people's room too?'

'The statue gallery?' Grant laughed. 'Of course—if you wish it.'

Lillian's insides were melting like candle wax. What better way to make the children feel this was indeed their home?

He caught her eye for a brief moment, but she could not discern if he meant to include her in his welcome. She suddenly turned again into that forlorn schoolgirl left at school, watching the other girls leave to celebrate Christmas with their families.

How absurd! It should be enough for her that he'd done this for the children.

'Let us start with the drawing room, shall we?' Grant led the children to the drawing room, with its walls covered in tapestry. They'd glimpsed it on their house tour.

This time the dust covers had been pulled from the chairs and sofas and the curtains were open. Light poured in from three huge windows, making the room sparkle with gold—the gilt of the tables, the sofas and chairs, the frames of the tapestries and the trim of the plasterwork on the ceiling. The room was perfect in its symmetry of pastel colours and design among the walls, carpets, ceiling and furniture, even the decorative items scattered about. Adding the vivid greens of holly, pine and laurel seemed like an invasion.

Lillian kept herself separate from the bustle of decorating, still feeling the outsider. Hannah, in her glory, took charge, directing the maids, Thompson, and even Grant and the children, ordering them all about, telling them what to put where. No one seemed to mind. The mood was festive.

For all but Lillian. For her, Christmas always brought sadness amidst the gaiety. When a schoolgirl, she'd yearned to share Christmas with family. When married, her husband's family planned all the festivities as if she did not exist. And now these people were becoming dear to her. She was even fond of Hannah and the other servants. But she did not belong with them. Soon she would be gone, perhaps as soon as St Stephen's Day. And what would be her fate then?

Hannah noticed her, and quickly set her to work. 'Fill this vase, Miss Pearson, if you please?'

That was the end of her idleness. Soon she was as busy as the rest of them—but still separate. Always separate.

They lined the windowsills and the mantel with evergreens tied with ribbons, and placed vases of evergreens, some with red berries, on the tables. They did the same in the hall, in the small sitting room where Grant ate his meals, and in the grand dining room where the greens complemented the yellow of the room. Grant directed the children or let the children direct him. Together they performed whatever task Hannah assigned them, including several trips to the stillroom to replenish their supply of greenery.

As they surveyed their handiwork in the dining room,

Hannah said, 'The table lacks a centrepiece, but we shall leave that to Cook. She has a plan for it.'

'You have all done excellent work,' Grant said to Hannah and the maids. 'Why not leave the decoration of the gallery to the children and me? Have a cup of tea and a rest before returning to your other duties. And be sure to take time to decorate your rooms, as well.'

As the servants left cheerfully, the children hung about Grant's side. Lillian stood a distance apart.

Grant clapped his hands. 'Come, children. Let us gather the baskets and make our way to the gallery.'

The baskets of greenery were too big for Anna to carry, so she skipped ahead, leading them all to the stone people's room.

'Tell us what to do, Anna,' Grant said once they were in the room.

She walked around as if she were an artist surveying a canvas. She stopped in front of a bust of the Emperor Augustus. 'Look. He has a crown of leaves.' She turned to Grant. 'Did they wear leaf crowns on their heads in Roman days?'

He gave an almost inaudible laugh. 'Yes. Some did. They were called laurel wreaths.'

Anna's eyes lit up. 'Let's make leaf crowns for all of them!'

Grant tossed a helpless look to Lillian. 'We'll need a ladder to reach the heads of the statues.'

He was speaking to her. When throughout the morning he'd barely glanced at her.

'You are right,' she replied. 'Some are much too tall. Let's make wreaths for the ones we can reach, and we can put evergreens at the feet of the others.'

She picked up a branch of laurel and twisted it into a

circle, then entwined another around it so that it stayed together. 'Try this.'

Anna happily took the wreath and ran over to the bust of Minerva. Grant lifted her so she could put the wreath on Minerva's head.

She laughed in delight. 'Make another one, Miss Pearson!'

Lillian tried to fashion the next one out of holly, but the leaves pricked her skin so she used ivy instead. Soon they were all working. William put sprigs of spruce, holly, pine, cypress or fir at the base of the large statues while Lillian made wreaths from laurel or rosemary or ivy for Grant and Anna to crown the white marble busts of Romans who had never celebrated Christmas. There was little talking, and Grant had returned to essentially ignoring her, but Lillian, in this brief time with Grant and William and Anna, felt the togetherness for which she'd so often yearned.

When they were done they gathered what they had not used into one of the baskets and stood at the entrance to survey their handiwork. Anna clapped her hands in glee and William wore a proud expression. Grant shared an amused glance with Lillian. The statues looked quite ridiculous. Lillian's heart soared at the shared moment.

As they sauntered to the hall carrying the baskets, Grant spoke to the children. 'Before supper you must come to light the yule log. We can eat supper together. Would you like that?'

'Yes!' cried Anna.

William only nodded, but his eyes sparkled with pleasure.

Grant turned to Lillian, but his expression had turned bland. 'You will come, too, Miss Pearson.'

As soon as they entered the hall Hannah bustled in.

'M'lord! One more thing. I've made the mistletoe into a ball. It must be hung in the doorway of the drawing room. There is a nail already there for the purpose.'

She handed Grant the mistletoe and just as quickly left.

'Well, I see we have one more task to perform.' He put down his basket and carried the mistletoe to the drawing room door.

'Can you reach it?' Lillian asked, forgetting that he'd seemed to shut her out again.

Grant was tall, but the doorway was so much taller that his hands barely reached the top.

'With William's help.' Grant handed Lillian the mistletoe.

Anna laughed as Grant put William on his shoulders. Lillian handed the boy the mistletoe and William hung it on the nail.

When Grant put William down, Anna ran to stand beneath the mistletoe.

'You have to kiss me, William,' she demanded.

He stepped away quickly. 'I'm not going to kiss you!'

'You have to kiss somebody who stands under the mistletoe. That is what you said.' Her voice rose. 'I'm under the mistletoe!'

'No!' William shot back. 'You're my sister. I'm not going to kiss you.'

'But you said—' She was wailing now, the sort of wail that preceded tears.

Lillian moved towards her, ready to scoop her up before she fell apart, but Grant got to her first.

'I will kiss you,' he said.

He picked her up and gave her a big kiss on the cheek.

She squealed in delight, then turned and kissed his cheek back.

Smiling, Lillian moved so that Grant and Anna could walk before her.

Anna turned around and her eyes lit up again. 'Now Miss Pearson is under the mistletoe! Lord Grantwell, you have to kiss her, too.'

His amused expression fled.

'You must! You must!' Anna persisted.

'Leave him alone,' William cried.

'No.' Grant turned to the boy. 'No, it is all right.'

He approached Lillian, who could sense his reluctance. He leaned down and gently placed his lips on her cheek, as he had with Anna, but his lips lingered a bit longer.

'You have to kiss him back, Miss Pearson!' Anna cried. 'Kiss him back.'

He stood so close she could smell the scent of pine and juniper on him from their day's work. She stood on tiptoe and he leaned down. She pressed her lips against his cheek. The taste of him brought back their night of tangled sheets and heated skin.

The contentment she'd finally managed to feel broke into pieces of grieving want.

As she moved away, her gaze caught his.

Did she see desire in his eyes? Or had she only hoped for it?

Before the supper hour, Grant and one of the stable workers dragged in the yule log and placed it in the drawing room fireplace. Grant himself packed it with kindling and readied it to be lit. He was enjoying this day, enjoying all the activity around preparing for Christmas. He'd forgotten the special pleasures of the season. He'd not been a part of them since a boy.

If it weren't for the children, he'd probably have treated

the day like any other. Had he remained at the house party he would have seen all these traditions as mere social obligations. He shuddered to think of what the tradition of hanging mistletoe would have meant for him there.

Although no kiss under mistletoe at a house party could have affected him as much as Lillian's lips upon his cheek.

It was becoming more and more difficult for him to remember her duplicity. How could he reconcile that duplicitous French spy with the caring woman who exhibited such joy at finding gifts for children? Sharing the search for toys with her had been...peaceful. An interlude in which everything had seemed as it should be.

Because of toys? It seemed absurd, thinking of it now, but Lillian had brought the joy of the holiday to him perhaps for the first time, and she'd only been concerned about giving that joy to William and Anna.

Without her, would he have thought of the children who were now his charge? He doubted it. Lillian, by thinking of the children, even brought back his old memories of traipsing into the woods to collect greenery, and of helping the maids and footmen decorate. Those were happy parts of Christmas and he'd almost forgotten them.

The tradition of the yule log brought fewer fond memories, though. His parents always had guests for dinner, and he and his brother George had been put on display and required to sing the wassail song for them. Much fuss would be made over his brother's singing voice and his brother was always invited to witness the mummers play some of the guests had performed. No one ever seemed to notice Grant slip away.

His good cheer plummeted for a moment.

Perhaps he could teach the children some of the songs

he used to sing in the servants' hall or maybe next Christmas they might perform a mummers play of their own.

Next Christmas.

Lillian would not be a part of Christmas next year, though.

That should not bother him, but it did.

Thompson entered the room, bearing a tray. 'The wassail, m'lord.' He placed two punch bowls on a table, a small crystal one and a larger silver one, along with their matching cups.

Grant grinned. 'I remember. The crystal one is for the children. The silver for adults.'

The crystal bowl would contain a hot spiced punch of apples and other fruit. The silver would hold the same, with the welcome addition of some brandy and port.

The butler nodded. 'You remember well.'

He gave his old retainer a conspiratorial look. 'I used to steal drinks from the silver punch bowl.' Because no one had paid him any mind.

Thompson gazed heavenward. '*I* remember well.'

Of course. How comforting. Thompson had noticed.

Grant smiled and hoped his fondness towards the butler came through.

Thompson gave a knowing nod and left the room.

His good mood somewhat restored, Grant gazed out the windows as he waited for Lillian and the children to come for the lighting of the yule log. Snow fell again, but not as thickly as the day Lillian had arrived—had it really only been five days ago? If the snow continued, there would be no attending of the Christmas church services tomorrow. This time, however, Grant did not mind the impassable roads.

Thompson returned with Cook and the maids. They lined themselves along the wall. Grant had invited all the servants who'd stayed in the house to celebrate this part of the festivities with them.

He heard the children's voices before they, too, entered the room.

As soon as Anna saw him she skipped to him and gave his legs a hug. 'When do we light the yule log?'

'In a moment.' He laughed.

The children looked polished, in what must be their finest clothes. Lillian stood apart, looking as beautiful as ever in a plain day dress of pale yellow. Befitting a governess, he supposed. In his boyhood, his parents' lady guests would have been dressed in glittering evening finery for this night's supper. He'd never seen Lillian dressed so. When he'd known her in Lisbon, she'd been wearing widow's black.

His heart hardened again at the memory.

'It is cold in here,' William said with a glance to the fireplace.

Grant walked over to him and tussled his neatly combed hair. 'Indeed, it is. Let us get to the lighting of the log.' He led them to the fireplace. 'First we pour wine over the log.'

'Why?' asked Anna.

'I do not know why.' Grant shot a helpless glance to Lillian, but she stood apart, her shawl wrapped tightly around her. He looked towards Thompson.

'That is simply how we did it when you were a boy,' the butler said.

Grant picked up a wine bottle and handed it to Anna. 'Would you do the pouring, Anna?'

The girl took the bottle and enthusiastically poured the wine over the log. The maids tittered at the endearing sight.

'Next we light the log,' Grant said. 'William, would you do the honours?'

'Me?' the boy said.

'You.' Grant handed him a taper. 'Light the taper from one of the lamps.'

William carried the taper to a lamp, lifted the glass and touched the taper to the flame. Grant stood next to the fireplace. He gestured William to come to him.

William looked uncertain. 'Where do I put it?'

'Place it in the kindling under the log,' Grant told him. 'You can light more than one place.'

William followed his instructions with the utmost seriousness. Grant inwardly shook his head. Did the boy know how to have fun?

Gratifyingly, the kindling leapt into flames and a satisfied sound of approval came from the servants. The wine helped the flames curl around the log, which would take longer to ignite and would burn more slowly.

The children stared into the fire as if they'd never seen such a sight. Poor tots. At least his boyhood Christmases had not been as bleak as theirs must have been.

'In the old days,' Grant told them, 'a whole tree would be brought in and they would have kept it burning until Twelfth Night.'

Anna turned to him with a sceptical look. 'How could they get a whole tree into the house?'

Grant tossed an amused glance towards Lillian. This time she met his gaze with a small smile.

He turned back to Anna. 'I suppose they had bigger houses.'

Her eyes twinkled. 'And bigger doors.'

'Maybe they lived in castles,' William offered.

'Maybe they did.' Grant touched the boy's shoulder.

He clapped his hands together. 'Now the next part.' He turned to the servants. 'Do you have the candles, Mrs Bell?'

'Right here, m'lord.' The cook pulled out two huge candles from her apron pockets.

'And I have the candlesticks!' cried Hannah. She brought the silver candlesticks used only for this occasion over to the table in front of the fireplace.

Cook handed the candles to Grant.

He walked back to the hearth where the children still stood. 'When I was a boy, I was charged with lighting the candles. Do you know why?'

'Why?' Anna blinked her big blue eyes at him.

He bent down to her ear. 'Because I was the youngest.' He did not explain that he'd shared the ritual with the servants, not his parents and their guests. 'The youngest lights the candles.'

'I'm the youngest!' she cried.

Anna reached for the candles, but Grant held on to them. 'Listen very carefully to my instructions.'

She nodded, bouncing from foot to foot.

'First we must extinguish all the lamps in the room.'

He turned to Thompson, who gestured to the maids to extinguish the lamps. As the room darkened the flames of the yule log seemed to brighten.

'Now, Anna, you must light the candles from the yule log, and while you are lighting them everyone must make a wish—'

'A wish?' She stood still.

'But do not say your wish aloud,' he warned. 'Or it will not come true.'

'I will tell nobody,' she whispered.

'These candles must burn out before any other candle can be lit in this room.' He handed the child the candles and stood. He turned to the others. 'Prepare to make your wishes.'

Anna approached the fire warily, so Grant stayed with her to guide her hands.

'Hold the candles low, under the fire,' he told her, helping her place them where they could catch the flame.

The wicks of the candles caught the flame and Anna turned around triumphantly. Everyone clapped. Hannah helped her put the lighted candles in the candlesticks.

Grant raised his voice. 'Now, who would like some wassail?'

Anna tugged at his coat. 'What is wassail?'

'Spiced punch.' Had these children never had wassail?

William spoke up. 'Our governess used to give us spiced punch at Christmas.'

Thompson served the children from the crystal punch bowl first, before serving everyone else from the silver one.

The children sipped their punch and looked from the yule log to the candles.

Grant stepped back and stood next to Lillian. She leaned towards him. 'You did well. Look how happy they are.'

The children were silhouetted against the flames of the yule log and bathed in the soft light of the candles. They did look happy.

He glanced back at Lillian and basked in her approval, feeling almost as much pleasure as the children showed.

Sod it. Why not believe in her? Simply for tonight.

He smiled at Lillian, and warmth showed in her eyes. His spirits rose even higher.

'You are forgetting something, m'lord,' Thompson said.

'Forgetting something?' He was puzzled. 'What?'

'The wassail song,' Thompson said.

Anna's face fell. 'I do not know the wassailing song.'

'No?' Grant touched her cheek. 'We will sing it for you.' He began and the servants joined in.

We've been a while a-wandering,
Amongst the leaves so green.
But now we come a-wassailing,
So plainly to be seen.
For it's Christmas time, when we travel far and
near,
May God bless you and send you a Happy New
Year....

He paused. 'Miss Pearson, why are you not singing?'

She shook her head. 'That is not the song I know.'

'That is the wassail song,' he insisted.

'No,' she countered with a smile. '*This* is the wassail song.'

Here we come a-wassailing
Among the leaves so green;
Here we come a-wand'ring
So fair to be seen.
Love and joy come to you,
And to you your wassail too;
And God bless you and send you a Happy New Year
And God send you a Happy New Year...

'No. No. No,' he protested. The words were slightly different. The tunes were slightly different.

He led the servants in the second verse.

We are not daily beggars,
That beg from door to door,
But we are neighbours' children,
Whom you have seen before...

Lillian stopped them. 'That is the third verse,' she said. 'Here is the second.'

Our wassail cup is made
Of the rosemary tree,
And so is your beer
Of the best barley.

He joined her in singing the refrain—his refrain along with hers—then they all continued singing verses with identical lyrics, Lillian's differing version making a sort of harmony while the refrains sung together became a jumble.

He and the others ended the song, but she kept singing. One last verse.

Her singing slowed and she held her gaze on his.

God bless the master of this house
Likewise the mistress too,
And all the little children
That round the table go.

When she mentioned children she walked over to William and Anna and put her arms around them. Grant joined them as they sang the refrain one last time, with the children trying to join in.

And God send you a Happy New Year...

Lillian, the children and the servants all broke into laughter when they finished. Grant hesitated a moment before he could join them.

In the New Year she would be gone...

Chapter Ten

The gay spirit they'd managed in lighting the yule log and singing the wassail songs continued through their Christmas Eve supper, which they ate in the sitting room near the kitchen. Grant was certain he had not dined with children since he'd been at school. He'd not held conversations with children since then either, but he was surprised at how comfortable it was.

Had he ever sat at the same table as his parents when he'd been William and Anna's ages? He had not. Not until well into his adolescence. William and Anna were surprisingly good company, though. Of course, Lillian helped them keep up the conversation.

William might have been content just to ply him with questions about the war, but Lillian turned the conversation to Christmas, and what each of them remembered about celebrating the holiday.

The children's remembrances were even bleaker than Grant's. Their holiday seemed to have been completely arranged by and spent with their governess, with strict admonitions to stay away from their grandfather and his guests. At least Grant had been allowed to make an appearance for his parents and their guests.

Lillian's turn came. 'Well, I spent most of my Christmases at school in Reading.'

'What did you do at school?' Anna asked.

'We played games, mostly,' she said. 'Like Bullet Pudding or Hoodman Blind or Rats and Rabbits. The teachers who stayed with us—those of us who did not leave school for the holidays—tried to make it fun. And it was.'

'You did not return to Portugal for Christmas?' Grant asked.

She averted her gaze. 'After…after my father died, my mother thought it better I stay at school.'

'Where is Portugal?' Anna asked.

'It is on the Iberian Peninsula, on the Atlantic Ocean bordering Spain,' William answered. 'Napoleon tried to conquer it, but he never did.'

That was close to how it was.

'When I was a very little girl I did spend Christmas in Portugal,' Lillian went on. 'We used to have our Christmas meal on Christmas Eve. We called it *Consoada* and we ate codfish with green vegetables and boiled potatoes.'

'I am sure I would like codfish,' said Anna.

Lillian laughed. The sight and sound still filled Grant with delight.

'You would both like our *Bolo Rei*,' she said. 'It is a cake with fruit and nuts.'

That started talk of cakes, which lasted until ginger cake was served for dessert.

By the time the children had finished their cake they were becoming visibly tired and, because the supper had been served much later than they were accustomed, Lillian pronounced it time to ready themselves for bed.

Grant followed them from the room, and Thompson began to clear the table.

When they reached the hall, Anna plopped down on the marble floor. 'I'm too tired.'

'Get up, Anna!' William chastised. 'You'll make Lord Grantwell cross.'

The little girl glanced up at Grant, her blue eyes filling with worry.

How might it have been for these children for them to worry about their every step?

He exaggerated the tone of his voice. 'Indeed, you shall make me very cross!' Anna's eyes widened even more as he bent down. 'Now I shall have to carry you!'

He picked her up and swung her round until childish giggles burst from her again.

Laughter. Anna's. Lillian's. Even William's, so faint one could barely hear it. Laughter made everything better.

He exchanged a glance with Lillian. There was approval in her eyes. Odd that her approval gratified him almost as much as the laughter.

He carried Anna up the stairs, all the way to the nursery wing and the children's room. Amidst her giggles he plopped her on her bed, turned, scooped William up and plopped him on the other bed.

'There you are. All ready for sleeping.'

Anna still giggled. 'No! We have to dress in night clothes and have a wash first!'

'Oh? I must leave, then.' He started for the door. 'Sleep well. Tomorrow is Christmas, you know.'

'Christmas!' Anna cried.

'Goodnight, Lord Grantwell,' William murmured.

Before he left the room, he turned to Lillian. 'Meet me in the library?'

She nodded.

* * *

Grant had asked Thompson to put some brown paper and string in the library for wrapping the gifts. He'd already brought down the bounty he and Lillian found in the attic, hiding it beneath his desk, out of view, just in case the children should come snooping through the servants' passages like before.

Like the day Lillian arrived.

He did not wish to think too much upon Lillian's arrival. Then he must think of her leaving as well. Or of the reasons she'd fled Portugal or of whether she might have told him the truth all those years ago. Was it possible?

He poured himself a brandy and wandered to the window, peering through the drawn curtains at the snow falling in large gentle flakes outside. Would the weather prevent Rhys and Helene from coming for Christmas dinner? He'd invited them before…before Lillian.

He must include Lillian in the Christmas dinner, must he not? Rhys knew of her now and he would have told Helene who would certainly question her absence. Helene would have an abundance of questions about Lillian—questions Grant either did not wish to answer or simply could not. At least if Lillian were present Helene would not ask her questions out loud. She'd lift her brows at Grant and he would know the questions were there.

But what if he invited the children to Christmas dinner? They'd be a distraction, would they not? Would it be too much of a scandal to include small children at such an event?

He and his brother had always been rushed off to the nursery before his parents and their guests dined, but those were big important parties, filled with people his father wished to impress. Christmas dinner here with his two good friends, cooked and served by the few servants who remained for the holiday would not be such a grand affair.

Why not include the children? They behaved excellently at dinner tonight. Besides, had the children not been hidden away long enough, as if they were something shameful? How shameful could they be? Their grandfather's executors had assured him that they were the product of his sister-in-law's first marriage. How much shame could be attached to legitimately born children? Indeed, he would not care if they'd been born on the wrong side of the blanket. He actually liked them.

His mind made up, Grant finished his brandy and turned back to the desk.

He pulled the crate of toys out of its hiding place. They were all here except the doll which Lillian had kept with her. How to wrap them? The toy soldiers would be easy. He'd always kept them in the same box he'd opened that long-ago Christmas when he received them. He'd found another box that might fit the doll, but what about the rest? How the devil did one wrap a game of ninepins without something to contain them?

He lifted out the box of tin soldiers, placed it on the desk, and removed the lid to examine his boyhood treasure one more time. His tin men could do with some polishing, so he took his handkerchief from his pocket and started rubbing them, one by one. He was still polishing when Lillian entered the room.

He glanced up at her. His breath caught.

He was transported to another room, another time when he'd looked up and had seen her by candlelight. He'd hardly known her then, but at the time it had not mattered—not to either one of them. They'd been awash in the pleasures of lovemaking. Nothing else had mattered.

The sensual mist that had enveloped them had been blown away with the force of a gale when she'd stolen his military papers. But it seemed as if the mist was seeping back now. Was it making it difficult for him to see her clearly?

Surely with the children she was not merely playacting when she treated them so kindly and anticipated their needs so sensitively? And with him—she'd not feigned her response to him. Indeed, she'd done nothing he could object to since she'd come here.

A puzzled look crossed her face. 'I—I have brought the doll. I was able to make a few new clothes for her.'

She approached the desk. He pushed aside the box of soldiers and she placed the doll before him. She'd sewn a new cap to cover the doll's hair, and a dress that was very similar to the one she wore, the pale yellow muslin with just a little lace around the neckline and hem.

He could not help but notice. 'You and she match.'

She glanced down at her dress and gave an embarrassed laugh. 'Hannah brought me this dress after I'd made the one for the doll. I think it is the same fabric.'

Realising he was staring at her, he quickly glanced back at the doll. 'She looks very stylish, indeed. Quite a transformation.' He bent down to the floor. 'I have found a box that might do for her.'

By God, he sounded so stiff. Lillian was turning wary, he could tell. Gone was the ease with which they'd shared dinner in the company of the children. With which they'd rubbed along together in the attic when they found these treasures.

He placed the doll in the box. She fit with room to spare.

Lillian handed him another bundle, this one wrapped in fabric and ribbon. 'Here are her clothes.'

He took the bundle from her. 'The original ones?'

She nodded. 'And some other pieces.'

He weighed the item in his hand. 'There feels like quite a few pieces in here. How did you manage it?'

She smiled wanly. 'Lamplight and little sleep, I am afraid.'

How kind of her. The mist thickened again. Was it clouding his vision or wrapping around him like a warm, safe blanket?

He mentally blew it away and lifted the doll out again. 'Let us see if it all fits.' He placed the bundle of clothes in the bottom of the box and put the doll on top. The box closed.

'Success.' He smiled. He motioned for her to come behind the desk. 'If you wrap the doll, I will wrap the soldiers.'

She picked up one of the little tin men and examined it under the lamp on the desk. Her voice turned soft. 'William will love these.'

'They will do, I hope,' he responded. 'The doll, too.'

Why had he summoned her to come closer? Fleetingly he imagined the lovemaking that so attached them to each other, but he shook it off, suddenly wanting merely to be with her, sharing this ordinary task as if what was between them was ordinary. For the moment he chose the warm blanket.

She wrapped the brown paper around the box and tucked the ends underneath.

'May I please have the string?' she asked.

He handed her the ball of string and she wrapped it around the box so that it held the paper in place. She tied the string in a knot.

'I need your finger.'

He placed his finger on the knot and she tied the string again and cut it off from the ball. She finished by tying it into a bow.

'There!' She picked up the parcel. The brown paper stayed in place.

He dipped his head in approval. 'Well done. I take back what I said before. You should wrap the tin soldiers, as well.'

She glanced into his face and smiled. He wanted to freeze the moment and keep it, like a treasure.

They'd done very little talking when together in Lisbon, but suddenly he wished he could share his thoughts with her. He wanted to tell her how much he enjoyed this ease between them, but that he did not entirely trust in it and it saddened him.

But how could he confide such a thing to her? It would place the wall between them again.

So he merely lent his finger again, while she tied the string around the wrapped box of tin soldiers.

That task complete, he pulled out the other toys. 'I cannot see wrapping these in brown paper,' he told her. 'And I despaired of finding boxes.'

Her elbow touched his as she looked down at them. 'Perhaps we should leave them in the crate. Let the children see them first before they open their big surprises.'

'Just leave them in the crate?' It did not seem festive enough.

They remained side by side and he was acutely aware of where they touched.

'Do you think there are any evergreens left?' she asked after a long pause. 'We could decorate the crate.'

'There might be some evergreens left in the stillroom.' He made a decision. 'Let us take the toys to the drawing room. We should have the children come there before breakfast. You and they will eat breakfast in the sitting room where we ate dinner tonight, will you not?'

Her eyes searched his face. 'If you wish it.'

He felt a flash of desire as his gaze met hers. He glanced away. 'I will go to the stillroom and see what is there.'

'And I will find some ribbons,' she added.

He quickly lifted the crate. She picked up the wrapped parcels. They walked through the hall to the drawing room, put the toys down, and went in search of decorations.

Lillian released a tense breath as she left the drawing room. It was still so difficult to be alone with Grant when her body betrayed her and reacted to his every gesture and expression.

This had been a near perfect day, spoiled only by the sensation that she was a spectator watching what she yearned to be part of. A place to belong and people to belong to.

When her mother had called her back to Portugal after her schooling was complete, Lillian had hoped to feel part of a family again, but it soon became clear to her that her mother considered her a tool to enhance her stepfather's place in the Portuguese aristocracy. Her mother had expected her to marry well, but the best she and her stepfather could do was fob her off on the younger brother of a Portuguese baron, a man who benefited more from his connection to her aristocratic stepfather than her stepfather to him.

Lillian had been a mere seventeen when her mother left Portugal for Brazil. She'd only been married three months, but she'd hoped her marriage would provide her with the home and family she wanted so much. Her husband's ardour had cooled considerably after the advantages of marrying her sailed away with her mother. It only became worse when she failed to give him a child. Then there was the accusation that she was spying for the French. Even her mother had stopped writing to her after that.

Lillian had been so alone for so long—except for that brief interlude with Grant. Losing him was perhaps the worst of all.

For brief moments with him, like when they searched for the toys from the attic, she had not seemed so alone.

She sighed. Enough of feeling sorry for herself. Christmas was promising to be another lovely day. She could not wait to see the children open their gifts. She would enjoy every moment while she could.

Lillian retrieved the basket of ribbons and lace she'd left in her room for adorning the doll's clothes and returned to the drawing room. Grant was already there, placing more logs upon the fireplace to burn before the yule log was used up.

He turned at her entrance and paused, staring at her as he'd done when she'd entered the library before.

Finally he stood. 'There you are.' He pointed to a few cuttings of holly and spruce. 'There was not much left.'

She walked over to him and picked up a sprig of holly. 'It should do.'

In the centre of the room, between a sofa and the fireplace, was the tea table upon which the yule candles still burned. Grant moved the wrapped boxes under the table and placed the crate holding the other toys near it. Lillian knelt down next to it and tied the spruce and holly cuttings to the crate with ribbons.

Grant stood next to her as she worked. 'When I was a

boy we always found our Christmas gifts in this room,
below this table or around it. My parents always had
plenty of guests present to witness the unwrapping of
gifts. My brother, of course, received the most. The
guests knew that gifts to George greatly pleased my parents. I always received something, enough so the guests
would think well of my parents.' He touched the box
containing the tin soldiers. 'Not these, though. My uncle
gave me these because he knew I would treasure them.'

Her heart hurt for that little boy. 'I suspect Anna and
William will be delighted with everything we've gathered.' She glanced up at him. His face in the candlelight
reminded her too much of their time in Portugal. The
memory impaled her heart like a knife. 'They have you
to thank,' she managed.

He shrugged. 'I'd not given gifts a thought until you
mentioned making a doll.'

She tied the last sprig of holly with a red ribbon. 'I
spend more time with them.'

'Poor babes.' He made a self-depreciating sound.
'Landing with me.'

'But you have been so good to them,' she protested.

He shook his head. 'I hardly know what to do with
them.'

She stood. 'May I make a suggestion?'

He remained close to her. 'Please do.'

'Search for their old governess who was dismissed
when they were sent to school.' It should not be too difficult to find her. Someone in their grandfather's employ
should know where the woman went. 'Hire her. Lure
her with more money if you have to. She was their main
stability.'

'That never occurred to me,' he said with feeling.
'But of course. It is the very thing I should do. I shall

send someone in search of the woman as soon as…as the weather clears.'

As soon as the weather clears. Then she would be gone, on the run once more.

But she refused to dwell on that in this moment. She had his ear about the children.

'See if you can also employ a footman William was fond of,' she went on. 'See how many of their favourite servants might be willing to come here. The children can give you their names.'

He touched her arm. 'Thank you, Lillian.' It was the first time he used her given name since she'd arrived. 'It surely is the right thing to do for them.'

He moved his hand away almost as quickly, but she still felt his fingers on her flesh.

He stepped back. 'Would you like some refreshment? Some tea or port or sherry?'

She shook her head. 'I confess I would like very much to go to bed—' Her face grew hot at her words and she saw he averted his gaze. 'I—I had little sleep last night. Working on the doll's clothes, you see.'

And, if she were very truthful with herself, yearning for him as well.

'Of course. I will not keep you.' He picked up the basket of ribbons and handed it to her.

As they walked to the door, she asked, 'What do you wish of the children tomorrow?'

He swept an arm towards the gifts. 'For them to come here first thing,' he said. 'Then we shall all share breakfast. I suspect that afterwards they will want to play.'

She smiled at him. 'I suspect you are right.'

'You and the children must attend Christmas dinner as well,' he added as they reached the doorway.

She halted. 'Are you sure?'

He faced her. 'Very sure.' His voice grew soft.

Of course. She understood. If not for her and the children, he would be eating Christmas dinner alone. A dismal prospect for anyone.

She started to move again, but he stopped her, capturing her arm. She gave him a puzzled look and his gaze rose above them.

To the bough of mistletoe.

He smiled an uncertain smile. 'Anna would insist.'

She swallowed, nodding slightly before lifting her face to him.

He touched her cheek before slowly lowering his lips to hers. The kiss was gentle and loving, if she could believe that. It also set her treacherous body aflame.

Let him deepen the kiss, something buried inside her demanded. *Let him take you to your room and make love to you. It is what you yearn for.*

He exhaled with a groan that was almost as warm as his lips, but he backed away.

His eyes turned dark and stormy. 'My apologies. I took advantage and I promised I would not do so again. I bid you goodnight.' He pushed past her and strode away.

By the time she'd collected herself enough to walk to the hall he was out of her sight.

Chapter Eleven

'Happy Christmas, Miss Pearson!' Hannah's voice was full of cheer as she bustled into the room.

Lillian sat up in bed. Usually she was awake and half-dressed before Hannah tapped at her door, but it had taken her a very long time to fall asleep the night before.

'What time is it?'

'The clock struck eight a while ago,' Hannah replied.

'Eight!' She had slept late. Lillian bounded out of bed. 'Are the children awake?'

'They are awake and I've seen to their washing and dressing.' Hannah carried a gown in her arms. 'I've brought you a lovely dress to wear today.'

The children were up and dressed already! She felt even guiltier. She hurried through her toilette.

Hannah lifted the gown. 'Do you approve?' The dress was long-sleeved and unadorned, but sewn of deep red-and-green-striped silk. 'You'll match the holly.'

Lillian smiled inwardly. Hannah took the same pleasure in dressing Lillian that she hoped Anna would find in dressing her doll.

'It is beautiful.'

Lillian fled Portugal with plain dresses—ones befitting a governess, dresses no one would notice, but in truth she loved fine clothes almost as much as Hannah did. And Lady Grantwell's dresses were very fine indeed, more beautiful than those she'd once owned.

Hannah helped her with her corset and helped her into the dress. When Lillian sat down at the dressing table and started to brush out her hair Hannah took the brush. 'Let me arrange your hair today.'

'Something quick,' Lillian said. 'I do not know when Lord Grantwell wants the children downstairs.'

'Oh, he is waiting already, miss.' Hannah gathered Lillian's long dark hair into one hand.

Oh, dear. Had he specified a time for them to be ready? She did not recall.

'Something *very* quick, then,' she said.

'A plain chignon, but I have a ribbon to put through it.' The ribbon was also red-and-green-striped, much like the dress.

When Hannah finished, Lillian had to admit the ribbon was a fine complement to the dress. 'Thank you, Hannah.' She stood and pressed her hand into Hannah's. 'You are a marvel.'

Hannah beamed.

Lillian hurried out the door and down the hallway to the children's room. She opened the door and was immediately taken aback. 'You are dressed for out of doors!'

They both wore hats and coats and boots, and carried mittens.

'Hannah told us that Lord Grantwell said to wear our coats,' William told her.

'That I did, miss,' Hannah called out as she walked by.

Hannah had not told her to wear a coat, so she surmised she was not part of whatever he had planned.

She bustled the children out of the room. 'Let us go, then. Lord Grantwell is waiting.'

The children ran down the hallway and clopped down the stairs, making noise enough for a horse stampede. They reached the anteroom before Lillian made it to the first landing.

By the time she entered the hall the children were already clustered around Grant, who was smiling and laughing with them.

He looked up at her. His smile faded only a little. 'Happy Christmas, Miss Pearson. We have another Christmas tradition to fulfil before we can go into breakfast.'

Breakfast? She'd thought he'd wanted the children to open their gifts first.

'What tradition is that?' she asked.

'Something green must enter this house before anything else comes in.' He put his hands on the children's shoulders. 'But something green will not walk in on its own, so we must send these children outside to find something green to bring in.'

'What something green?' asked Anna.

'Anything. Whatever you may find.' He walked with them to the door. 'But it may be a bit difficult because of the snow.'

He opened the door. It was snowing again, soft, big flakes that covered the drive, the lawn, the shrubbery. Heedless of the weather, the children ran out through the door, their footprints appearing behind them in the pristine snow.

William circled a few times before shouting, 'The shrubbery!'

He ran to the hedges bordering the circular drive that

led to the house's front entrance. Anna was right behind him.

William shook off the snow. 'Green!' he cried, breaking off a sprig and handing it to Anna.

'Here it is!' Anna ran for the door. 'Something green!'

She waited for William on the threshold and, holding the green-leafed sprig out in front of her, made certain it entered the house before the two of them. She handed the sprig to Grant.

'Excellent work!' He spoke with exaggerated enthusiasm. 'Now our house will have good luck all year long.'

Such luck would not hold for Lillian. She would be gone.

She shook the thought away. 'Take care, children,' she said. 'Your boots are packed with snow.'

Hannah appeared carrying two pairs of shoes. 'Here are your shoes. I'll take your coats and other things.'

Coats and hats and mittens and boots soon filled Hannah's arms. She left the hall by the servants' stairway, the same one Anna had fallen down that day Lillian arrived.

If Anna had not fallen, what might have happened? Perhaps none of this. Perhaps she would have wound up in a guest bedchamber far from the nursery to await passable roads alone.

'Are you ready for breakfast?' Grant asked the children. He glanced over to Lillian and smiled.

'I am hungry!' Anna still bounced with excitement.

William pushed at her. 'You are forgetting!' He turned to Grant. 'We need to get something first.'

'Oh! I know!' Anna cried.

They ran up the stairs.

They were getting Grant's gifts, Lillian surmised. They'd worked so hard creating them.

'It is as if they do not expect any gifts for themselves,' she said, more to herself than to Grant.

But he responded. 'I expected them to fuss about eating first. To ask about their gifts. They must have received *some* gifts at Christmas time, do you not think?'

'They said their governess gave them gifts.' Whatever those were , could not have been much.

The children noisily returned, each carrying three small packages wrapped with brown paper and string.

William handed one package to Grant, one to Lillian, and one to Anna. Anna did the same, giving the last gift to her brother.

Lillian's hands shook as she fingered the gifts handed to her. They'd thought of her all on their own. How had these children become so generous when life had never been generous to them?

'Open them!' William said.

Grant stared down at the gifts in his hands. 'I will. I will. Let us open them in the drawing room, though. That is the place for opening gifts. And we must check to see if the candles are still burning.'

The children ran ahead of them to the drawing room.

'I did not expect—' Grant said to her, his voice raspy.

Lillian nodded. 'Anna was the first to think of giving a gift to you.'

When they approached the drawing room door, William was already in the room, but Anna stood on the threshold.

'You have to kiss me, Lord Grantwell.' She giggled.

'With pleasure,' He bent down and kissed her on the cheek.

She kissed him back. 'And you have to kiss Miss Pearson, too, when she walks under the mistletoe.'

'With pleasure,' he murmured again. He straightened.

Lillian stepped forwards, remembering his kiss of the night before. Best to get it over with, though. She stood under the mistletoe and Grant slowly leaned over to place his lips on her cheek. She inhaled the scent of him, felt the warmth of him—and the yearning—but the moment passed swiftly and they entered the room.

William stood near the table that held the yule candles, mere pools of melted wax now. Next to them sat the gifts Lillian and Grant had wrapped the night before, but William seemed not to notice them. Instead he stared at the crate of toys and turned back to Grant, a puzzled look on his face.

'Yes,' Grant said in a low voice. 'Those are for you and Anna. Happy Christmas.'

William put his gift from Anna on the table and pulled out the box. He tentatively examined the toys. 'Look, Anna!'

Anna, who was rarely reluctant about anything, stood still for a moment before walking over to the crate.

'Oh!' she cried. She took out a top and twirled it.

William looked back at Grant again. 'All these for us?'

'Those and more.' Grant placed his gifts on a nearby chair and walked over to the children. He picked up the wrapped boxes. 'You also have these.' He handed one to William and one to Anna. 'From Miss Pearson and me.'

How generous of him to include her.

He stepped back next to Lillian as William, too carefully, unwrapped his gift. Anna clutched hers to her chest but waited for William to finish first.

The boy removed the paper and opened the box cover. His face lit up like a thousand yule candles. 'Toy soldiers!'

'They were Lord Grantwell's when he was a boy,' Lillian told him.

He glanced at Grant with an awed expression. 'They were yours?'

'When I was about your age,' Grant replied. 'I am afraid they are a bit old-fashioned—'

'I don't care,' William said quickly. He picked up one soldier and rubbed his finger along the tricorn hat. 'I love them.' His expression turned uncertain. 'Are they truly mine?'

'They are truly yours.' Grant's voice was raw with emotion.

Lillian felt tears stinging her eyes.

Grant turned to Anna. 'Your turn, Anna. Do you not wish to see what is in your box?'

Anna looked almost afraid. She tried to take the wrapping off as carefully as her brother had.

'Just rip it,' Grant said. 'It won't matter.'

She ripped the paper and held the box in her little hands. Slowly she opened it. And gasped. 'A doll! A doll!'

She lifted out the doll and touched the doll's hair and smoothed her dress. Then she hugged the doll, pressing her cheek against the doll's head.

'A doll,' she said again, with a sigh.

William put the tin soldier back into the box and closed it. He turned to Lillian and Grant. 'Now you must open your gifts.'

Grant, blinking rapidly, said, 'You've forgotten your gifts to each other.'

'Oh!' William picked up his gift and untied the string. It was a handkerchief Lillian had helped Anna make. She'd embroidered the letter 'W' on one corner. 'Thank you, Anna,' William said with genuine gratitude.

Anna smiled and opened her gift from William. It was a little wooden doll, about the size of her hand. 'Oh, William! It can be a doll for my doll!'

'Rogers made it a long time ago, when he was show-ing me how to whittle,' William explained. 'Now I want you to have it.'

Grant glanced at Lillian. 'Rogers?' he asked.

'A footman,' she responded. 'The one I think you should hire.'

He nodded.

Anna skipped towards them. 'Now it is your turn. Open your gifts now!'

'Ladies first,' Grant said.

Lillian opened Anna's gift, guessing what it was. A handkerchief hemmed all round, as she'd shown Anna how to do, and with crude letters embroidered on it spell-ing *Anna*.

Lillian blinked. 'You made one for me...'

'I put my name on it so you will remember me,' Anna said.

Eyes blurred, Lillian went to Anna and hugged her. 'I will never forget you. Or William.'

'Now mine,' William said.

She unwrapped the other small parcel. A carved dog, much like the one the footman had taught him to make. 'Oh, William. I will keep it always.'

He beamed, but sobered when turning to Grant. 'Will you open yours, sir?'

Lillian saw on Grant's face that he was as touched by these children as she.

He opened Anna's gift first. 'A handkerchief!' Grant smiled. 'I was hoping I might receive a handkerchief when I saw William's and Miss Pearson's.'

His was a more skilfully sewn one, Lillian having helped her with it. It was monogramed with a 'G'. He examined it closely, as if it were a precious item.

'I like it so much I shall be loath to blow my nose in it.'

Anna giggled.

William watched intently as Grant next opened his gift.

'A wooden soldier.' Crudely made, but unmistakable. He held it up. 'An infantry officer, by the looks of it.' The carving had an officer's sash.

'It is you,' William said in a quiet voice.

'Me?' Grant examined it again. 'You've made me into a very fine soldier indeed.'

He went over to the children, knelt down and simply hugged them. They hugged him back, and Lillian's tears finally rolled down her cheeks.

She loved them. She loved all three of them. How was she ever to bear leaving them?

As he hugged the children Grant's throat was so tight he could not speak. He'd not expected gifts from the children. Nothing from them. How much of it had Lillian inspired?

He dared a glance at her. She was dabbing at her eyes with her new handkerchief. He could not help but grin at her. He'd been fighting tears as well.

Through her tears she caught his glance and returned an embarrassed smile back at him.

Imagine that he, who'd fought in battle after battle, who'd needed to keep a cool head when cannon fire or musket fire or cavalry was flying towards him, could be brought to the brink of tears by two children who'd been thrust unwanted upon him. He was in danger of breaking into guffaws of laughter at the absurdity of it all.

The laughter was even harder to contain. Grant finally let it loose while he tucked both children under his arms and picked them up like luggage.

'Arrghh!' he cried. 'Look at Miss Pearson! We've turned her into a watering pot.'

'Why?' Anna managed as she trilled with laughter.

Even William laughed, and the joyous sound of it nearly undid Grant again.

'I think Miss Pearson is hungry,' he said. 'Is that not right, Miss Pearson?'

'Famished!' she responded, looking lovely, her nose pink from weeping.

'That settles it!' Grant headed for the door. 'I am taking you children to the breakfast room.' He turned his head to Lillian. 'Miss Pearson, follow us if you wish to stuff yourself full of Bath buns and black pudding.'

'I don't like black pudding,' Anna said through her giggles. 'Wait!' she cried after they'd passed through the doorway.

Grant stopped, puzzled. 'What?'

From her position under his arm, Anna looked up at him as if he were daft. 'Wait for Miss Pearson. When she is under the mistletoe you must kiss her!'

Just reaching the doorway, Lillian halted at Anna's words, a look of alarm crossing her face.

Grant was not about to make a fuss over this. He walked back and, still carrying the giggling children, leaned down, this time kissing her directly on her lips.

He'd intended the kiss to be playful, more of the silliness he was promoting, but his lips lingered.

She did not move away.

For that moment he forgot all else besides Lillian, the press of her lips against his, the taste of her, the scent of evergreen that lingered about her.

'Enough kissing!' William covered his eyes with his hands. 'Let us get breakfast.'

Grant came to his senses, but his gaze met Lillian's briefly before he moved away. 'Right you are, William.'

The children squealed all the way to the sitting room where the breakfast sideboard would be filled with food. Thompson was there awaiting them.

'Happy Christmas, Thompson!' Grant, his arms tired, put the children down. 'We are quite hungry this Christmas morning, as you can see.'

'Indeed, m'lord.' Thompson wore his version of a smile, which was a mere softening of his typically bland expression.

The sideboard was filled with Bath buns, cooked eggs, bread for toasting, butter and jam, bacon and sausages. And black pudding.

They sat in the same chairs they'd sat in at dinner the night before. Thompson asked each what they would like and served them.

When he served Anna, she said, 'William and I brought in something green this morning.'

'Did you, now?' responded the butler.

'And we opened presents,' she went on. 'William got toy soldiers and I got a doll. Two dolls. Because William gave me a doll, too.'

'A happy Christmas, then, miss?' Thompson glanced over at Grant.

Was that approval Grant saw in Thompson's eyes? It gratified him as much as it had done when he was a boy.

Anna went on to describe all the gifts, ending with, 'And you and Cook and Hannah and the others will get yours tomorrow.'

Thompson's lips quivered. 'Will we? How very good, miss.'

Grant sipped his tea as Thompson served the rest of the food. He felt more relaxed than he had in weeks—

certainly more relaxed than he'd felt since Lillian arrived. They'd created this Christmas together, for the children, and the joint effort made it more gratifying somehow. How bleak this day would have been if Lillian had not thought of gifts for the children and given him the idea to search in the attic for forgotten toys.

Later, when they'd finished breakfast and returned to the drawing room, Grant sat in one of the gilt chairs that would have been forbidden to him as a child. He watched William examine his toy soldiers, picking them out of the box, one by one, looking them over and standing them in formation.

Lillian sat with Anna on the sofa opposite Grant. They'd unpacked the doll's clothes and were looking through them.

Lillian picked up the doll's original dress, showing it to Anna. 'This was the dress that was on your doll when Lord Grantwell found her in the attic,' she said. Lillian was giving Grant more credit than he deserved. 'Did you know your doll belonged to one of his ancestors, who probably lived one hundred years ago?' She touched the dress. 'See how old-fashioned it is.'

'Like the ones on the ladies in Lord Grantwell's paintings!' Anna said.

'Yes,' Lillian responded. 'We should search the house to see if we can find a painting of a lady wearing something similar.'

Anna leaned against Lillian. 'I do not want to look for it now.'

Lillian put her arm around the girl. 'Neither do I.'

Grant felt a pang in his heart. He would never have guessed that such a peaceful scene would fill him with contentment. Why should it? He could not remember ever playing with his toys while his parents looked on.

Certainly never in this room. He could not remember this room ever being used unless guests were present.

The peaceful scene was Lillian's doing, Grant admitted. She'd shown him the children through her eyes and he'd seen himself in the children as well—the boy who'd never played at the feet of admiring parents.

But all this domestic calm was transitory, was it not?

Chapter Twelve

Grant was seized with an urge to pace the room. He pushed himself from his chair and strode over to the window. The snow had stopped but had covered everything in a beautiful pristine white. Why stay in a cage, he thought, with—what had Anna called it?—all that winter *fairyland* out there?

He spun around. 'Who fancies a walk in the garden?'

William immediately started to scoop up his soldiers and put them back in the box. 'I will go with you, Lord Grantwell.'

Anna gazed at her doll. 'I do not want to leave my doll.'

'May we still go?' William asked with a hopeful expression.

'Of course we may!' Grant told him.

Lillian had not responded, Grant noticed, but she would stay with Anna, he knew.

Lillian rose and put some of the toys back in the crate. 'I can take these toys to the nursery, if you like,' she said.

Yes. As pleasant as this morning had been, the drawing room was not a playroom, even though the time they'd spent together there had done it no harm.

'I suppose you must take the toys to the nursery eventually,' Grant responded. 'But you and Anna are welcome to stay here if you like. Or take however many toys you wish to take to the nursery now, and William and I will carry the rest when we return.'

Anna slipped off the sofa. 'Let's go back to the nursery,' she said. 'I want to make my doll a blanket. And a shawl.'

'Excellent idea,' Grant said.

As Lillian and Anna packed up the doll's things, Grant, his hand on William's shoulder, walked out of the room.

When they reached the hall, he said, 'Come with me first to the library for a minute.'

William nodded.

In the library, Grant took from his pocket the wooden soldier William had carved. 'I want to put this on my desk, so I might see it when I am working on my correspondence.'

William's eyes filled with unmistakable pride.

Grant felt the boy's emotion deep in his bones. His throat tightened again. He cleared it.

'I expect Hannah has put your coat and boots below stairs in the boot room. Mine are there as well. Shall we go?'

'Yes, sir.' William's voice was lighter than usual.

Behind the house stretched a long expanse of lawn as wide as the roads in London, but bordered by trees and shrubs instead of buildings. They set off on this snow-frosted thoroughfare, trudging through snow that reached William's calves. The boy had to step high to make it through.

'Is it too deep for you?' Grant asked.

'No, Lord Grantwell.' William continued with determination.

A part of Grant cringed whenever the children called him Lord Grantwell. In Grant's mind Lord Grantwell was still his brother or their father before him.

'I think you should call me something else. Not Lord Grantwell,' he said to William.

'Like what?' the boy responded.

'Like…' He thought about it. 'Like Uncle Grant. How would that be?'

The boy's brows knitted. 'But you are not our uncle. You are not related to us at all. That's what my grandfather's men said when they brought us here. I heard them talking. They foisted us on you, they said.'

That was about the gist of it, Grant admitted. But how awful to feel foisted upon someone, as if no one would have them unless tricked into it.

'I could have said no,' Grant said, although, really, it would have meant the children would have had nowhere to live and no provision made for them. 'I chose to have you and Anna stay.' It was better than leaving them on the streets.

'You did?' William's eyes grew huge.

'Of course I did.' Although, if not for the snow, he would have been willing to put Lillian out on the streets with nowhere to go and no money.

They trudged on.

Grant spoke again. 'You and Anna are somewhat related to me, you know. My brother was your stepfather.'

William's voice turned agitated. 'He did not know us! He never saw us!'

Grant put his hand on William's shoulder again. 'I know. It was very foolish of him.'

'Grandfather said he did not want us.' William's breathing came faster. 'Grandfather said nobody wanted us.'

Curse the old man! And curse his brother, too.

'Your grandfather could not speak for me. I am happy you and Anna are here.' Well, he was happy now. When they'd come he'd thought little beyond what the devil to do with them. 'And I prefer to think of you as my nephew and my niece. So I think you should call me Uncle Grant.'

William gazed up at him with awe. 'Very well… Uncle Grant.'

Grant rubbed the top of William's hat. 'Want a ride?'

The boy looked puzzled.

Grant lifted him onto his shoulders. 'Like this. Easier than slogging through the snow.'

William laughed. 'Not for you!'

They walked on, William riding on Grant's shoulders, until they reached the end.

'Time to turn around,' Grant said.

When they neared the house, Grant put William down again.

After a few steps, William asked, 'Are you going to send me and Anna to school after the holidays?'

'School?' He had never considered it. William seemed a little young at eight years old. Anna certainly was at six. Grant had been sent to school at age ten. 'I'd not planned to,' he replied. 'Would you wish to go?'

'No!' cried William.

'Then you do not have to,' Grant said. 'When you are older you might change your mind, though.'

They were almost to the door when William spoke again. 'Could we have Miss Pearson as our governess, then?'

Grant's insides clenched. 'She will be leaving. She

has somewhere else to go.' No. She had nowhere to go, if she was to be believed.

William glanced up at him, his eyes hopeful. 'I'll wager she would stay if you asked her.'

'Would she?' Grant's heart beat faster.

No. Wait. He did not want her to stay, did he? Both because of what she'd done to him and for what her presence still did to him. But he could not explain all that to the boy.

He felt as if a grey cloud had come down and enveloped him.

'I'll tell you what, William,' Grant said when they reached the door. 'Miss Pearson may stay until Twelfth Night, if she wishes.'

The boy looked up and smiled. 'Thank you... Uncle Grant.'

Lillian smiled to herself when Grant and William left for their walk. Grant was no longer an ogre in William's eyes. The boy worshipped him. And Grant did not fail him. Over and over again Grant proved himself worthy of William's esteem.

And hers.

She and Anna folded the doll clothes again and put them in the box. 'Would you like to bring any of the other toys up to the nursery?' Lillian asked.

The girl shook her head. 'Just my dolls and the doll clothes.'

Lillian carried the box and Anna held her dolls as if they were the most precious items in this house full of priceless treasures.

'May we sit in the room where we eat our meals?' Anna asked. 'I like the chairs there.'

It was a comfortable sitting room, and its fireplace kept it warm and cosy.

'Of course we may,' Lillian responded.

'May we make my dolls some blankets and bed linens so they can sleep?' Anna hugged the antique doll. 'They are very tired.'

Lillian wished she and Grant had found a doll's crib in the attic. 'Yes, we may.'

She stopped by her bedchamber and picked up the basket of fabric and the sewing box, and soon they were settled in the sitting room, hemming squares of fabric to serve as bed linens.

'I am going to make the box their bed,' pronounced Anna.

Lillian thought of the trunk full of fabric up in the attic. There was some cotton wool in there that would make a perfect mattress for the box. It would not be difficult to make—

Except she did not know how long she would be here. The new snow might have earned her another day or two, but after that she would have to leave. Leave the children. Leave Grant.

She paused, her needle poised above her work.

She thought of making love with him, how glorious it felt and so comforting in its familiarity. Comforting and thrilling. It seemed to have erased the seven years they'd been apart. The scent of him; the feel of his hands against her skin; his lips against hers. The heights of delight. It had all come back to her.

And she would lose it again.

She pushed her needle through the fabric. She did not want to think of this now, not when it had been such a lovely day. Idyllic. The sort of Christmas she'd used to dream about when she was a child.

'Shall we make up a story about your doll?' she asked
Anna. That should keep her mind off Grant.

'Oh, yes!' responded Anna. 'Make her be Cinderella!'

'Oh, I do like the story of Cinderella.' A down-trodden
maiden rescued by a prince. A lovely fairy tale indeed.

But only a fairy tale.

'Miss Young read it to me.' Anna's voice had a tinge
of sadness. 'She was my governess.'

Grant simply had to find the woman and bring her
back to Anna and William.

Lillian took a breath. 'Once upon a time, long, long
ago, Cinderella lived with her wicked stepmother and
sisters...'

An hour passed, the story finished, and they had almost enough bed linens and blankets sewn to satisfy
Anna when they heard William's and Grant's voices in
the hallway.

'They are back!' Anna popped up from her chair and
skipped to the door. 'We're in here!' she called to them.

William, pink-cheeked and smiling, walked in carrying his box of soldiers.

Grant held the crate of other toys. 'Where do you want
these?' he asked.

The question took Lillian aback. She had no right to
say where to put toys. She was not really the governess.

'Bring them in here for now.'

He entered the room and put the crate down.

She could smell the out of doors on him. 'Did you
have a pleasant walk?'

'A very pleasant walk,' Grant responded. 'Did we not,
William?'

'The best!' gushed William. 'We walked all the way
to the end of the garden and the snow was deep, so I had
to lift my legs up high. And on the way back I rode on

Uncle Grant's shoulders.' He turned to Anna. 'He said we must call him Uncle Grant, because he is almost our uncle and he wants us to stay and not be sent to school.'

Grant had said all that? What a lovely walk, indeed.

Anna skipped over to Grant and hugged his legs. 'Uncle Grant!'

He picked her up. 'Cook is making you and William some milk and biscuits. It will be here soon.'

She put her small arms around his neck. 'Warm milk and honey?'

He grinned at her. 'Warm milk and honey.' Putting her down, he added, 'Tea for you, Miss Pearson.'

'Will you join us, m'lord?' Lillian asked, her heart melting. How good of him to make it clear that the children would stay with him.

He sat in the chair next to hers.

William turned to Lillian. 'Uncle Grant said you can stay, too, Miss Pearson. You can stay until Twelfth Night.'

Grant opened his mouth in what appeared to be the start of a scold but he shut it again. Finally he said, 'If Miss Pearson wishes to stay, I said, William.'

Stay until the sixth of January? Did she dare? Surely Dinis would be searching for her soon. It was too much to hope the roads would stay snow-filled until January sixth. And what about money? She had none.

She felt the fear creeping back, covering over the pleasant events of the day.

She tried to push it away. 'Thank you, m'lord,' she murmured.

Anna's happy squeal drowned out any further words. The little girl ran over and hugged her. 'I wish you could stay for ever!'

Lillian glanced at Grant. He averted his gaze.

At that moment one of the maids brought the tea, milk

and biscuits and Lillian busied herself serving the children and pouring tea for herself and for Grant.

When the children reached for their second biscuits, Grant said, 'Be sure to save some appetite for dinner. Cook is roasting a goose—'

William interrupted. 'We saw the goose. It was turning on a spit.'

Grant went on. 'And we'll have mince pies and the Christmas pudding which Cook has been tending since Stir-Up Sunday.'

'I'll still be hungry,' William vowed, taking a third biscuit.

'I'll be hungry, too,' Anna added.

'I will count on it, then.' Grant's tone was good-natured. 'I will also count on your good behaviour in front of our guests.'

Guests? This was the first Lillian had heard of guests.

The children seemed to shrink in their seats.

'We are not allowed around guests. Grandfather had guests.' Anna crossed her arms over her chest.

Grant reached across the table and touched her cheek. 'Well, you are allowed around these guests. In fact, they will want to see you. Do you remember Mr Landon who helped us gather evergreens?'

'He was an officer with you in the army,' William said.

'Yes. He's my estate manager now. He and his wife will join us for dinner, assuming there is no more snow and they can walk the short distance.'

Mr Landon? Who looked at Lillian with so much curiosity she was certain he knew everything about her? And his wife, who surely would know of her, too?

'Perhaps it would be better for the children and me to eat Christmas dinner up here,' Lillian said.

Grant gave her a direct look. 'Rhys is my friend more

than my employee. More than a friend. He and Helene will certainly not stand on ceremony. They will welcome you.' His gaze encompassed all of them. 'I want you to come. Miss Pearson, you can borrow a dinner dress. Have Hannah help you.'

At least he was smart enough not to mention the children's mother. Did he not realise she was already wearing Lady Grantwell's dresses every day?

What she really wanted to ask him was why? Why allow her to stay until Twelfth Night? Why want her to attend a dinner with friends? And, while asking why, why had he kissed her again last night? Was it merely the carnal urge that flashed through them both, or had his heart softened towards her?

Or was this invitation to Christmas dinner merely because of his growing attachment to the children? Yes. That was the most likely. She would be attending the dinner as the children's temporary governess, not Grant's former lover.

'We will be eating early,' Grant added. 'At six o'clock. Come to the drawing room.'

Comfortable again, Anna went back to tending her doll. William busied himself removing his toy soldiers from their box.

He looked up at Grant. 'Uncle Grant, would you show me how to put the soldiers in a proper formation?'

'Certainly.' Without a glance to Lillian, Grant walked over to William and sat with him on the floor.

Anna brought her doll to sit closer to them. They made a charming family scene that both touched Lillian's heart and broke it at the same time.

Because she must leave them.

Even before Twelfth Night.

Chapter Thirteen

Hannah had insisted on using all her resources and skills on Lillian's dinner attire. She brought out the most beautiful dinner dress of crimson satin, with a three-quarter-length overdress of silver-striped gauze that shimmered in the candlelight. The bodice and hem of the dress were edged with crimson and white ribbon and ornamented with clusters of silk flowers.

'Oh, no, Hannah,' Lillian exclaimed. 'It is too fine a dress for a governess.'

'No, it is not,' the maid protested—although it clearly was. 'Her Ladyship never even wore it. And it goes so well with your colouring. I have ribbons to put in your hair.' She stood with arms akimbo and feet wide apart. 'Besides, there is not time enough for me to ready another dinner dress and you cannot wear a day dress to a Christmas dinner.'

Lillian doubted all that was true but there was no point to distress Hannah over a dress. 'Very well, but can we remove the flowers? It is simply too ornate.'

Hannah lifted her chin. 'If you insist.'

'I do, Hannah. Please.'

The two of them snipped the threads holding the silk

flowers but instead of making the gown plainer, it simply made it more elegant. The hairstyle Hannah fashioned was equally unsuitable for a governess. She piled Lillian's hair into a chignon high on her head and wove the ribbon through it. She curled tendrils around Lillian's face. She even dusted her face lightly with Lady Grantwell's powder and tinted her cheeks and lips with the barest amount of rouge.

It was nearing six and Lillian wanted to look in on the children and ensure they were dressed. She started to rise from the dressing table.

'One more thing,' Hannah added a few of the small silk flowers to Lillian's chignon. 'There. That is the finishing touch.'

Lillian let the flowers stay for the sake of time. She rose and Hannah helped her don the dress.

'We should go to Lady Grantwell's full mirror so you can see how perfect you look!' Hannah said.

'There is no time.' Lillian peered as best she could into the dressing room mirror. She looked her finest, she thought. Nothing like a governess.

'It is very beautiful,' she admitted. 'Thank you, Hannah. You do excellent work.'

Hannah beamed.

They hurried to the children's room. William and Anna were playing with the spinning top and the ball and cup. William could catch the ball in the cup about every third try.

'Time to get dressed, children,' Lillian said.

They looked up at her and their eyes widened.

'Oh, Miss Pearson, you look pretty!' Anna said.

Lillian felt her cheeks flush. 'Thank you, Anna.'

Between her and Hannah they managed to dress the children quickly in their best clothes—which were looking a bit small on them, Lillian thought. She must tell Grant to send for the local seamstress to come measure them for new clothes once the roads cleared.

When Lillian would be gone.

The children were putting on their shoes when the clock struck six.

'Let us hurry,' Lillian said. 'This is the time Lord Grantwell wanted us in the drawing room.

Anna stopped fiddling with the buckle on her shoe. 'If the yule log has stopped burning it will be cold in there.'

Lillian buckled her shoe for her. 'I am certain Thompson will have seen to a fire. Let us go now.'

'At least the candles burned down. Our wishes should come true, then,' Anna said.

Lillian knew hers would not.

She and the children hurried to the top of the stairs.

William, a worried look on his face, asked, 'Should we run?'

It seemed both William and she were worried that Grant would be displeased with them being late. 'Lord Grantwell probably wants us to walk quietly,' she said.

Anna held back. 'I don't want to go!'

Lillian turned to her, trying not to show her impatience. 'Why not, Anna?'

'I don't like guests.' Anna stopped completely.

Lillian walked back to her and crouched down to her level. 'But these guests are Mr Landon and his wife. You remember how kind Mr Landon was to you when we gathered evergreens?'

Anna's eyes glistened with tears. 'But Grandfather said we must never let guests see us.'

'Oh, Anna!' Lillian gave her a hug.

William came to his sister's side. 'Uncle Grant is not

at all like Grandfather. He wants us there. And Captain Landon is his friend.'

'They will like you,' Lillian assured her.

'No.' Anna crossed her arms over her chest.

Before Lillian could react, William said, 'What if you bring your doll with you?' He turned to Lillian. 'That would be acceptable, would it not, Miss Pearson?'

'Of course it would.' It was an excellent idea, in fact.

'I'll get her.' William ran to their room and brought back the doll, dressed in one of the gowns Lillian had made her.

Anna clutched the doll, but still did not move.

'Come, Anna,' William said in such a kind voice it almost made Lillian cry. 'I will hold your hand.'

William continued to reassure Anna as they made their way down the stairs and through the hall to the drawing room. When they got to the doorway Lillian could see Grant sitting with Mr Landon and a lady who must be Mr Landon's wife. Anna halted again.

She pulled her hand away from William's and, clutching her doll even tighter, would not budge.

William poked her in the arm and pointed above them. 'Anna! Look where you are standing.'

She glanced up at the mistletoe, but her little chin remained set.

Then William did something that made Lillian's heart ache.

William rolled his eyes, gave an exaggerated sigh, then leaned over and gave his sister a kiss on the cheek. '*Now* you can move.'

Anna blinked in surprise but held out her doll. 'Kiss my doll, too!'

He did so, again acting all affronted. Anna smiled a little and William took her hand.

At that moment Grant rose from his chair. 'Here are the children. Come, William and Anna. Meet Mrs Landon.'

Lillian had not expected Mrs Landon, the wife of an estate manager, to be such a regal figure. She was a beauty, as well, with dark hair, pale skin and startling blue eyes.

The introductions were made and Mr and Mrs Landon immediately engaged the children in conversation.

'Is this your doll?' Mrs Landon asked Anna. 'She is so pretty!'

Grant gazed at Lillian who had remained a short distance away. He walked over to her. 'You look…quite elegant, Lillian.'

She did not know if that was censure or a compliment. One glance in the huge mirrors that hung between the windows showed just how unlike a governess she'd dressed. She looked elegant, indeed.

'Hannah chose the dress,' she responded, with a pang of guilt that she might be giving Hannah the blame instead of the credit.

He gave her a puzzled look, but eventually said, 'I almost laughed at William kissing Anna under the mistletoe.'

'I almost cried,' she responded. 'Anna was afraid to come in. William was being exceedingly kind to her.'

'Afraid? Why?' he asked.

'Apparently her grandfather made her afraid to be seen by guests.'

He made a disparaging sound. 'That old goat. I'd kill him if he weren't already dead.'

He walked back to Anna, picked her up, and fussed over her until she was giggling.

'How sweet she is,' Mrs Landon said to him. She glanced over to William. 'They both are.'

'I know it,' Grant said.

'And very good at collecting evergreens,' Mr Landon added, ruffling William's hair. 'Are you not, William?'

William smiled. 'I liked doing it.'

Mrs Landon's gaze turned to Lillian. It was certainly speculative.

Grant noticed. He extended his arm towards Lillian. 'Let me present Miss Pearson to you.'

She walked over and Grant introduced her.

'I understand you have been stranded here,' Mrs Landon said. 'How good of you to help with the children.'

Was she fishing for more information? Or simply trying to put Lillian at ease? Lillian could not tell for certain, although her manner was kind.

'I have enjoyed the children very much,' Lillian responded.

Thompson entered the room, carrying the tray of wassail, the silver punch bowl and the smaller crystal one. He set it on the table.

'I will serve it,' Grant said to Thompson.

Poor Thompson. He would have plenty to do this night without any footmen to help.

'Very good, m'lord.' Thompson bowed and left.

Lillian wished she could have left with him.

Grant turned to the wassail bowl, grateful for an excuse to focus his eyes on anything other than Lillian. She was a vision. Like some gossamer enchantress who'd come to put a spell on him.

Although the children saved him from making a complete cake of himself when they first entered the room. Their introductions gave him time to regain his senses again.

Not that he was very successful.

The children had captured Helene and Rhys's attention so perhaps they had not noticed his discomposure. Helene was rising to the occasion, as she always did, although this could not compare to what she'd done at Waterloo, tending to soldiers horrifically injured during the battle. She embraced the presence of the children and greeted Lillian in a friendly manner. Certainly Rhys had told his wife something about Lillian and Grant's past, although Helene gave no hint of it.

He poured Helene a cup of wassail first. Next he served Lillian. No possibility of avoiding the vision of her then. He caught her eye and she looked so wary and uncomfortable that he felt sorry for her. He gave her a reassuring smile, but that seemed to disconcert her even more.

He did not want her to end this fine day in discomfort. Everything that had made it a wonderful day was due to her, as far as he was concerned. Had he been selfish in wanting the children and Lillian to share in this special Christmas dinner as well?

Next he dipped the ladle into the crystal wassail bowl and served the children.

'Thank you, Uncle Grant,' William said.

He grinned. 'You are welcome.'

The boy did not miss a chance to call him uncle. He was glad he'd proposed it, if only to avoid hearing *'Lord Grantwell'* so many times.

He lowered himself to Anna's level and handed her the cup. 'In this house, Anna, you need not fear anyone, guest or not.'

She clutched her doll in one arm and took the cup in her other hand, looking unconvinced.

Helene had taken a seat on the sofa. She patted the

space next to her. 'Anna, come and sit by me and tell me more about your doll.'

Grant poured two more cups from the silver bowl and handed one to Rhys, who had been somewhat cornered by William.

'Is William asking you army questions?' he asked, handing Rhys the cup.

'He is, indeed,' responded Rhys. 'Intelligent ones.'

Because his gaze seemed to find her wherever she was, Grant saw that Lillian had chosen a chair apart from the rest of them. In Portugal, she'd seemed quite at ease at the formal entertainments the few aristocrats left in Lisbon had invited the British officers to attend. Why not here, in what seemed to Grant more like a family gathering than one that posed any social risk?

He'd meant this as something nice for her, no matter what had happened in the past.

His thoughts were interrupted by William. 'Uncle Grant, would you and Captain Landon tell me what it was like to fight in the Battle of Waterloo?'

He and Rhys exchanged glances and Rhys looked as stricken as Grant felt. The sights, sound, *smells* of the battle returned in that moment, as if it had been yesterday their companies stood in square while wave after wave of cavalry attacked—

He pushed the memory away. 'Talking of a battle wouldn't be quite right in front of the ladies.' Although Helene had witnessed as much carnage on that day as Rhys and Grant had.

William looked stricken, as if he'd done something wrong.

Grant ruffled the boy's hair to reassure him. 'Maybe one day soon Rhys and I can use your tin soldiers to show you the formations Wellington used in the battle. Just us men.'

William's eyes lit up again.

'Tin soldiers?' Rhys piped up. 'Tell me about these tin soldiers.'

William happily described them. In great detail.

Grant's glance drifted over to Lillian again. She at least appeared composed now, but still separate.

They finished their wassail, and each had a second cup before Thompson announced dinner.

Grant led them all to the dining room. They could have eaten in his sitting room, where he took all his meals, but he'd thought this day deserved the formal room—even if there were children eating with them. He had Thompson seat them informally, though. He sat at the end in what he still thought of as his father's chair. Rhys sat on one side of him and Helene on the other. William was next to Rhys, and Anna, who might need some assistance, was between Helene and Lillian. The seating did set Lillian apart again, he realised, seeing them all in their places, and he wished he'd chosen the smaller room and a round table instead.

Still, he refused to let the dinner be anything but happy, putting on his most light-hearted self.

The laughter grew, increasing with the number of glasses of wine they consumed. The children joined in the conversation when invited to and remained very mannerly the whole time. Someone had taught them how to behave. That governess Lillian had spoken of.

Lillian did not talk much, unless someone addressed her directly or she needed to say something to the children. Grant supposed this was precisely as a governess should behave, but he remembered how she had once laughed and actively joined in his fun.

Everyone tried to make poor Thompson's job easier, serving themselves second helpings. Cook had outdone herself. Her centrepiece of holly, spruce, apples and pears had taken a lot of work, but she also had prepared a feast of green pea soup to start, fried gudgeon, cardoons with mushrooms, mince pies, potatoes, parsnips and, of course, the roast goose. And the last course included not only Christmas pudding, but an apple pie as well.

By the time the pudding was served, the children were visibly flagging even though they made a herculean effort to finish both pudding and pie.

'I should take the children to bed,' Lillian said.

At that moment, though, Hannah appeared. 'I'll put the young ones to bed tonight.' The maid smiled.

'I—I do not mind.' Lillian left her chair.

The children immediately rose.

'You must stay at the party, Miss Pearson,' Anna said.

'We do not mind Hannah putting us to bed,' William added.

This looked like something Hannah and the children had contrived, Grant thought. How nice of them. He'd not thought about whether Lillian would stay or leave after the children went to bed. He'd not even considered that the children would need to go to bed before the party ended.

Rhys and Helene bade the children goodnight as Anna and William walked over to Hannah, waiting by the door.

'Goodnight, Anna and William,' Grant said.

William turned back to him. 'Goodnight, everyone. Goodnight, Uncle Grant,' William said. 'Thank you for our nice Christmas.'

He would have hugged the boy had he been close enough. 'I think I must thank you and Anna and Miss Pearson.'

He glanced at Lillian, who had followed them to the doorway and did hug them both. Would she leave anyway?

He realised he wanted very much for her to stay.

Lillian wished she could leave with the children. It was difficult to be with Grant, who appeared especially handsome in his evening attire, a superbly fitted dark blue coat, pristine white neckcloth and waistcoat. He easily looked as handsome as he had in his regimentals. She envied his cheerfulness, as well. And how at home he felt among his friends when she felt so very out of place.

'The children are lovely,' Mrs Landon said when the children disappeared from sight.

'They are quite good children, are they not?' replied Grant. 'Poor tots. I have not a clue what to do with them. They would have had no Christmas at all if not for Miss Pearson.'

Lillian returned to her seat but Mrs Landon gestured for her to sit next to her in Anna's chair.

'You must be very good with them,' Mrs Landon said to Lillian.

'She is,' her husband responded. 'I could see that on our evergreen-gathering expedition.'

'Thank you,' Lillian managed, disliking the attention placed on her.

Thompson returned to remove the pudding dishes and poured glasses of Madeira wine.

Lillian took a sip, even though she'd consumed enough wine throughout the dinner.

'How did you come to be so good with children?' Mrs Landon asked her.

Was she seeking information?

'I used to spend time with the little ones at school.'

Especially the little ones who were left at the school for the holidays as she was.

How much had Grant told this woman?

Lillian changed the subject. 'Do you have children, Mrs Landon?'

The woman smiled and her blue eyes shone with pride. 'I have a one-year-old son. Too young to bring to dinner.' She put a hand on her stomach. 'And another on the way.'

'How happy for you.' Lillian genuinely meant it. She suspected the Landons were a lovely family. From the looks she and her husband tossed each other, they seemed quite devoted to each other. 'Tell me about your son,' she said. 'What is his name?'

Mrs Landon smiled. 'We named him John.'

Grant's given name.

'Is he walking?' she asked, keeping the attention off herself.

'Running, more like it.' Mrs Landon's eyes looked heavenward. 'He is more like his father every day...'

Lillian let Mrs Landon's words wash over her.

When she'd been a mere schoolgirl she used to dream of having a family and a husband—especially after her father died and she no longer saw her mother. When she married Estevo she'd known it was not a love match. Still, she'd hoped it would grow into something resembling what the Landons obviously had. Now, after years of unhappiness, her husband was dead and she was being pursued as his murderer.

Did Helene Landon know all that?

She glanced up at Grant, who was laughing at something his friend had said. She remembered being happy with him like that.

She looked away, only to notice Mrs Landon regarding her.

The woman smiled. 'Should we leave the men to their port and take tea in the drawing room?'

'If you wish,' Lillian managed.

Grant and Mr Landon stood as Mrs Landon rose from her chair. 'When you have finished your important conversation—' They had been merely joking with each other. 'We will be in the drawing room.'

As soon as Lillian and Mrs Landon left the room, Helene grabbed Lillian's arm. 'Please excuse me! I am desperate to refresh myself.' She touched her stomach. 'One of the hazards of being with child, I'm afraid.'

'Of course,' Lillian replied. 'I—'

The lady was already hurrying away. 'Do not worry. I know the way. I will see you in the drawing room. Just a few minutes.'

Lillian could use this moment simply to disappear, but she hated to do that to Mrs Landon who was trying to be nice to her. Instead she went down to the kitchen. Poor Thompson was so overworked, she could at least bring up the tea for him.

When she reached the door of the kitchen, Cook looked up. 'Why, Miss Pearson! Look at you, looking so beautiful.'

Lillian's cheeks grew hot. 'Thank you, Mrs Bell. Hannah did wonders.'

'She did indeed!' Her expression turned puzzled. 'But what are you doing down here, miss?'

'I came to carry the tea to the drawing room. Thompson has been so busy.'

'No. No. No.' Cook shook her finger. 'You will risk spilling on that lovely dress. Mary or Sally can do it.'

'I'll carry the tea,' Mary piped up. 'It is nearly ready to go.' She poured water from the kettle on the fire into the teapot and picked up the tray.

Lillian walked ahead of her.

'How was the party, miss?' Mary asked. 'Did the children like it?'

'Everything has been perfect,' Lillian told her. It was true, even if Lillian felt she never should have been a part of it. 'The food was delicious, thanks to all your hard work. The children were delighted. And well-behaved.'

'Aye, they've been little angels since you arrived, miss,' Mary said.

They reached the drawing room and Mary placed the tray on the table where the punch bowls had been. Someone had cleared all the cups and bowls from the room.

'Thank you, Mary,' Lillian said.

'That is all right, miss,' Mary responded. 'I like seeing this room. It is so pretty.'

'Happy Christmas,' Lillian said.

'See you tomorrow for St Stephen's Day!' The girl grinned.

Chapter Fourteen

Mrs Landon returned to the drawing room right after Mary left. Lillian was still standing next to the tea service.

'Oh, tea already?' Mrs Landon said. 'How nice!'

'Shall I pour for you?' Lillian asked.

'Please.'

Mrs Landon told her how she preferred her tea and settled on the couch.

After Lillian handed her the cup and poured her own tea, Mrs Landon said, 'Come sit by me.'

Lillian reluctantly did as she asked.

The lady smiled. 'I am going to pry. It is not usually my nature, but I cannot help it this time.'

Just as Lillian feared.

Mrs Landon charged ahead. 'I know you and Grant have a past together in Portugal. I confess I was prepared to see you as a villainess, but now, meeting you, I do not think so. You are in love with Grant, are you not?'

Lillian felt pain wash through her. She could refuse to answer. Should refuse to answer. 'I—I do not know,' she responded honestly.

She did know that her senses heightened every moment she was with him. She knew her body craved him. She knew her heart grew to bursting when she witnessed his kindness to the children. She knew her heart would break when she had to leave him and never see him again.

'He is...' She searched for the right words. 'He is the finest man I have ever known.' She felt compelled to go on. 'I assure you, ma'am, I am not a villainess. I do not know what you have been told, but I am innocent of the wrongs of which I am accused.'

'But Grant does not believe you?' Mrs Landon posed this as a question.

Lillian shook her head.

'Then why come here?' Mrs Landon asked.

Lillian averted her gaze. 'I was desperate.'

Mrs Landon grasped her hand. 'Tell me, Miss Pearson. Tell me why you were desperate.'

Lillian told her the whole story. Of her husband's murder. Of being accused. Of running to her old headmistress. Of almost being discovered there by her brother-in-law who had vowed to avenge her husband's death. Of Dinis being right at her heels.

'My money was running out.' Was gone, actually. 'I needed somewhere to hide, someone to help me, so my brother-in-law could not catch me. Grant did not want me to stay. I think he still does not, but he is waiting for the snow to clear enough to make the road to the village passable. Then I must leave, but I do not know where to go next without any money. The children asked him to let me stay until Twelfth Night and he agreed, for the children's sake. I do not think it was what Grant wished, though.'

Mrs Landon squeezed Lillian's hand. 'Then why did he invite you to Christmas dinner?'

'Oh, that was for the children as well,' she responded. 'He did not want to leave them out.'

Mrs Landon looked sceptical. She released Lillian's hand and took a sip of her tea. 'Then why does he look at you the way he does?'

Thompson left the bottle of port on the table after pouring the first glasses for Grant and Rhys. Grant twirled the stem of the glass with his fingers.

Rhys took a sip. 'So, what is the current situation with Miss Pearson?'

Grant looked up in surprise. 'Current situation?'

'She remains here.'

Grant gave him a sour look. 'The roads are still bad. Besides, do you think I am despicable enough to toss her out at Christmas?'

'Foolish enough, perhaps.' Rhys grinned. 'Or scared enough.'

'Scared enough?' What the devil did Rhys mean by that? 'No. She's here because of the weather. And the children. They want her to stay until Twelfth Night.'

'And of course you said yes.' Rhys smirked. He leaned towards Grant. 'Face it, my good friend. You are still besotted with her.'

Grant downed the contents of his glass and poured himself another. 'There is…there is still a definite attraction.' He consumed the second glass. 'But she must leave.'

Rhys sipped his port. 'What if she really didn't spy for the French? She hardly seems the sort.'

Grant had to agree with him. 'I confess, I begin to wonder.' Or had it simply ceased to matter?

Grant poured another glass.

They turned the conversation to estate business. And to remembrances of friends lost in battle. But it did neither of them any good to tear open the grief of over all the good men who'd died. Instead, as if by mutual agree-

ment, they rose to join the ladies for tea before they fell
into that abyss.

In the drawing room, Lillian and Helene were seated
together, talking companionably, which surprised and
somewhat disconcerted Grant. What might they be discussing? Him, no doubt.

Rhys grinned at his wife and leaned down to give
her a kiss. He seemed to be especially feeling the effects of all the wine they'd consumed. Grant was a little
unsteady himself.

He wandered over to the window and glanced out.
'More snow falling.' Not thick, just enough to further
enchant this night.

'Snow?' Rhys walked over to stand next to him. He
groaned. 'I am heartily weary of snow. We had better
leave before it gets heavier.'

Helene rose. 'Yes. We should be off anyway. It grows
late.'

It was ten o'clock. Grant and Rhys used to drink the
night away and still rise early to drill their companies.

Helene turned to Lillian, who had also risen from her
seat. 'It was lovely to meet you.'

Lillian merely nodded.

Helene walked over to Grant and kissed him on the
cheek. 'Thank you for a lovely evening, Grant. Please
stay and finish your tea. And do not bother Thompson.
Rhys and I will find our cloaks and boots in the cloak-
room. We know our way out.'

Helene took Rhys's arm. When they reached the doorway, Rhys pulled her to a stop and pointed to the mistletoe above their heads. Helene laughed as Rhys planted
a deep, sensual kiss upon her lips. When they finally
broke apart, they continued out of the room arm in arm
and seemingly oblivious of their audience.

Grant glanced at Lillian. She'd seen them too, of course. She avoided his eye.

Rhys and Helene's kiss had roused a deep longing in Grant. Not necessarily for its sensuality, but for the bond that existed between them. He envied them. Helene had been born a lady, but she'd given up that distinction and that life to marry Rhys. Rhys had given up the army for her. And they were blissfully happy.

What would Grant be willing to give up to have that sort of bond?

He remained by the window but his gaze drifted back to Lillian. He'd felt that bond briefly with Lillian, when they rummaged through the chests in the attic looking for toys for the children and when they wrapped the gifts together, planning for this day. Was he willing to give up his old anger at her?

She cleared her throat. 'Now your guests have left, I should retire as well.'

And leave him alone? He had no desire to end this day alone with nothing but a glass of brandy for company.

'If that is what you wish.'

She started for the doorway.

'Lillian?'

She turned towards him.

'You look very beautiful tonight.'

The compliment did not seem to please her.

'It upsets you for me to say so. Why?' he asked.

She shook her head as if exasperated. 'Hannah dressed me as if I were one of your guests, not the children's governess.'

He took a step towards her. 'But you are not the children's governess. You are a guest.'

'I am not a guest. I am a woman from the past whom you did not wish to see ever again, but who is desperate for help.' Her eyes flashed in annoyance and pain. 'A fact your friends are quite aware of.'

'Yes. So what would be the point of you pretending to be the governess?' His own temper was beginning to flare. The dinner was meant to be something nice for her. 'Neither of my friends were unkind to you, were they?'

'No,' she admitted. 'Mrs Landon was particularly kind. Although she seemed to think you and I again could be—' She stopped herself. 'She did not comprehend the breadth of the breach between us.'

More like a wall. A wall that could not be breached.

Grant ignored the wave of sadness that thought brought on, preferring anger instead. 'Did you expect me to say nothing about you to my friends? Rhys is closer to me than my own brother ever was. I do not hide information from him.' Not much information, that was.

She pressed a hand to her forehead. 'Oh, what does it matter now? Please grant me your leave. I wish to check on the children and then go to bed.' Her eyes widened slightly, as if she feared he would take her words as an invitation.

But Grant knew it was no invitation. The other time they'd made love had been a moment of weakness when their emotions were raw with pain, not anger.

There was one thing he could feel good about. Watching William soak up kindness as if he were the very driest of sponges. Seeing him smile.

That was Lillian's doing.

'Goodnight, then, Lillian,' he murmured.

His gaze followed her as she crossed the room. The candlelight caught on the silver threads of her dress and the ribbons in her hair, making her shimmer, making her into even more of an ethereal figure. But it was not only her beauty that made him ache with longing. He simply wanted to be with her.

She reached the doorway.

'Lillian, wait!' he called out.

She turned back to him, her expression confusing—one of pain? Wariness? Anger?

He walked over to her so he would not have to raise his voice from across the room. She waited.

He came perhaps too close, close enough to inhale that scent of evergreen around her, as if she herself were a creature of Christmas.

'I—I simply wished to thank you,' he managed. 'To thank you for this Christmas. On—on behalf of the children. And me.'

'Oh, Grant.' Her expression softened, but he still saw pain there. 'Do not give me credit when you did so much.'

He opened his mouth to protest, but twisted it into an ironic smile. 'We could argue all night about who made this a happy Christmas.' Better than arguing about his friends—or the past.

She lowered her gaze for a moment, before raising her eyes to him again, with a small smile. 'I will agree to share the credit, then.'

They stared at each other, neither moving.

Finally she blinked and shook her head a little. 'Well, I shall say goodnight, then.'

He smiled at her again, although sadness at being alone filled him. 'Goodnight, Lillian.'

She turned to go.

'Wait!' The command burst unbidden from him.

She turned back.

He cast his gaze above him, to where the mistletoe hung on its festive ribbon.

Her eyes widened, but she did not move.

He took a step closer, leaning down to her. 'I meant it,' he murmured. 'Thank you, Lillian.'

Lightly touching her cheek with his thumb, he pressed his lips very gently to hers, wanting more, but willing to let her go if she so chose. Instead she stayed in the kiss. He promised himself he would remember the softness of her lips against his, the taste of tea and Christmas pudding on them. Another memory to intrude, along with more sensual ones. And the heartbreaking ones.

Her arms slid up his chest and he felt her hands caress the back of his neck. A sound escaped her. Something like a sigh. Or a moan.

She deepened the kiss and it was like lighting tinder inside him. He flared with need. He wrapped his arms around her and pressed his body against hers.

'Grant…' she murmured against his lips, her voice urgent.

He moved to kiss her cheek, her delicate ears, her neck. Sadness, regret, anger, all fled from him, chased by the joy of having her in his arms again.

But he let her go, easing himself away. He'd sparked the carnal urge that now flamed between them. He knew they both could barely resist giving in to it. He'd led her into making love three nights before and knew he'd taken advantage of her then. They'd had enough nights together in Portugal for him to know she'd be powerless to refuse him.

At arm's length, he gazed at her. 'Do you want this, Lillian? I will not force you.'

'You did not force me before,' she responded.

'Not physically, but I know what happens between us.'

She met his gaze. 'I know as well. I also know that soon I will never see you again—' Her voice cracked and she did not continue.

'I want you,' he murmured. 'I want you above all things at this moment, no matter what else lies between us.'

Lillian inhaled a deep breath and released it slowly. 'Let us walk upstairs. Then we will see. Perhaps the fever will leave us.'

In a way, the fever had already left him. Grant filled with a peacefulness that was unexpected. He suddenly wanted whatever she wanted—even if she did not want him. The absurd notion felt freeing.

He glanced up at the mistletoe above her head and quickly stepped forward to touch his lips to hers again. He ended the kiss after the lightest touch.

He grinned at her. 'I believe Anna would be pleased. Two kisses under the mistletoe.'

She smiled back. 'I believe you are correct.'

He took her hand. 'Let us go.'

Instead of a frantic rush to the bedchamber, they sauntered into the hall.

'I liked your friends, by the way,' she remarked as they crossed the hall. 'They were good to the children, were they not?'

'I knew they would be.' He laughed. 'Although I am certain my mother—my father, too, perhaps—is turning over in the grave because *children* dined in her dining room. And the *estate manager* was an invited guest.'

'I confess when I spent Christmases in Reading among my school-fellows, I would not have known such a formal dining room.'

'Christmas here was for parties,' he said. 'My brother and I were merely part of the entertainment. We ate in the nursery, while my parents and their guests feasted on elaborate dinners. Even when I was old enough I only dined here with guests a handful of times. I was bored to tears.'

She laughed, a musical sound.

They reached the first floor.

'I preferred this dinner to those,' he said, his voice low.

They continued down the hallway that led to the nursery rooms.

'I just want to check on the children.' She walked a little faster, away from him.

'I'll get a candle.' He stopped in her room and used a taper to light a candle from the fireplace.

She waited at the children's door until he brought the light. Quietly opening the door, she peered in while he held the candle.

'They are like angels,' she murmured.

Both children were curled up in their beds. Anna's arm was wrapped around her doll. William's box of tin soldiers was on the table next to his bed. That they treasured those old toys made Grant's heart ache for their lives up to today. How could anyone not have wanted these children?

They backed out of the room and Lillian closed the door.

Without Lillian, how long would it have taken Grant to pay attention to the children?

'I am grateful to you for them,' he told her as they walked back to her room.

They stopped at her door and, although he yearned to enfold her in his arms, he also knew he would accept her refusal if it meant keeping this momentary peace between them. He felt no walls needing to be breached. They were together for at least this space of time. He did not feel alone and would not feel alone even if she bade him goodnight.

* * *

Lillian gazed up at his face, illuminated by the candle. Had she ever felt so calm in his company? His handsome features still set her heart to racing, but she felt entirely in control of herself and her emotions.

He waited and she knew he waited for her to decide, but she sensed no pressure from him, as if it was really fully up to her whether or not they made love. She was used to being swept away by him, like last time, when her emotions had been bursting and she'd felt unbearably hungry for him.

'This is strange,' she said. 'I feel as if I could say goodnight to you and be content with it.'

He nodded. 'I feel the same.'

She knitted her brows. 'Do you wish me to say goodnight?'

He regarded her with a soft smile. 'I desire you, as always, but I want nothing to destroy this…this tranquillity.' He touched her cheek. 'I assure you this is quite a new experience for me.'

'And for me,' she responded. 'We are not in a passion, but we are not arguing either.'

His smile broadened. 'Imagine that.'

'So I am to decide?'

'Yes,' he said. 'You are to decide.'

She took a breath and smiled back at him. 'Lord Grantwell, would you like to share my bed this night?'

His eyes twinkled as he pretended to deliberate. 'Miss Pearson, I would be honoured.'

She opened her bedchamber door and they entered the room. Grant put the candle on a table and its light joined with the fireplace to illuminate the room. He touched her cheek again and drew her into a long kiss. When they parted their gazes held.

'Come,' he murmured. 'I will act as lady's maid.'

She presented her back to him so he could undo the row of buttons. She slipped out of the dress and it pooled onto the floor. At other times, other dresses had been left where they lay, but she picked up this one and draped it carefully over a chair. He next untied her corset, and with that garment gone she stood only in her shift and stockings.

She turned to him, helping him out of his coat, unbuttoning his waistcoat, hanging both neatly on another chair. She untied his neckcloth and laid it with the coat. As she did so, he kicked off his shoes and pulled his shirt over his head. It joined his other clothes. She unbuttoned his pantaloons and pulled them down to his feet. He shrugged out of them, now dressed only in his drawers and stockings.

He took her in his arms again and kissed her. When he released her, she took his hands in hers and led him to her bed.

She felt as if they were under a spell which took away everything but this time together. There was no past. No future to fear. No one else to think about. Just she and Grant together.

She climbed onto the bed and he followed her, lounging beside her.

'Shall I take your stockings off?' he asked.

She put her arms over her head and presented one leg to him, relishing the feel of his hands against the skin of her leg. One stocking gone, she gave him her other leg. And afterward she pulled her shift over her head. This garment and the stockings she dropped to the floor.

He stared at her, lying before him. His eyes slowly travelled over every inch of her and she felt his gaze as acutely as his fingers removing her stockings.

'You are still too dressed,' she said, unfastening his drawers and pulling off his stockings to join hers on the floor.

There was no hurry, no urgency between them. Lillian had the notion they could have stopped even at that moment without distress. She had no desire to stop, though, but also no need to rush.

He touched her, his hand gentle as it stroked her. All of her. Arms. Legs. From her neck to just short of the most private part of her. She knew how a cat must feel when someone stroked its fur. The need in her grew, a tiny flame, seemingly content to burn slowly, not too hot, not too cold.

She urged him onto his back, returning to him the pleasure he'd given her. His skin was taut against his muscles and rough from scars of battle.

She fingered one of them, just under his ribcage. 'What happened here?'

'A French sabre,' he responded, his voice languid, as if it were a trifle. 'At Salamanca. Not deep enough to do any real harm.'

There were other scars as well—scars that had not been there when they'd had their affair in Lisbon. When he'd left her, feeling angry and betrayed, he'd gone on to fight battle after battle and if that one scar was any indication he might easily have lost his life.

She leaned down and kissed it. 'What happened to the French soldier?'

'My sword went deeper.'

She laid her head against his chest and, not wanting to think of all the death from that war, listened to the very alive beating of his heart.

She sat up enough to be able to look him in the eye. 'I'm glad you survived.'

He pressed her head against his heart again and laughed. The sound was glorious, like some fanciful drumbeat coming through his chest.

'I am glad, too,' he murmured.

He lifted her above him and entered her, that oh-so-familiar feeling of him filling her, filling the empty spaces inside her.

She moved slowly, happy to bestow the pleasure upon him and to set the pace herself. She did not hurry. She wanted to remember every stroke, every sensation of this night.

He groaned and fixed his hands on her hips, but joined her rhythm.

He groaned again and the flame inside her grew hotter and hotter still. She looked down at him as they moved together. Their gazes caught. She saw the arousal in his face, the loss of coherent thought, the giving up of everything to the sensation created between them. It built in her until her release erupted inside her, then erupted again. And again.

Only then did he arch his back, and she felt him convulse inside her. She slid to his side and snuggled next to him, his scent filling her nostrils, his warmth warming her. His presence comforting her.

Chapter Fifteen

Grant knew by her soft, even breaths that Lillian had fallen asleep. He was afraid to move lest he wake her. Never had he bedded her so…quietly. The pleasure of it was unique and would stay with him a long time. He felt sated. Settled.

And bereft, because this was all so temporary.

Even if what had happened in Portugal no longer mattered quite so much to him, she could not stay. She would need a better place to hide than with a former lover. People talked. It would become known she was here and eventually her brother-in-law would think to look for her here.

No, he must release her. For her sake. Send her somewhere safe. To some remote estate in Scotland. Or better yet the Colonies where any chance of him seeing her again would be gone.

The thought was like a death blow.

He tried to contrive some other plan, one that would keep her in his life, but he knew he was fooling himself. That wish would never come true.

He must have slept, because when he opened his eyes again, she had rolled over. The candle had burned down to its nub, the fire in the fireplace was low, and through the window he could see the sky's first light.

He eased himself from the bed, hoping he'd not jostle her. There was a definite chill in the room. He hurried to gather his stockings and to don his drawers. He was buttoning them when the bed linens rustled. He turned.

Lillian's eyes were open. 'You are leaving?' she murmured.

'It's nearly dawn. I presume you do not want Hannah or the children to find me here.'

'Nearly dawn?' She stretched and sat up, covering herself with the blanket. 'If you say this was a mistake, I shall throttle you.'

He leaned down to kiss her but it merely made him want to crawl in next to her and savour her a bit longer.

'No mistake,' he said. 'No regrets. It was quite astounding.'

She smiled at his words, but he pulled himself away from her and put on his pantaloons and shirt.

He placed another log on the fire and started for the door, but turned around abruptly and returned to her kiss her one last time.

One last time—for the moment. She would stay at least until Twelfth Night, would she not? There would be other nights like this one before the end came.

That was some comfort.

Grant slept only a couple of hours in his own bed. He rose near his usual time and dressed himself. It was St Stephen's Day. He'd told Thompson to let the servants know they should each come to see him in the library that morning and that they were to do as little work as possible that day.

Rhys, with Helene's help, no doubt, had prepared the

boxes for the servants and the stable workers. Modest bonuses and some sweet treats. It seemed that everyone but he had thought about Christmas and prepared for it. Perhaps some day he'd get used to the duties of being Viscount Grantwell.

He walked to the window. The day was grey and the cold from outside seeped through. There would be scant melting of snow today. What did it matter? All was well.

He pulled on his boots and left the room lighter in spirits than he'd felt…since that winter in Lisbon.

He hoped he was early enough to take breakfast in the kitchen and save Cook and Thompson some work. This was their holiday and they certainly deserved a rest, carrying the load for all the servants who'd been given time to visit their families.

He reached the kitchen, where Cook was fussing with something on the stove.

'Mrs Bell. Do not tell me I have caught you working.'

She turned and gave an embarrassed laugh. 'I was just making some porridge.'

'Porridge sounds precisely what I have a hunger for.' He walked over to the stove. 'But you sit. I'll stir it.'

She swatted his hand. 'No, you will not, you scamp. You will ruin it for sure. Sit and I'll dish it out for you. It is almost ready.'

He knew his way around the kitchen from hanging about when he was a boy. 'I'll make some tea if you will sit with me and have a cup.'

'Lawd, boy,' she said in a scolding tone. 'Your father would be tanning your hide if he were alive.'

'Mrs Bell, I have probably spent more time in your company here in this kitchen than with my own mother, certainly more time than with my father. I can think of no one I'd rather share a cup of tea with.'

She harrumphed. 'If you insist.'

He fixed the tea and she spooned out a bowl of porridge for him.

'Where are Mary and Sally?' he asked.

Mrs Bell made a disapproving sound. 'Asleep, most likely. Some around here do not know their duty.'

He gestured for her to sit. 'Now, you and those two have taken on more than you bargained for, staying here for Christmas. Let the girls have their day off.' He pointed to her. 'As should you.'

She settled into a chair and frowned. 'You would all go hungry if I did not make you some food.'

He poured her tea and handed the cup to her. 'You are right, Mrs Bell. You take very good care of us all. I do not know what I would have done without you. Especially since the children arrived here.'

She took a sip from her cup. 'I understand the children had a very nice day yesterday?'

Thompson and Hannah must have told her.

'They did. As did I. I think it was the most pleasant Christmas I have ever passed in this house.'

She laughed. 'That is not high praise.' She took another sip. 'And Miss Pearson? Did she enjoy herself?'

He immediately thought about sharing her bed. 'I believe so. Mostly, anyway.'

'Hannah said she looked very elegant.'

He nodded. 'She looked beautiful.'

'She should stay.' Mrs Bell gave a firm nod. 'You should ask her to stay. She's a charm with the children.'

And with him.

He glanced away. 'She has reasons she cannot stay.'

'Well, it is a shame, I say. You should talk her into it.' She lifted her teacup. 'She's a treasure.'

When Grant was a boy, he'd always marvelled that the

servants all seemed to know everything that was going on in the family. How much did they know about Lillian? He doubted they knew any details, but could they fail to see there was some connection between them?

In any event, he'd have a harder time concealing that connection after last night.

Lillian rose when the clock struck seven. She washed and dressed and pinned her hair into a simple bun, all the time thinking of Grant. It sent tears to her eyes to recall how tender and loving their night had been. Not the emotionless coupling she'd endured with her husband. Not the frantic, passionate lovemaking she'd shared with Grant before. Something elevated, more than carnal desire, something that felt as comforting as it had been sensuous. To think she might have gone her whole life without ever experiencing such glorious sensations and emotions.

She must remember it always.

She hurried to the children's room.

The little dears stirred and rubbed their eyes, the sound of her opening the door apparently waking them.

'Time to wake up,' she said.

Anna sat up and stretched her arms over her head. 'Is today the day we give our gifts to the servants?'

'It is, indeed,' Lillian responded. 'It is also the day when they rest and we must take care of ourselves as best we can. So rise from your beds. Let us get you dressed.'

'Wait!' Anna cried, looking all around her. 'Where is my doll?'

William jumped out of bed and picked up the doll from the floor. 'Here she is.'

Anna hugged her, then frantically looked around again. 'Where is her doll?' She looked in her bed and found the wooden figure William had made for her under her pillow. 'I have found her. And the rag doll, too. I have three dolls now!'

Rich with dolls, Anna was content to get dressed, and soon they were all ready to go.

'Shall we walk down to the kitchen so Hannah or the maids won't have to bring the food to us?' Lillian asked the children.

'That is a good idea,' William responded.

'We will save them work!' Anna cried.

How had Hannah ever found these children troublesome? They were so eager to please.

As they neared the staircase Lillian glanced at the closed door to Grant's bedchamber. Was he there? In his bed, sleeping, his skin warm and the beat of his heart slow and rhythmic?

No, his habit was to rise early. Was he even in the house or was he off on some business with Mr Landon? Was he thinking about their lovemaking as well?

As they reached the hall, there he was, entering on the other side, looking slightly rumpled, as if he'd made a choice of comfort over a pristine appearance.

'Uncle Grant!' Anna ran to him and was gathered in his strong but gentle arms.

'Good morning!' He greeted her with a smile.

William hurried up to him as well. 'Good morning, sir. Did you sleep well?'

Grant laughed and ruffled the boy's hair. 'Very well.' He shot a glance to Lillian and his smile widened. 'Very well indeed. And you?'

'I slept very well, thank you.'

Lillian felt her cheeks go warm under Grant's smile. 'We are off to the kitchen to save the servants from bringing breakfast to us.'

'Excellent plan,' Grant responded. 'I was just there myself. I'll go back with you, though. I know the kitchen backwards and forwards and maybe we can save Cook any work at all.' He gestured with the hand that was not holding Anna. 'Lead the way, William.'

To Anna's delight, he carried her all the way down the stairs, as effortlessly as if she'd been made of feathers. Lillian simply savoured the memory of those same arms holding her.

In the kitchen, Cook was busy at the oven.

'Mrs Bell,' Grant admonished. 'You are supposed to have the day off.'

She wiped her hands on her apron. 'Well, I had to make bread, didn't I?'

He looked heavenward, as if exasperated. 'You are hopeless. Sit, Mrs Bell,' he told her. 'I'll serve this lot. Have another cup of tea.'

The kitchen was warm and comforting with its aromas of porridge and baking bread. And the novelty of a man bustling about the space made Lillian smile. Mrs Bell engaged the children in telling her all about their Christmas. Lillian poured herself a cup of tea and watched it all with unpredicted contentment. And an uncoiling fear.

For when this time would end.

When they finished eating, Grant commandeered the children to help him wash the dishes. At Lillian's insistence, Mrs Bell told her what cold foods could be served this day, most left over from the Christmas dinner.

When the dishes were done and the surfaces wiped clean, Mrs Bell rose from her chair. 'You children deserve a biscuit for all that hard work.' She opened a tin from a nearby counter.

They also needed a change of clothes having splashed as much water on themselves as on the dishes.

'Thank you, Mrs Bell,' they both said.

As they were leaving, Grant reminded Mrs Bell, 'Do not forget to come to the library today for your Christmas box. I'll be there directly.'

'We have gifts for you, too,' William said.

Grant turned to William. 'I heard you had gifts for the servants. You are welcome to bring them to the library and give them out as I do. You may bring some toys to entertain yourselves as well.'

Lillian's heart swelled with love for him. Including the children. Feeding them. Caring for his servants.

'May we?' William asked her.

'Of course you may,' she replied. 'After you change into dry clothes.'

Grant directed his gaze to her. 'You may come as well, Miss Pearson.'

She felt the colour rise in her cheeks again. 'Let me do some of Hannah's chores first. Make the beds. Tidy the rooms. Take care of the clothes.'

Once out of the kitchen, the children ran ahead. Grant fell into step with Lillian and took her hand, squeezing it before letting go. He released her quickly, but she'd felt his message.

At this moment they were as together as they had ever been.

By the time Grant had set up the Christmas boxes in the library, the children appeared in dry clothes. William carried a basket that held wrapped gifts and his box of tin soldiers. Anna brought her doll and all the doll's things.

William set the basket on the floor. 'Miss Pearson told us she must tend to Hannah's duties, but she might come down if she has a chance.'

Rhys sat behind his desk, the boxes lined up in front

of him, names affixed, so he'd give each to the proper person—Helene's efficiency, no doubt. William's wood carving of the soldier was also prominently displayed.

'Find yourselves a chair or play on the floor,' he said to the children. 'We will have plenty of time.'

William immediately sat on the carpet near Grant and opened his box of soldiers.

Anna asked, 'May I show my doll to the stone people?'

'You may.' Grant would forever more think of his grandfather's sculptures as the stone people. 'Have you named your doll?'

Anna nodded. 'She is Lady Charlotte. Like the Queen.'

'That is a silly name,' William said.

'It is not!' protested Anna. She turned to Grant. 'I shall call her Lottie.'

'Good choice.' He suppressed a grin.

They passed a calm morning, with the household servants appearing one by one to receive their gifts and bonuses.

The kitchenmaids and housemaids came first, although they did not tarry there and left before opening their boxes or unwrapping the gifts from the children.

Hannah was next, but Hannah opened her box immediately. She looked into the purse inside and her face lit up. 'Thank you, m'lord.'

Rhys must have guessed the proper amount of coin to give her. How the devil he knew such a thing, Grant could not say. 'Thank you, Hannah, for all your hard work.'

She tore into the wrapped gift from the children. 'Oh, now I know why you were wanting to find fabrics and lace and things. I can do a lot with these. Thank you, Miss Anna, Master William.'

'Miss Pearson helped us,' Anna piped up.

'Did she, now?' Hannah responded. 'I will thank her as well.'

She made a quick curtsey to Grant and breezed out through the door.

Cook bustled in and made the biggest fuss over the wrapped package the children gave her. 'Now is that not the nicest thing, you making a gift for me? I am thinking it was a very happy day when you came to live with us.'

She could not have said a kinder thing to them, Grant thought.

Cook went on. 'I believe I will make a meat pie for your dinner. Can't have you all eating cold meat on such a cold day. Perhaps I'll bake you something as well.'

Grant almost laughed. There was no stopping Mrs Bell, even on her day off. 'Do not forget to take a rest,' he said to her.

She gave him a puzzled look. 'I am resting. I have hardly anything to do.' She lifted up her box. 'You can be certain I'll be looking inside this one, m'lord. I know you will be generous. You were generous last year. Much more than your brother.'

Rhys had only been the manager for a few months before last Christmas had come up, but Grant had been stuck in London and had not given any thought to Christmas boxes. That had all been Rhys. Grant thanked God his friend had accepted the position as his estate manager. Between the two of them they'd been able to weather the financial chaos left by his brother and his brother's manager, who had probably kept part of the Christmas bonuses for himself, come to think of it. The thief.

Cook rushed out as quickly as she'd arrived.

Throughout the morning the stable workers and the tenants came in. The snow was packed down enough to make getting around the estate possible. The roads would be passable soon too and Twelfth Night would come all too quickly.

Grant frowned at that thought.

Thompson was the last to come in.

'I hope you have been resting today, Thompson.' Grant greeted him with a smile.

'I have indeed, m'lord,' Thompson replied. 'With a particularly fine book.'

'I am glad.' He handed Thompson his box. 'Yesterday was very busy for you, I am afraid.'

Thompson took the box. 'Not too busy. It was especially a pleasure to see the children enjoy themselves.'

Anna and William stood up from where they were playing on the floor and stood beside Grant. 'We did enjoy ourselves, Mr Thompson,' William said. 'Thank you very much.'

Thompson's mouth quivered. 'You are welcome.'

'We have a present for you.' Anna held out the wrapped package.

'This is an unexpected surprise,' the butler said. He put down his box on the desk and took the wrapped gift. 'Shall I open it now?'

'Yes!' cried Anna.

Thompson's wrapped gift looked different from the others, given to the female servants. Theirs had been flat and his was cube-shaped.

As he unwrapped it, Anna told him, 'William made it himself.'

It was a wooden box, about six inches square. The boy must have worked hard on all the items he created. What a worthy skill. Grant picked up his wooden soldier and rubbed his thumb against it. Perhaps Dawson could be on the alert for good carving wood. Keep William in good supply.

Thompson held the box up high and examined it. 'Now, that is the finest wooden box I have ever owned.'

Grant was filled with affection for the butler. How dear these old retainers were to him. So important in his childhood and never a disappointment now.

Thompson looked William in the eye. 'Thank you, Master William.'

Grant thought William would burst with pride.

'Well,' Thompson said, 'I must take my leave. Thank you, m'lord. Thank you, children.'

'Enjoy your day, Thompson.'

After the butler had left, Grant stood and stretched his legs. It was near noon, but the day did not look any brighter.

'That went well, did it not?' he asked the children.

'They liked our gifts!' Anna said.

'Mine too.' Grant grinned.

Lillian finished Hannah's chores with renewed appreciation for all the maid accomplished in a day. She descended the stairs and made her way to the library. When she entered the room, William was putting his toy soldiers back in their box.

'We are all finished, Miss Pearson,' William told her.

'I missed it all?' She glanced at Grant and her heart lightened at the mere sight of him.

'You missed it *all*!' Anna responded.

'They liked our presents,' William added.

'The presents were indeed happily received.' Grant met her eye.

She held his gaze. 'I am glad of it.'

His smile did not falter. 'Shall we go down to the kitchen for some refreshment? I am certain these children have earned something sweet.'

'Very well.' Lillian returned his smile.

William and Anna ran ahead.

Grant took Lillian's hand and kissed it. Sensation flared through her. How unique it felt to be so comfortable in his presence yet so filled with excitement.

'I have one more bonus to give,' he said.

'Oh? I thought you said you were finished?'

He fished in a pocket and pulled out a purse. He took her hand again and placed the purse in it. It was heavy with coin. She gazed into his eyes, a question on her lips.

He spoke first. 'There should be enough there to keep you safe until you are settled. And if you need more you need only to write to me.'

'Grant—' She could not make herself speak. He had rescued her!

He touched her cheek. 'When it is time for you to leave, you cannot go without a penny in your pocket.'

She lifted the purse. 'This is more than a penny.'

He enfolded her in a quick embrace. 'It is less than you have given me.'

They broke apart, lest someone in the household see them.

'How can I ever thank you?' she asked as they walked.

He grinned at her. 'Well, you could curtsey to me. That is what the maids did.'

She skipped ahead and dipped into a curtsey fit for the Queen's drawing room.

He laughed.

She took his arm again. 'Were the others happy with their bonuses?'

'They seemed to be,' he replied. 'I have Rhys to thank for that. I am getting a great deal of credit for this Christmas that truly belongs to others.'

She jostled him. 'Do not keep saying so.' He could not

see all he'd done, especially the way he'd included the children in everything. And then there was his gift of money for her. All she needed now was a position some place far away and she would be safe.

'They were all surprised and touched by the children's gifts,' he went on, sliding her a glance. 'The gifts you arranged.'

She had done no more than any good governess would, had she not? 'I did not arrange William's gifts,' she remarked. 'Those were his own doing.'

'William is a constant surprise,' Grant said with pride in his voice. 'He is a fine boy.'

By the time they reached the kitchen William and Anna were already seated and Cook was fussing over them. Lillian felt she could truly relax for the first time. The nagging fear of being destitute had disappeared. She had the means to escape her pursuer.

Because of Grant.

There was a clatter in the hallway and Grant left the kitchen to investigate. Lillian followed him. A man had entered the house, his boots caked with snow, his face bright red from the cold.

'Smith!' Grant cried.

'M'lord…' The man sounded out of breath. 'I thought I'd try making it back from the village. The roads, though, are still difficult. Near impassable. I need some men to help. Two fellows. Stranded. Not from around here.' He shivered. 'Horse ran off. One man worse than the other. They were out in the cold a long time. Couldn't help them alone.'

'Let's get you out of those boots and coat and get you into the kitchen where it is warm.' Grant took his arm.

The man protested. 'We must see to those fellows.'

He looked up and noticed Lillian. His expression turned puzzled.

'This is Miss Pearson,' Grant told him. 'A—a stranded traveller. She has been helping with the children while she is here.' Grant faced Lillian. 'Miss Pearson, this is Smith, one of my footmen, come from the village.'

'Smith.' She nodded. 'I'll see if we have something hot for you in the kitchen.'

She hurried back to the kitchen. 'Mrs Bell, Smith is returned. He needs something warm to drink.'

'Hot cider!' she said.

Smith was soon settled at the kitchen table, a blanket around his shoulders. Grant stood in the doorway. 'I am off to help the stranded men. Smith, you stay here and get warm.'

'Stranded men?' Cook cried.

'On the road,' Smith said. 'They are closer to here than to the village.'

William popped off his chair. 'May I go, too, Uncle Grant?'

Grant looked to Lillian.

'It is up to you,' she said.

Grant nodded. 'Very well, William. You may come—if you are dressed for the weather and in the stables before we have the sleigh ready.'

'Yes, sir!' William ran off.

Lillian shuddered. An unexpected sense of foreboding washed over her. Because of who those two strangers could be.

Chapter Sixteen

Grant, William and two of the stablemen made up the rescue party. His horses had no difficulty pulling the sleigh, although the road looked as if it had received very little traffic since the snowstorm. The surface was still slippery, though, and it would be easy for the sleigh to slide off the road into the hedges or a ditch. It was definitely too soon for traffic going any distance, so what the devil were these two strangers doing on the road?

One of the stablemen drove the sleigh. William sat next to him.

They travelled about three miles from Grantwell House when William called out, 'I can see them!'

They were indeed in a ditch, in what had once been a curricle but now was in pieces. The poles to which the horse had been hitched were broken off. How foolish could a man be to take a curricle out on roads this bad? As they got closer they could see the horse's hoof marks in the snow, clearly it had dragged the broken pole back to the village.

'I hope the horse has made it back,' one of the stablemen said.

Both men were huddled together. Unable to speak.

Unable to walk. The two stablemen carried them into the sleigh.

'William, get their luggage,' Grant said.

William jumped down from the sleigh and picked up two travelling bags that had tumbled out of the carriage. The bags, their clothes, denoted quality. What were two men of quality doing on a nearly impassable road in an area where they were unknown?

'You are safe now, gentlemen.' Grant covered them with the blankets he'd brought along. 'We'll take you somewhere warm.'

One of the men nodded; the other seemed incapable of even that. One of the stablemen sat in the back of the sleigh with the two men. Grant sat with the driver and William.

On the ride back, all Grant could feel was a sense of disquiet. The presence of these strangers would disrupt the idyll he'd planned to share with Lillian and the children over these next few days, but it felt like a bigger bad omen than that.

Could they be Lillian's pursuers?

When the sleigh neared the house, Grant leaned down to William's ear. 'Do not speak Miss Pearson's name to these men. Or say anything about her. If you must speak of her, only call her your governess.'

William turned to him. 'Why, Uncle Grant? Are these bad men?'

'I do not know,' Grant admitted. 'I do know she wants to stay secret, so we'll do this for her. And tell her to stay in the nursery. Better not to be seen. Do I have your word?'

William looked solemn. 'Yes, Uncle Grant.'

Almost two hours after they'd left, Lillian looked out of a window in Lady Grantwell's bedchamber that faced the driveway in front of the house. She saw the sleigh approaching.

She crossed the room to the doorway, to call out to Hannah, who waited in the hall. 'They are here.'

Two guest rooms in a wing on the opposite side of the house from the nursery had been made ready for the men. Who were they, though? Smith had said they were not from this area. Why had they been on the road, then? She was afraid of who they might be.

She watched the sleigh pull up to the door. William hopped down before anyone else and ran inside the house.

She met him at the top of the stairs.

'Miss Pearson!' he cried. 'Uncle Grant said you should stay in the nursery wing. He said you'd want to stay a secret from the men. I'm not to speak to them of you or tell them your name.'

'Did Grant say why?'

'No,' William admitted. 'But you should do as he says.' He took her hand and pulled her towards the hallway leading to the nursery. 'I think they will bring the men upstairs.'

She quickened her step. When they were out of sight. Lillian stopped William. 'Did the men give their names?'

'They could not talk.'

'Oh.' She put a hand on his shoulder. 'Let's get you out of that coat, hat and scarf. Do you need something warm to drink?'

'No, miss,' William said.

'Anna is in the sitting room, sewing for her doll. I am going to check on her. Will you come in after you take off your coat?'

'Yes, miss.' He started for his bedchamber, but turned around when he reached the door. 'The men did not give names, but one of their bags had a crest on it.'

She stiffened. 'What kind of crest?'

He closed his eyes, as if seeing it in his mind. 'It was red, with a white and black cross on it and a lion on top. At least I think it was a lion.'

The Coval crest.

Her brother-in-law, Dinis Carris, the Baron de Coval. Her pursuer.

The stablemen helped bring the two strangers up to the guest rooms, which had fires burning in the fireplaces and plenty of blankets. Cook prepared hot cider and had it at the ready. Smith took care of one man; Thompson the other. They removed their coats, boots and stockings, but did not try to undress them fully. The sooner they were in bed under the blankets, the better. Hannah had warmed the beds with warming pans and Grant found clean stockings for them. They helped them sip the cider, then put each man in a bed under blankets.

'Obrigado, senhor,' one of the men said.

Grant froze. He recognised that language. What other Portuguese men would travel on the road to his estate?

Lillian's pursuers.

But he must not let on. He could hide her. Send them on their way. In a day or two the roads should be clear enough to take them back to the village, where they would hopefully catch a coach to search for her elsewhere.

When they were finally settled, with Smith nearby to attend to them, Grant hurried to the nursery. He found the children in the sitting room, sitting together, their arms around each other, looking distressed.

'What is it?' he asked. 'Where is Miss Pearson.'

'We think she left,' William said, sounding distraught.

'We saw her carry her bag and go down the servants' stairs. It is my fault. I told her about the crest.'

'What crest?' Grant asked.

'The one with the cross and the lion on the stranger's bag.'

Her brother-in-law's crest? She must have recognised it. 'It is not your fault, William,' he assured the boy. 'How long ago did she leave?

'I don't know.' William lowered his head but raised it again. 'The clock has chimed since then.'

Grant glanced at the clock. It was ten minutes to the hour now. 'That helps, William.'

'Is she gone forever?' Tears glistened in Anna's eyes.

'Not forever,' Grant said. 'I'm going to find her. I'll bring her back.'

'Why did she go?' Anna was about to break into full weeping.

Grant went to her, picked her up and hugged her. 'She became afraid, I suspect.'

'Why?' Anna asked. 'Should we be afraid?'

What was he to say to that? He'd be damned if he'd tell these children that the men in the guest rooms thought Lillian had murdered her husband, or that Lillian had once been a thief and a spy.

'You do not need to be afraid.' He tried to sound reassuring. 'But I do not have time to explain it all. Miss Pearson is in trouble, but we are going to help her.'

He placed Anna back on the sofa with her brother and hurried out the room. He'd left his coat, hat and gloves in the hall, but when he looked they were gone. Efficient Thompson. He'd probably hung them in the boot room.

On his way there, he met the butler coming out of the kitchen. 'Thompson. I must go out again. I need you to do something.'

'Yes, m'lord?'

'Tell all the servants not to speak of Miss Pearson being here. Never say her name. Act as if she was never here. As if they'd never heard of her. I cannot tell you the whole of it, but she has run off and I must find her and make certain she is safe.'

'Yes, m'lord.' Thompson's eyes were wide with alarm.

Lillian focussed on putting one foot in front of the other, even though her feet were so cold she could hardly feel them. But she could make it to the village, she was sure of it. If Smith made the trek, she could. Sometimes she came upon his footprints and it comforted her that she could see the marks in the snow from the sleigh's runners. It was like following in Grant's and William's tracks.

A gust of wind blew her hat off so that it dangled from its ribbons on her neck. She stopped to put it on again and to retie it more firmly in place. Even though it was not snowing this time, it was so much colder than when she'd walked the same distance only a few days ago to reach Grant's estate.

Only a few days? It seemed so much longer…as if she had lived half a lifetime in those days.

It was a lifetime she would acutely miss. Each step away from it was like a shaft pressed deeper and deeper into her heart. How was she to bear life without Anna and William?

Without Grant?

How had she endured life without Grant in the past? She'd let her anger at him fool her into thinking he no longer mattered. Then she'd always tried to convince herself that their main attachment had been carnal. Now, even after only a few days, she realised it was so much more.

Before she'd only sensed the man; now she knew him.

Grant was a good man. Strong, but kind. Fair and loving. She thought of the heavy purse in her pocket—he was generous, too. He'd revealed himself through those dear children. She'd left them without a goodbye, left them as so many others had. That pain rivalled the pain of losing Grant.

But she must move forward. One foot in front of the other. To the village. To the first coach out of the village, wherever it was bound. With luck she'd be on it before Dinis and the man with him could return.

Grant had given her the means to go anywhere.

Her boot slipped and she dropped her portmanteau to keep herself from falling. The portmanteau felt heavier than before, but that was impossible. The only additions she'd accumulated were Grant's purse full of coin, Anna's handkerchief, and William's carved dog. Those were upon her person. She paused for a moment, wrapping her cloak around her as if that would give her more warmth. Then she picked up the portmanteau and trudged on up a gentle hill.

As she reached the crest she saw a broken curricle in a ditch at the side of the road. Dinis's carriage, she suspected. She was surprised it made it this far. It must have been hard going for the poor horse. The snow was soft enough to make the wheels difficult to turn. When she came closer to it, the damage was clear. It must have slid off the road and broken its poles.

From behind her she heard the clomping of hooves. The curricle's horse, perhaps? She turned to see.

Over the hill came a small sleigh, pulled by one horse with one driver. Fear waved through her. There was nowhere to hide.

As the sleigh came closer, though, she could see it was Grant.

He pulled up near her and climbed off the sleigh. 'Lillian! What the devil do you think you are doing?'

She stood her ground. 'Do not try to stop me, Grant. I am going to the village. It is my brother-in-law you have rescued. I need to get away. I cannot let him find me.'

'Don't be daft.' His voice rose. 'It is too cold. You will freeze before you get there.'

She lifted her chin. 'Smith did not freeze. If he can walk the distance, I can as well.'

'Smith was a soldier. He'd endured more than one winter in Spain and he's well used to long marches.'

'I can make it to the village,' she insisted. 'I am almost halfway there already.'

She wished he would go on his way. She wished he'd never come after her. It hurt to see him after she'd believed she'd never see him again.

He reached out his hand. 'Come. Get on the sleigh.'

She shook her head. 'Please, Grant. Let me go. Dinis believes I killed my husband, and I have no way to prove I did not. My only hope is to flee him until I reach a place he will never find me.'

'No.' His expression was firm. 'Come back with me. We'll hide you until he leaves and then I promise I will take you somewhere safe. But you cannot risk this weather.'

He walked closer, close enough to touch her. He extended his hand again.

'Please, Lillian.'

Another gust of wind wailed through the landscape, as if to emphasise his words. The chill worsened. Became painful.

She put her hand in his. He picked up her portmanteau and led her to the sleigh.

* * *

Grant stowed the portmanteau under the seat and helped her onto the sleigh. He climbed in next to her and took the ribbons. The wind picked up and she scooted close to him. Carefully he turned the sleigh around, but it still slipped on the slick road. Luckily the horse and sleigh stayed upright, and they were soon headed back to the estate.

He'd been fairly frantic about her venturing onto the village road alone in the cold. It was hard to shake those emotions.

'What did you think going to the village would do?' he snapped. 'It is equally as snowed in as we are. No coaches will be braving these roads.'

'I realised that,' she responded in a tight voice. 'But I would have taken the first coach that was going anywhere.'

'If your brother-in-law did not return there and find you first.'

She sniffed. 'I assumed you wouldn't return him to the village until the roads were better.'

He shook his head in dismay. 'He'd still discover what coach you went on. Someone would remember such a thing. He'd track you down.'

She was silent for a while. Perhaps she'd heard what he said and was considering the logic of it.

Finally she spoke. 'Dinis has been tracking me ever since I left Reading. I deluded myself thinking he would never guess I would contact you. He'd only have had to hear your name to figure out where I had gone. I should never have come to you, Grant. Now I've involved you and the children and everyone at the house.'

He glanced over at her and his voice became quiet. 'I

do not credit that, Lillian. The risk is only to you. I will keep you safe, though.'

Nothing was more important.

Grant turned his attention to the road ahead and they rode in silence. When they passed through the gate, Grant headed away from the house.

'I'm taking you to Rhys and Helene. You can hide there until we decide what to do next. With any luck I can rid us of your brother-in-law in a day or two.'

Chapter Seventeen

Rodolfo Santos stood at the window of the fine room he'd been given, a blanket wrapped around him and a mug of hot cider warming his hand.

'May I assist you in any way?'

Santos turned to face the man standing in the doorway. His guard, disguised as a footman.

'Não, obrigado.' Santos smiled ingratiatingly and switched to English. 'No, thank you. You have met my needs very well.'

The footman nodded. 'I am near if you need me to attend you.'

Santos made a little bow. 'I am grateful.'

The servant turned to leave, but Santos stopped him. 'May I enquire as to the health of the Baron de Coval?'

'He seems to be sleeping comfortably at the moment,' the man responded.

'Excellent,' Santos said. 'Do inform me when he wakes, if you will be so good.'

'I will do so,' the servant said and disappeared from the doorway.

But not to go far, Santos thought.

He turned back to the window which looked down on

the outer buildings including the stables. He'd told Coval that the roads would be treacherous, that they should wait a day or two, but the baron refused to listen to him. Now they'd lost the element of surprise. And they'd almost lost their lives, either when the curricle slid into the ditch, or by nearly freezing to death.

But it would do no good to say such a thing to the baron.

Santos liked to think of himself as the Baron de Coval's most valued assistant. He liked the word assistant better than servant, although on this trip he also was acting as the baron's valet. And chief investigator. It was he who discovered that Senhora Carris had taken a coach to this village and, while they'd been stranded there and unable to find her, it was he who'd heard about the new Viscount Grantwell.

She had to be here. There was no more logical explanation.

He wondered what that burly fellow of a guard would do if he walked out of the room to search the house. No need to find out quite yet. Wait until Coval was awake to distract him while Santos searched. Or sneak out of this room at night.

He took another sip of hot cider and savoured the feel of it warming his throat and chest as he swallowed. From the window he spied a man walking from the stables. He looked very much like their host. Viscount Grantwell.

Santos had been able to maintain some of his wits when they were rescued. He recognised Lord Grantwell from all those years ago in Lisbon, when the man had been in the British army and had engaged in that affair with Senhora Carris.

Senhora Carris. So widely shamed for cuckolding her husband. So despised for being a French spy. And now a murderess as well. Who else could have killed her husband the Portuguese hero, Baron Coval's brother?

Her shame would be complete after they returned her to Lisbon and the justice of the courts.

All he'd need do was find her.

Grant entered through the servants' entrance, leaving his outer garments and boots in the boot room.

Thompson met him as he entered the hallway. 'M'lord?'

'I found her,' he said. 'She is safe for now.' Better not to tell where she was.

Thompson's face relaxed.

Grant continued down the hallway. 'Gather the servants together in the servants' hall. All except Smith. Is he still watching over our guests?'

Thompson kept pace with him. 'He is, m'lord.'

'Good. I need him to stay for a bit.' He'd speak to Smith separately. He'd already talked with the stablemen. No one else on the estate knew of Lillian—except the woodsman, but it was not likely that her brother-in-law would encounter Dawson. 'I'm going to see the children and I'll be down directly.'

He used the servants' stairway to reach the nursery wing the fastest. The children were still in the sitting room. William and Anna remained on the sofa, but William was showing his sister a book. Hannah sat in a chair near them.

'There you are, m'lord,' she said as she rose to her feet.

William and Anna looked up, worry on their young faces.

'Hannah. I am glad you are with the children,' he said. 'And Miss P?'

He would have smiled at her effort not to speak Lillian's name, as he'd requested of her, but there was too much else to think of. 'She is safe.'

William and Anna's little bodies visibly relaxed.

Grant said to Hannah, 'Would you gather the maids and meet me in the servants' hall as soon as you can? I will be there to speak to all of you.'

'Yes, m'lord.' She hurried out.

Grant sat with the children on the sofa. Anna climbed into his lap.

'You do not have to worry about Miss Pearson,' he assured them. 'She is with friends and she is completely safe.'

'Is she still in trouble?' Anna asked.

'Yes,' he admitted. 'And we are still going to help her.'

'By pretending she was never here?' William asked.

'Yes, you are completely right, William,' Grant said. 'I'm going to ask Hannah attend the two men. I'll have Jane and Sophie look in on you as often as they are able, but you will stay on your own some of the time. Will you be able to do that?'

'We can do that, Uncle Grant,' William said solemnly.

'If you become frightened or lonely you may go sit with Cook in the kitchen.' He attempted a smile. 'But I warn you: she will put you to work.'

They nodded, expressions remaining serious.

'Avoid the two gentlemen who are our guests, if you can,' he added.

Anna's eyes grew wide. 'Will they hurt us?'

'No, no,' he assured them. 'Do not ever think so. They might ask you questions and it might be difficult for you to avoid answering them.'

'Do they want to hurt Miss Pearson?' William asked.

Grant so much did not want to tell these children the whole story. It seemed too much of a burden for them.

But would he have wanted to know everything when he was their ages? He would. Whenever adults kept matters from him, his imagination always made them bigger than they actually were.

He set his chin. 'I am going to tell you all of it.' Or at least most of it. He'd leave out what was between Lillian and him. He'd try to soften the rest. 'Miss Pearson ran away from Portugal because the people there thought she had caused her husband's death and they would not believe her when she said she did not.'

'She would not cause a death,' William said firmly.

'She wouldn't,' Anna piped up.

'I agree,' Grant said. 'She has said she did not and I believe her. One of these men is her husband's brother and he wants to take her back to Portugal to stand trial.'

'Would they hang her?' William asked.

A horrific image came to Grant's mind. 'They might. But she has become our…friend, and we will find her a place to hide where they will never find her and she will be safe.'

'Can she stay here with us?' Anna asked.

How Grant wished. 'That is the thing. They already suspect she is here, so this is no longer safe for her.' He placed Anna back on the sofa and hugged them both. 'I need to go down to speak to the servants, to tell them what I have told you. Do you want to come with me?'

'I want to come with you,' William said.

Anna jumped off the sofa. 'Me too.'

They descended the servants' stairway to reach the lower floor. The servants' hall was right near the kitchen.

Cook met them in the hallway. 'Ah, you have come, too, Master William, Miss Anna. Hurry back to the kitchen with me first. Let us find you some biscuits and milk. You must be very hungry.'

Grant had not even thought of food.

He invited all the servants to sit at the table and he joined them. When Mrs Bell returned with the children, he repeated what he'd told them.

'Don't talk about Miss Pearson even among your-selves. Pretend she was never here,' he said. 'It will only be for two or three days at the most. The roads are bound to improve and we can return these men to the village. This will be extra work for all of you, I know, but I prom-ise you may have time off when the others are able to make it back.'

He trusted them all, but it was a lot to ask of them to conceal their knowledge of Lillian merely on his word alone. He was careful not to tell them where she was so they would not have to lie about that even if they slipped up.

When he finished Thompson spoke. 'You've done right by us, m'lord. We will do right by you.'

The others nodded in agreement.

The housemaids and kitchenmaids were new to him, but Thompson, Mrs Bell, and even Hannah who had come here as a young girl before he left for the army, were like his family, more like his family than his parents or brother had ever been. They agreed to do this because he asked. None of them knew Lillian, except for these few days. They did not even question why he would extend himself so much for her.

'Thank you all.' Emotion caught in his throat.

'Come, now,' Thompson said. 'We must get back to work,'

When Cook walked past Grant she patted his arm. 'I'll have a dinner ready for the guests, m'lord. Just let us know where you'd like it to be served.'

'Next on my agenda is to look in on the gentlemen. I'll know more after I see them.'

William walked up to him, waiting patiently while the servants filed by. 'May Anna and I stay down here with Mrs Bell for a while?'

Grant squeezed William's shoulder. 'Certainly you may. I'll come and see you after I check on our guests.'

He left them and went to the guest wing of the house.

Smith stood in the hallway. 'The one fellow has been up for a while. The one who was worse off—he called him Baron de Coval—he has just roused. They are both in that gentleman's room.'

Grant knocked and was invited in.

Coval was seated at the table, his fingers wrapped around a mug of hot cider. The other man was standing at his elbow. Coval started to rise at Grant's entrance.

'Please, remain seated, baron. I am pleased to see you up. You gave us quite a scare.'

'Ah, you remember me, Grantwell,' he responded, his voice not quite smooth enough to hide hostility. 'I do not recall our meeting…back then.'

'My footman told me who you are. He was the one who found you.'

Coval smiled. 'But you must recognise my family name, Carris, no? From all those years ago?'

'Of course.' No point in pretending he could ever forget the woman he had known as Lillian Carris. 'I confess to some surprise to find you in Yorkshire. I assure you, you are welcome as my guest until you recover and the roads are passable again. Someone should have warned you not to attempt travel. I apologise for that on behalf of my countrymen.'

The other man—a servant, perhaps?—shot the baron an exasperated look.

Grant went on. 'Are you experiencing any difficulties? To your legs or feet? I fear we cannot summon the surgeon until the roads clear.'

'My legs and feet pain me, but I do not think there is—what do you call it? The damage from the cold?' His smile did not reach his eyes.

Grant did not bother to provide the word. 'I am glad of it.' It meant his health would not delay his departure. 'I must also apologise. You have found me short-staffed. Most of my servants were given a holiday and have been delayed by the snow. You have wound up here at a bad time, I am afraid.'

The baron's smile did not waver. 'No matter. You have brought me where I wished to be.'

Grant feigned a puzzled look. 'I do not understand.'

Coval's smile faded. 'Where is she, Grantwell?'

'Where is who?'

His eyes bore into Grant. 'Senhora Carris. As you well know.'

Grant summoned all the emotions he'd felt about Lillian at the time of her betrayal in Portugal. 'Senhora Carris.' He spat out her name. 'I know nothing of her and I am glad of it.'

Coval seemed to waver.

His servant spoke. 'A woman of her description was seen in the village nearby. She enquired of the whereabouts of your estate several days ago.'

'Well, she could have had no business with me,' he said with feeling. 'None of you can have any business with me.'

Some uncertainty still flickered in the baron's eyes, but he cocked his head. 'Can we not, sir?'

Grant glared at the man. 'I have no need of a French spy or for members of her family.' He took a breath, as if calming himself. 'But you will be offered every hospitality while recuperating in my home.'

'Perhaps you have offered hospitality to Senhora Carris as well?' the servant said.

'The devil I have!' Grant snapped.

'Come now, Lord Grantwell,' the man continued in a smooth silken voice. 'You were once quite devoted to her.'

'Until I discovered her to be a liar, a thief and a spy.' He made his voice rise. 'Do not speak of her to me. I will see you as comfortable as your situation allows, but that is all. I need to tend to other duties.' He gestured to the hallway. 'I'll instruct Smith to remain nearby in case you need anything.' He turned to leave.

'Do you not wonder, Lord Grantwell,' the baron said, 'why we search for Senhora Carris here?'

'No,' Grant said bluntly. He continued to the doorway but stopped and spoke over his shoulder. 'My cook is preparing dinner. Would you prefer to be served in your room or to dine with me?'

The baron's breathing accelerated. 'In my room, if you please. My servant will eat with me and attend me.'

'Very good.' Grant reached the door.

'Wait!' cried Coval.

Grant turned to face him again. The man tried to rise, but sat down again, pain pinching his face.

His servant spoke. 'I believe the baron would like you to know that Senhora Carris murdered her husband and fled Portugal. We have tracked her to here. It is our intention to take her back to Lisbon so justice may be served.'

'Her husband?' Grant scoffed—convincingly, he hoped. 'Are you certain the man is dead? As I recall, he made a miraculous recovery once before.'

Coval's eyes flashed in anger. 'My brother is dead. And I intend to make her pay.'

'You'll get no argument from me on that account, sir.' Grant bowed again and left the room, closing the door behind him.When he was out in the hall, he gestured for Smith to follow him. 'Did you hear that?' he asked, keeping his voice quiet.

'I did indeed, sir,' Smith responded.

'Was I convincing?'

'I thought so, sir, but I would not trust them.'

'I don't.' Grant gave Smith the same instructions he'd given the others. 'I cannot expect you to stand guard over them day and night, but keep your eyes and ears open when you are near and sleep nearby.' He gestured to the door across the hall. 'Choose any room. Hannah can make it ready for you.'

'I will, sir, but, sir, they speak together in Portuguese and I catch only a word or two.' Smith had been in Grant's regiment that first winter, before the army had marched on to Spain. He'd not known of Lillian, though. Not then. 'I've forgotten the language, I fear.'

'So have I,' Grant admitted. 'Do what you can.'

Smith nodded and returned to his post.

Santos moved quickly away from the doorway and closed the door. 'The footman is returning,' he told Coval.

'Could you hear anything?' the baron asked.

'No.' It was frustrating. 'But I do not believe for a moment that Grantwell has no knowledge of the woman.'

'He was very convincing,' the baron said uncertainly.

'Quite,' Santos agreed. 'Too convincing. I shall keep an eye on the matter. As your servant I should be able to move about. Tending to your needs.'

Coval released a stressful breath. 'Santos, you have been invaluable to me throughout this whole ordeal.'

That suited Santos very well. He intended to be indis-

pensable to Baron de Coval. Bringing the woman back
to Portugal should secure the regard in the baron's eyes.
They were close. She was here, he was certain. And he
would find her.

Chapter Eighteen

Lillian sat with Mr and Mrs Landon—or Rhys and
Helene, as they insisted she call them—in their warm,
comfortable sitting room. They'd welcomed her without
hesitation when Grant brought her there that afternoon,
sat her by a warm fire with a hot cup of tea, and readied a
comfortable bedchamber for her. Now they had finished
dinner. Helene had just put their darling son to bed, and
she'd brought some sewing for Lillian to do.

How kind of her to realise that Lillian needed to be
busy, to keep her mind off Dinis's pursuit of her.

Rossiter, the burly manservant whom Helene assured
would protect her, appeared at the door. She knew he had
been Rhys's batman during his time in the army. 'Captain Grantwell, sir—I mean, Lord Grantwell.'

Lillian's heart flipped at the sound of his name. And
swelled when he stepped into the room and his gaze immediately fell on her, piercing her with his hazel eyes.

Rhys rose at his entrance and crossed the room to
shake his hand. 'Grant. I guessed you'd come.'

Helene greeted him as well. 'Hello, Grant.'

'Is all well here?' he asked, darting a glance to Lillian.

When she'd walked towards the village on the cold, snow-packed road, she'd made herself accept losing him. She'd said goodbye in her heart. Now to see him again was more difficult than she could imagine. She tried to still her heart and keep her emotions tightly inside.

'As well as can be expected,' she heard Rhys reply. 'We've sworn everyone in our house to secrecy. They know we are hiding Lillian and not to speak of her to anyone.'

Grant asked, 'Do they know the whole?'

'The servants do not know all the details,' Rhys went on. 'Only what we want them to know.'

'We can trust them, though,' Helene assured both Grant and Lillian.

Lillian hoped so.

'What else do you need me to do?' asked Rhys.

'Nothing, I think,' Grant replied. 'Go about your routine as always. They will be gone as soon as the roads are passable.'

'A sleigh could make it to the village now,' Rhys said. 'I could take them back tomorrow.'

Lillian shot Grant a glance. He should have taken her on to the village instead of bringing her back and involving all these dear people in her problems.

'I do not think that is wise,' Grant said. 'They would find it suspicious if I rushed them away. Coval has not completely recovered. They will have to stay at least through tomorrow.'

His gaze returned to her.

Helene suddenly stood. 'Rhys, come upstairs with me. Let us leave Grant and Lillian alone for a while.'

Before Lillian could protest that it was not necessary, they walked out. Grant moved closer to her but she remained in her chair, her sewing on her lap as if it were some armour.

Against what? Her yearning for him?

She managed to speak. 'How are the children?'

'Frightened for you,' he responded. 'But they are good.'

It was painful even to think of them. 'I did not wish to leave them this way.'

'I know.' He made a gesture, as if to touch her but drew back again. 'I think it best you stay out of sight. Remain in your bedchamber, if you must. We cannot chance anyone else seeing you. I've not told the servants where you are, but if they give it half a thought they could guess.'

She lowered her gaze. 'I have put all of you in such a difficult spot.'

He sat in a nearby chair and leaned towards her. 'Do not think of that, Lillian.'

Did any of them believe she may have really murdered her husband? All those dear people she'd come to care about, did they now think her a murderer?

'Grant.' Her voice came out so quiet she was surprised he heard it. 'Do you believe me? I did not murder my husband. I swear to you—'

His gaze met hers again. 'I believe you. We all believe you.'

But what if Dinis provided Grant with the details, with how thoroughly it appeared she'd done it? What if he reminded Grant of the fiction Estevo had so enjoyed perpetuating? That she was an adulteress. A traitor. A spy for the French. There was no one in the Carris family who believed her to be anything else.

She was afraid to ask Grant if he also now believed that she had not stolen his papers. If he thought too much upon it, how much of a leap would it be to believe a spy could become a murderer?

He reached for her hand and curled his strong fingers around hers. 'I'll see you through this, Lillian. I promise. It is not beyond my means, financially or otherwise, to be certain you are safe for ever.'

She turned her hand so that she was now clasping his. How loving of him to say such a thing.

As true as it was that she should never have come here, she could not regret doing so. If she had not come, she'd never have had the chance to love Grant as she did. She'd never have loved the children. She'd not regret that, not ever.

Santos woke early the next day and watched out of the window of his room for a while. The night before he'd seen a man who could have been Grantwell carrying a lantern in the direction of the stables. It piqued his curiosity. Why was someone needing to go to the stables at night? Surely he was not hiding her in the stables?

He rubbed his face, still stinging from his razor. He would investigate. Santos excelled at discovering things.

The baron would likely not rise for a couple of hours, time enough for Santos to make use of his status as servant. He picked up the baron's coat and shoes and stepped out into the hallway.

As he'd expected, the footman stood guard. 'May I assist you?'

Santos smiled at him. 'Direct me to the valet's room, if you please. I must care for the baron's coat and shoes.'

The footman reached for the clothes. 'I can do that for you.'

Santos pulled them away. 'Oh, no. The baron is—

how do you say it?—*fussy* about his clothes. I must care for them.'

The footman frowned. 'I will show you, then.'

He led Santos to a servants' stairway that descended all the way to the lower floor. He could see hallways leading to the rooms on each floor. Handy to know if he wished to explore.

He'd accomplished a fair amount of exploration already. When the house became quiet late into the night and their guard had no longer been lurking in the hallway, he'd left his room and walked to his heart's content throughout the first floor.

He'd learned a few interesting things. There were children in the house. A boy and a girl. He'd seen them sleeping. He also saw another bedchamber nearby—for a governess, perhaps—that looked recently occupied. Two maids slept in another room near the children, but there was no sign of a governess. Of course, the governess could have been on holiday, like most of the other servants. Who the children were, he had no clue. Grantwell was not married, they'd said in the village.

In the servants' hallway Santos could hear kitchen sounds and inhaled the smell of baking bread. An older servant approached them. A worried look flashed through the man's expression. What was the cause of that? Santos wondered.

'Sir, should you be up and about?' the man asked.

Santos lifted the clothes in his arms. 'I am Baron de Coval's servant. As you know, there is no rest and recuperation for those in service.' He inclined his head. 'I am Santos. And you are, I believe, one of the men who assisted us yesterday.'

'Thompson,' the man said. 'Lord Grantwell's butler.'

He gestured to the clothing in Santos's arms. 'May we take care of that for you?'

'No. It is my responsibility,' Santos said. Besides, he wanted to be around the servants. Perhaps one of them could be persuaded to speak to him.

He tallied how many he knew of so far. The footman guarding them. The butler. The maid who tended their rooms. The two maids near the children. Obviously some in the kitchen, but he'd check them later. He did not wish to act too suspiciously.

No other servants revealed themselves while Santos finished brushing off the coats and polishing the shoes. Someone had cleaned and polished his boots and the baron's, though. He gathered those in his arms as well. When he walked out of the room the butler was nearby. A coincidence or was he being watched?

On the servants' stairway he met the maid who tended his room. He'd spied her when she'd rebuilt his fire that morning.

'*Bom dia.*' He smiled in his most charming manner. 'That means good morning.'

'Does it?' Her tone was unfriendly.

'I am Santos, servant to Baron de Coval.' He bowed as best he could with his arms full. At least it made it difficult for her to pass him. 'I suppose you have heard why the baron and I are here?'

'Because your carriage broke on the road,' she said.

He laughed. 'Correct. But there is a more important reason. We are searching for a woman.'

'Oh?' she said without curiosity.

He leaned closer as if imparting a secret. 'She murdered her husband, you see. The baron's brother. We must take her back to Portugal.'

She tried to step past him. 'I don't like murderers.'

He went on. 'I do not either. Will you help us? Have you seen her? She was once your lord's lover before she betrayed him.' Perhaps that would capture her interest.

He thought her eyes flickered. 'I do not know anyone like that. You are making me late. I'm needed in the kitchen.'

'Oh, forgive me,' he said in his charming voice. 'I will endeavour to make room for you to pass.' As she squeezed past him, he added, 'The baron will pay generously for any information about her. About where she is hiding.'

'Too bad I don't know, then,' the maid said and continued on her way.

Santos watched her descent with a frown. He thrived on the gossip of servants. That these servants seemed so...*protective* made him suspicious.

He purposely turned the wrong way and entered the wing where the children had been sleeping. As he'd hoped, he found one of the maids who looked surprised and frightened at his appearance.

He tried charm again. 'Forgive me, miss! I fear I have lost my way. I am Santos, Baron de Coval's servant.' He lifted the clothes as if that was proof.

'You should be in the guest wing,' she said.

'Would you be so kind as to show me?'

She walked him back to the servants' passageway. He thought he heard other footsteps but could not discern from where.

'There.' She pointed in the proper direction and turned to go.

'Wait a moment, miss.'

She stopped. Reluctantly, he felt.

'Do you know anything of the woman the baron and I search for?' he asked.

'No, sir.' She was not as convincing as the other maid.

He'd prime her with gossip. 'She was once Grantwell's lover, you know.'

Her eyes widened at that.

He was encouraged. 'The baron will pay generously for any information you can provide us.'

Another maid opened the door to the stairway. 'Jane!' she called. 'I need you.'

'I have to go.' The girl scurried away.

He'd learned nothing for certain, but he was just beginning. No reason to be disheartened.

He reached the proper hallway where the footman guarding them stood. 'I am returned, you see.'

'Any difficulties?' the footman asked in a perfunctory tone.

He responded cryptically. 'Everyone was *most* helpful.'

Let the man worry over what that might mean.

That morning Grant went to look in on the children first thing. They were not in their rooms, so he went down to the kitchen.

As he'd suspected, they were there, looking small and vulnerable at the table, eating their bowls of porridge.

He greeted them. 'I thought you might be here.'

The two small heads looked up without the smiles he'd come to expect of them.

'Good morning, Uncle Grant,' William said.

'Jane and Sophie got us up and dressed and we came down here for breakfast,' Anna explained.

'That is excellent.' He sat with them and bade Cook and the kitchenmaids good morning.

Cook placed a mug in front of him.

He inhaled its scent. 'Coffee?'

She nodded. 'I thought the foreigners might want it. You never know about those sorts.'

He poured milk into it. 'We used to drink this without milk or sugar in Spain.'

'May I taste some?' asked William.

Grant nodded and Mrs Bell poured a small amount in a cup. Grant added some sugar and milk to it and William took a sip.

He put the cup down. 'I do not like it.'

'Didn't think you would,' Mrs Bell said, removing the cup again.

Hannah entered the kitchen, curtseying when she saw Grant.

Mrs Bell gestured to her. 'Tell m'lord what you told me. About that foreigner.'

Grant's brows rose.

'That one—I suppose he's a servant, because he was on the servants' staircase, carrying clothes—he tried to get me to talk about...you know.' She was careful not to speak Lillian's name.

'What did he say?' Grant asked.

'He tried to tell me all about—' She paused glancing at the children. 'You know. What she did. Tried to gossip about it. I pretended to know nothing and to not be interested. Then he said he would pay for information.'

Bribery? He should not be surprised.

Grant addressed them all. 'Any of you—if they offer you money, say nothing. Come to me instead.' He added. 'If we get through this, there will be rewards for all of you.' He turned to the children, saying quietly. 'She is safe and well. I saw her.'

Anna simply stared at him with her wide blue eyes.

William spoke just as quietly. 'Anna and I saw one of them.'

'In the nursery wing?' Grant did not like hearing that.

Anna piped up. 'He said he was lost.'

William went on. 'And Jane said she'd show him the way.'

'We followed them into the servants' stairway,' Anna said.

'He offered Jane money, like he did Hannah,' William added.

'We were spying on them,' Anna explained.

Grant nodded. 'You were right to tell me, but I do not want you to spy on anyone. Your job is to continue your studies and take care of yourselves the best you can while Jane and Sophie tend to other duties.'

'And we can come to the kitchen any time we want?' Anna asked.

'That is so,' Mrs Bell called over.

Grant rose and gave each of them a quick hug. 'I must go now, but I'll check on you later.'

He met Smith out in the hallway.

'They want breakfast,' Smith said. 'And that servant fellow's been out and about. Down to the valet's room here and who knows where else?'

'So I heard.' He gave Smith an approving nod. 'I'll give them time to eat breakfast and then I believe I must speak to them.'

Later that morning Santos helped Coval dress and they settled down to breakfast in his room. The baron professed to feel better but fatigued from the day before. His legs still troubled him some. It was enough of an excuse for them to stay longer, if needed.

Even if the footman was eavesdropping, which Santos expected he was, he would not understand Portuguese, so they spoke freely.

Santos liked that the baron desired to eat his meals with him. He'd done so the whole journey. It was a rise in status Santos was determined to keep.

'I have begun my investigation, Baron. Last night and this morning,' he said.

The baron took a bite of ham. 'And what did you discover?'

'I better know the configuration of the house, which may come in handy. I discovered that Grantwell has two children and a governess's bedroom in the nursery wing that looks recently occupied.'

'By *her*?'

Santos knew precisely who he meant. 'I cannot say. The governess might simply be on holiday. I have not yet explored all the rooms, to see if she is hiding in the house, but I will.'

'Do you think she is in the house?' Coval asked.

Santos thought of the figure he'd seen walking towards the stable the night before. 'I do not think so. But Grantwell has hidden her somewhere. I would wager on it.'

The baron frowned. 'Can't you seduce one of the maids and find out? Make her tell you?'

'I am working on exactly that plan,' he told him. 'I've encountered two maids so far. So two possibilities.'

Let him think he'd been more successful with the maids than he had been. These English women were colder than his countrywomen, after all. It took some finesse. If need be, he would pursue that route. He was confident they'd not resist him.

'You must not recover too quickly, baron.' He took a sip of coffee. 'We need more time.'

There was a knock on the door and their footman guard announced Lord Grantwell.

The man barged in. 'I see you are not finished breakfast. I am sorry to intrude.'

Santos rose.

'I would not deny you entry,' the baron said smoothly, switching to English. 'We are your guests.'

'And my hospitality is yours,' the viscount went on. 'But I will not have your servant questioning my maids about Lillian Carris. You are frightening them with this talk of murderers.'

Santos made an ingratiating bow. 'My apologies, m'lord.' He spoke in his most subservient voice. 'I simply hoped they might know something, even though you do not.'

'They know nothing,' Grantwell said. 'They've been snowed in just as long as I have. Except for Smith—and you owe your lives to him, you know.'

'He will be rewarded,' Coval said.

'Give the servants whatever vails you want, but do not press them for information they do not possess.'

Santos bowed. 'It will be as you wish, m'lord.'

Except he had no intention of remaining prisoner in these rooms. Or even refraining from currying favour with the servants. He felt in his very bones that the woman was near. And he needed her to be caught and for him to have the credit of it.

All would be right when that occurred.

When their guard left his post Santos would slip out. He had a great desire to take a walk towards the stables and see where that night-time walker might have been bound.

Chapter Nineteen

Could this day be any longer?

Lillian stood back from the window of the small bed-chamber she'd been given. Its view spanned some out-buildings and the kitchen garden, growing parsnips, turnips, carrots and potatoes. Not the best vantage point if you feared someone coming for you.

She'd spent some of the morning playing with Rhys and Helene's dear little boy, a little over one year old and already able to run and climb and jabber up a storm. But then he needed a nap and later some time outside in the fresh air. Outside, where she could not go.

The household was adhering to its usual schedule, which meant everyone was busy doing their daily tasks and she had little but time and worry on her hands.

She wished Grant had allowed her to run. At least in flight she felt some control. This was how the fox must feel, hiding in its lair, hearing the dogs coming closer and closer.

She returned to the chair that was near enough to the window for light, but not so near as to allow her to be seen from the outside, not that anyone would even walk by to look in the window. Still, she did not know how secure her particular lair was. She picked up the mending Helene had given to her. Thank goodness for that. Without the sewing she might truly go mad.

As she sat she could hear every creak in the floorboards, every wisp of wind from the outside. Occasionally she'd hear a voice or a footstep. She'd stop then and listen. Was it from the household? Or were the dogs approaching?

At the moment all was deadly quiet.

Until she heard the faintest creaking of the door.

She whipped around.

In the doorway stood Rodolfo Santos. Dinis's servant.

Fear gripped her throat. He was between her and escape.

'*Senhora.*' He smiled that heartless smile that had always made her avoid him in her brother-in-law's household.

'Santos.' She lifted her chin. 'I should have known it would be you.'

He bowed and replied in Portuguese. 'At your service, m'lady.'

'English, please.'

He bowed ingratiatingly.

'I did not hear you enter,' she said.

His smile grew wider. 'Oh, I have a great talent to sneak into places without making a sound. I've put it to good use for many years. As recently as last night, as a matter of fact.'

What did he mean, last night? Her thoughts immediately went to the children, to Grant. She did not wish him to see her fear, though.

'A handy talent, I am sure,' she responded coolly. 'Had I heard you I would have had a weapon ready.'

He scoffed. 'What weapon would you have?'

She reached into the sewing basket and pulled out a pair of large scissors.

He flinched, but quickly recovered. 'Scissors?' he mocked.

'If you are lucky, before I use them on you, there is a large manservant here, a former soldier, who will come at my first cry.'

His smile was replaced by malevolence. 'But you will not use your weapon, nor call the former soldier. Not when you see what I have.'

He took something from the pocket of his topcoat and opened his hand to reveal it—a tin soldier and a small wooden doll.

Lillian felt herself go pale. 'How did you get those?'

'Quite easily.' He smiled again. 'What fine children. I wonder what you thought when you learned Grantwell had children. It must have been quite a surprise.'

'Leave the children out of this.' Her heart pounded faster.

'Ah, you are attached to them?' He nodded. 'I suspected you might be, being as barren as you are.'

She regretted revealing so much. 'I would say the same about any children.'

'But especially your lover's children, is that not right? I chose wisely. They give me my advantage, you see.'

'Your advantage?' She feared what he meant.

His dark eyes turned sinister. 'You will come with me now or harm will come to them. I am more than capable of seeing to it.'

'You wouldn't. They are innocent children.' At this moment, though, she thought he looked perfectly capable of it.

'What do I care about two English children?' He put the toys back into his pocket. 'You do not know what I

am capable of, *senhora*, what I have already done. But
you will come with me now. To Baron de Coval. You will
become our prisoner and we will take you back to Portugal where they will surely hang you.' He paused. 'Or
the children will die.'

She needed to get to Grant. Grant would protect the
children.

But if she managed to escape Santos now, could she
reach Grant before Santos reached the children?

She could not depend on it. There was nothing to do
but go along with him. Let him take her to Dinis. Surely
she would see Grant then, and could warn him.

'Very well, Santos. You force me.'

Santos's ability to sneak in and out of places was not
mere bluster, Lillian discovered. He led her out of Rhys's
house without anyone seeing them. As they walked the
distance to the great house, the enormity of her situation struck her.

She would now be Dinis's prisoner and she would
have to go with him. Grant could no longer protect her,
not without creating great trouble for himself. Harbour-
ing a murderer. For all she knew that might put him in
jeopardy.

Or if Santos brought violence to the situation, someone might be hurt. Killed, perhaps. She could not allow
that. She could not be the cause of someone dying or the
cause of someone murdering another person.

No, she was already caught, already doomed to ac-
company Dinis back to Lisbon. Her only hope would be
to escape from him while on the journey.

'I have another requirement of you,' Santos said as
they neared the stables.

'Are you changing the bargain already?' She moved

her portmanteau from one hand to the other. Santos had made her carry it.

'Call it an…addition,' he sneered. 'You must admit aloud to Dinis and to your Lord Grantwell that you killed your husband.'

Why did he consider that necessary? 'But I did not kill Estevo.'

'You must say out loud that you killed him. And also admit that you spied for the French.'

'I did not spy either!' she snapped.

Why bring up the spying? The only person who would care about that now would be Grant and he already believed it.

'Nonetheless, you will admit to both or I will harm the children.' He stopped to look her in the eye. 'And do not suppose you can warn anyone—especially your precious Grantwell—because I will reach the children before that can be accomplished.'

If it were only her life at stake she would never admit to the spying or to murder; she'd die protesting her innocence. But she would not risk the lives of Anna and William. Or Grant. Or anyone on the estate. For a brief time they'd all become the family she'd dreamed of having.

She did not respond. Let him worry that she might not do as he demanded.

Instead, she said, 'Hurting children seems like an extreme measure, Santos. Why go to such extremes? Why risk the consequences of being caught?'

'Oh, I am never caught.' He gazed off into the distance. 'I am ambitious, however. The Baron de Coval will be so grateful to me for delivering you to him. I expect he will see that I become so much more than a mere servant. I expect to be elevated to assistant, perhaps, then to other positions of authority. This is my opportunity and I have waited a long time for it.'

'I am your gift, then?'

'A gift for which I expect a reward,' he clarified.

Was this ambition enough for him to harm children? What sort of man was Santos? He'd been in the baron's employ for as many years as Lillian could remember, certainly since her marriage to Estevo. She'd never noticed anything remarkable about him. When she and Estevo had lived in a set of rooms in Dinis's palace in Lisbon, Santos had never seemed to be anything but the more unpleasant of the servants.

They reached the house and, again, Santos managed to bring her inside without anyone seeing them. He led her to a hallway of guest bedchambers. Smith stood in the hall. His eyes widened and his posture straightened when he saw her.

Santos murmured to her. 'Our guard will undoubtedly bring Grantwell. But our bargain still holds.'

Lillian caught Smith's gaze. As they walked past him, the footman took the portmanteau out of her hand. Santos merely smirked.

He knocked on a door.

Lillian heard a voice say, 'Enter.'

Santos put his hand on her back and pushed her ahead of him into the room.

Dinis sat on a chair with one leg resting on a footstool. He tried to rise, but, she suspected, out of surprise not courtesy. He slumped back down again.

Santos swept his arm dramatically. 'I have found her, as you can see.' He spoke in Portuguese.

'Dinis,' she said.

Her brother-in-law's eyes filled with hatred. *'Senhora.'*

He would not even speak her name.

She turned to Santos and spoke in English. 'Am I to fulfil our bargain now?'

'Later.' Santos switched to English as well. 'When we have another witness.'

Grant. Her heart thudded at the thought of him witnessing what she must say.

'Where did you find her?' Dinis asked, as if she were not standing in front of him.

'I explored,' Santos replied. 'Grantwell was hiding her in a house nearby.'

Lillian spoke up. 'You make an assumption. I was a guest, yes. But you do not know that anybody was hiding me.' She was determined not to cause trouble for anyone but herself.

Santos made a gesture that rendered her point inconsequential.

She tried again. 'Dinis, do not make any of these people responsible for my actions. I hid from you, that is true, but that does not mean anyone was hiding me.'

It was Dinis's turn to wave a hand. 'I care nothing about that. It is you I mean to make pay for my brother's murder.'

Grant had just left the children in the nursery when Smith appeared. The children were not being as well-behaved as Grant would have wished. They spent more time avoiding Jane and Sophie than doing as they were told.

'Sir!' Smith looked alarmed.

Bad news? Grant certainly did not want the children to hear it, if so. He signalled Smith to walk away from the children's door.

'What is it?' he asked when they were out of earshot.

'That servant,' Smith said. 'He must have sneaked out. He came back with Miss Pearson!'

Grant's spirits plummeted. 'He has found her?'

'Apparently, sir,' Smith responded. 'She was carrying her bag. He didn't even carry it for her.'

'How the devil did he find her?' Grant said, more to himself than to the footmen.

'He must have sneaked out when I took the dishes down to the kitchen.' Smith frowned. 'I am sorry, sir.'

'I never expected that you could guard them all the time,' Grant reassured him, while quickening his pace. He needed to see for himself.

He and Smith hurried to the guest wing.

'Stay near,' Grant told him as he opened the Coval's door.

The servant spoke. 'Our witness has arrived.'

Grant stepped into the room, his gaze finding Lillian. She looked pale, but unharmed. And her spine was straight, her head proud. He wanted to know how this servant had found her and why no one had stopped him.

Coval pointed to his leg. 'I will not rise, Lord Grantwell. As you can see, we have found your hideaway.'

'I am no one's hideaway,' Lillian said.

Coval ignored her. 'You do not seem surprised that your former lover is here, Grantwell. Perhaps you knew of her existence after all.'

How was he to play this? Best to say as little as possible. 'So you found her. What now?'

'Transport back to the village?' asked Coval. 'We will take over matters from there.'

'The roads are not ready.' Not for carriages, but the sleigh could make it.

Coval's brows rose. 'They were passable enough for

your horses to pull a sleigh to where our carriage broke. We should be able to reach the village.'

'I am not risking my horses,' Grant said, all the time aware of Lillian standing so near. 'Perhaps tomorrow.'

'Then we will need a room we can secure her within,' the servant said.

'And Santos must guard her,' added Coval. 'We cannot trust any of your servants.'

'My servants have done nothing,' Grant retorted.

Santos spoke. 'She has something to tell you. You are our witness, you see.'

Grant glanced towards Lillian.

Her eyes were full of defiance but she turned to address both Coval and him. 'I am compelled to tell you that I killed my husband.'

Grant's stomach turned to lead. No. It could not be. He'd been certain she could not be a murderer, that she could not conceal such a black sin in her character. She'd duped him again. Lied to him. Pretended to be someone she was not.

'How?' pushed Santos.

'Poison. Was not poison found in my room?'

Coval did rise then. 'You did indeed poison him, as you very well know! My brother! He was nothing but good to you. Better than you deserved. And you killed him.'

She did not flinch. Nor show any remorse. Grant frowned. Was her heart truly that hard?

Coval went on, leaning close to her face. 'Why? Why kill my brother?'

Her glance went immediately to Santos.

He answered for her. 'Perhaps he discovered you with another lover?'

Her gaze slid away from the man.

Santos turned to her again, though, demanding, 'You must say it all, *senhora*.'

She simply gazed into the air—avoiding looking at him, Grant suspected. At least she was not gloating over his gullibility.

She took a breath. 'I am to say I really was a spy for the French.'

This was another punch to Grant's gut. She finally admitted it. Admitted she was a spy and a murderer. To think he'd been halfway to believing her about the spying too.

Grant's vision burned as he stared at this stranger in front of him. Where was the Lillian who'd cared so much about William and Anna as to make Christmas special for them? Where was the woman who'd made love to him two nights ago? Had that all been playacting?

He trembled with anger. What a fool he was.

She darted a glance to him, but he could not read the expression in her eyes. His vision was too blurred by his anger.

'Repeat yourself, *senhora*,' the servant insisted. 'Show the baron and Lord Grantwell precisely who you are.'

'I lied before.' She turned her head and gazed directly at Grant. 'Everything I said was a lie.'

'An admission!' Santos cried. 'She admits to lying about murdering Estevo Carris and about being a French spy! The woman is a liar. She deserves her fate.'

'You will hang,' Coval said to her, spittle flying from his mouth. 'And I will watch you die.'

She'd certainly murdered something inside Grant. She'd almost killed his spirit all those years ago, and now it was as if she struck the final blow.

He could hear her plan.

Make him believe in you again. Make him fall in love

*with you. Use him to help you, a murderer and a spy,
to get away.*

He'd fancied himself in love with a murderer and a
spy, a liar skilled in deception.

Damnation, he wished the ground would open up and
swallow him and everything around him and take the
pain along with it.

He managed to turn to the servant. 'I will find you a
suitable room and provide you with the key.'

He turned on his heel and walked out .

In the hallway, Smith waited, obviously eager to know
what transpired.

'Come with me to the kitchen,' he told the man. 'I
might as well tell all of you.'

They would all feel betrayed by her as well, he knew.

It was all Lillian could do to remain standing. If she
had thought there could be no pain greater than Grant
not believing her when she'd told him she had not stolen
those papers from him, it was nothing compared to the
pain of him *believing* what she'd said now.

She'd so hoped he would read between the lines and
see what was truly happening. Not that it would have
made any difference in what her fate would be but facing death would be so much easier if Grant knew she
had never betrayed him or her husband. Nor either of
her countries.

'Get her out of my sight!' Dinis yelled.

Santos bowed to him and took her arm, forcing her
out of the room and into another that reeked of his scent.
Smith no longer stood in the hallway. She felt completely
at the mercy of this malevolent man.

He shut the door behind him and shook his finger
at her. 'You thought you would be so clever with your

words, did you? Well, your lover was too obtuse to catch on. You are lucky indeed.' He tossed her a meaningful glance. 'As are those children.'

'I have your word on that?' she asked.

He laughed. 'Oh, yes. My word.'

She would not rest until they'd left this estate and he was safely far away from the children. If she could even rest then.

All she wanted to do was run, get as far from Dinis and Santos as she could, but that would have to wait. If she ran she could never come back here, though. Perhaps the children would not be safe if she ran anywhere. What was to stop Santos from coming back here and slaying them in their beds?

She shuddered at the thought.

He pulled a chair in front of the door and sat. 'You will not mind me resting a bit. It has been quite a morning.' He waved his fat fingers. 'Feel free to seat yourself as well.' He chuckled. 'You have nowhere to go.'

She had no wish to do anything he requested of her. 'I am restless. I will stand.'

He closed his eyes and continued to chuckle. She wondered if she could knock him out with something and run out.

No, when he regained consciousness he might harm the children. And even if she could reach Grant and explain to him what Santos had threatened, would Grant even believe her now?

She paced the room. Something nagged at her—something elusive, like a missing puzzle piece. She pored over it in her mind. What was it?

'Santos.' Her voice was demanding.

'Hmmm?' he responded, too casually.

'It bothers me that you and Dinis—' and Grant, especially '—so easily accept me as Estevo's murderer. If I were, would I hide the poison in my room? Surely I would throw it into the sea, or somewhere it could never be found.'

He opened his eyes and sat up straighter. 'Are you attempting to make a point?'

'Why did none of you think someone else might have killed him? The murderer might be walking about, endangering other members of the family this very day. Why presume it was me?' Her ideas were coming faster now. 'You said I had a lover. You know I did not. The only time I took a lover was when I thought Estevo was dead.'

He glowered at her. 'You claim that, but you might have had a lover.'

'There were no secrets in Dinis's palace. Especially among the servants.' The servants always knew everything. 'If I'd had a lover, you would have known. I had no reason to kill Estevo. Why would I kill him then and not the year before, or the year before that? My days were all the same there.' She continued to pace. 'You knew I had no reason to kill him. You invented one for me.'

'It matters not.' His voice was clipped. 'The poison was in your room.'

'But someone could have sneaked into my room—' She stopped and felt the blood rush to her face. 'You!' She faced him directly. 'You killed him!'

Hatred gleamed in his eyes. 'Yes, I killed him. He discovered something about me. Something that would foil my ambitions. Make me lose my employment. It was easy to throw suspicion on you. You were already so despised for being a French spy.'

'I was never a French spy!' she cried. 'Someone else stole those papers from Grant—' She glared at him. 'You stole the papers.' It all made sense now. 'You crept into my room while I was with Grant and you stole the papers.'

He shrugged. 'I believed the French would rule Portugal. I wanted their favour. If that stupid courier had not been caught...'

'Was that what Estevo discovered? That you were the spy?'

'I doubt he would have cared about that,' he said. 'No, he found out that I was the one who had tried to get him captured and killed.' He sighed. 'We thought he was killed.'

'It all makes sense now,' she murmured.

He came towards her. 'Yes. I stole the papers. I killed your husband. But no one will believe you if you say so.'

She backed away and her eye caught a crack in the wall and a glimpse of two little faces. Her heart pounded in fright. She tried to lead him away, so his back was to that wall, but there was a creak and he whirled around.

'Run!' William cried, closing a secret door of which she'd had no knowledge.

Santos crossed the room. 'They heard all that! That is it for them.'

'No!' Lillian grabbed his arm to stop him, but he flung her off. She fell to the floor.

He pressed against the wall until the door popped open and dashed through.

Lillian scrambled to her feet and ran after him.

'Where are you?' he growled. 'I'll find you!'

She heard panicked cries and the pounding of the children's feet against the wooden floor. The passageway was in near darkness, the only light coming from what she supposed were mere slits in the doors to other rooms. She blindly followed the sounds and the voices. She must stop him!

The footsteps sounded as if they were descending stairs. Good. Maybe someone would hear them—although she'd never heard any sounds from these passages she'd not known existed.

'Grant!' she shouted as loud as she could. 'Help us!' Could he hear her?

Chapter Twenty

Lillian found the staircase and climbed down as quickly as she was able. She could make out shapes in front of her. Santos had reached the children. He had hold of Anna, who was screaming for him to let her go. William pulled and pounded at him.

Lillian launched herself at Santos, landing on his back. He tried to shake her off, but she hung on tight.

'Find Grant!' she cried to William. 'Quick.'

William dashed off, the darkness soon enveloping him.

Anna flailed her arms and kicked with her feet, but Santos did not let go. Neither did Lillian. He dragged them both to a part of the passageway that was wider and lit by rush lights.

They'd reached the top of another staircase. This must be near the door that opened into the hall. Someone would be able to hear them.

'I'm going to throw her down,' Santos growled, but Anna had her little fingers clinging to the fabric of his waistcoat and Lillian was desperately trying to pull him away from the top of the stairs.

*   *   *

Grant fled to a chair in the library with a decanter of brandy after telling the servants Lillian would be taken back to Lisbon.

He downed the first glass, but the brown liquid did nothing to ease the anguish inside him.

It did not add up. It did not add up. The words reverberated in his brain.

He downed another glass.

She was a vile murderer and traitor to both England and Portugal. She'd hang for it. She deserved to hang for it.

His gaze wandered to the doorway of the statue gallery. He remembered her coming to look for a book, rushing into his arms in fright from the statues. He remembered her fashioning wreaths so that Anna could place them on the statues' heads. He averted his gaze, but the memory of them wrapping the children's gifts filled his mind.

Could he let that woman hang? Was that woman a murderer, a traitor, a liar, a deceiver?

It did not add up.

He poured another glass of brandy but stared into it, the fire in the fireplace shooting gold through it. All her protestations of innocence, back in Lisbon and here. Why tell the truth now? Simply because she'd been caught?

Grant despised lies. Lies doubled the betrayal. Doubled the pain.

'Everything I said was a lie.'

She'd said it. Clearly. Finally admitted it. But why? Why?

'I lied before. Everything I said was a lie.'

He dropped the glass and its contents spilled on the carpet.

He heard her words again, this time with their meaning. She'd lied when she'd admitted to the murder and to spying. That meant she'd told the truth before. She *was* innocent. Santos and Coval were wrong.

Grant finally believed her.

Rumblings and voices reached his ears. Within the walls. He was listening, trying to make sense of it, when the servants' door burst open.

It was a frantic William. 'Uncle Grant, come quick! He has Anna!'

He followed William into the passageway to where Lillian and Anna struggled with Santos. The man smashed Lillian against the wall and she fell, just catching herself before tumbling down the stairs. Grant reached Santos as he was raising his arms to throw Anna to the bottom of the stairs. Grant seized him from behind, knocking him off balance.

He dropped Anna, but Lillian caught her.

Grant spun Santos around and landed a punch directly onto his cheekbone. He threw another punch and another until Santos was teetering on the edge of the stairs. William ran up next to Grant and pounded his fists into Santos's stomach. Grant pulled his arm back and used all his strength to hit Santos in the jaw.

The man lost his footing on the stairs and tumbled to the bottom, landing with a loud thud. Lillian and Anna wrapped their arms around William and Grant until the four of them were tightly bound together, one big roll of humankind.

'I believe you, Lillian,' Grant said to her. 'I believe you.'

Later that night Grant and Lillian put a shaken Anna and William to bed and sat with them until both children finally fell asleep.

Santos, who had survived his tumble down the stairs, was safely bound with ropes and guarded by Smith. Baron de Coval was contrite, if not apologetic, that he'd not recognised the viper in his employ and had accused Lillian of the heinous crimes. Tomorrow they'd send for the magistrate who would make the final decision whether to keep Santos in England or let Coval take him back to Portugal to be tried for treason and murder.

But tonight it was finally quiet.

They stepped into the hallway outside the children's door and Grant wrapped his arms around Lillian and held her tight.

He could have lost her. Lost her and William and Anna if Santos had been successful in completing his treachery. How barren the winter would be then, *'with its wrathful, nipping cold...'*

He laughed even while he held her.

She pulled away and gaped at him. 'Why are you laughing?'

'I'm quoting Shakespeare.' He repeated it, *'"Barren winter, with his wrathful, nipping cold..."'*

'Oh,' she said. 'From *Henry VI Part Two.*'

'You know it?'

She took his hand and led him towards her room. 'Of course I know it. We studied it at school. But you've left out the rest of the quotation.'

He opened the door to her room and followed her in. 'You know the whole quotation?'

She smiled at him and recited.

'"Thus sometimes hath the brightest day a cloud, And after summer evermore succeeds Barren winter, with his wrathful nipping cold; So cares and joys abound, as seasons fleet."'

'"Joys abound"?' he repeated. 'Joys indeed abound.'
He enfolded her in another embrace and leaned down
to place his lips upon hers.

Epilogue

Yorkshire, December 24th, 1818

The entire household was gathered in the drawing room. All the servants. That included Rogers, the new footman, hired away from the heir to the children's grandfather, the footman who'd taught William how to carve wood, and Miss Young, the children's beloved governess. It had taken Grant some months to locate her, but she had jumped at the chance to be governess to William and Anna again.

Most important to Grant, though, was the presence of Lillian, his wife, standing next to him, her belly swelling with the baby she had not thought herself able to conceive, and the children—their children now—William and Anna.

On the table was a small crystal punch bowl and a large silver one with plenty of cups to match. All was set.

'Are we ready to light the yule log?' Grant asked.

There was a resounding 'Yes!' throughout the room.

Anna stepped forward. 'First we pour wine on the log.' He handed her the wine bottle. 'Yes, we do.'

'Next we light the log,' William said. He already held

a taper and lit it from a lamp. He carried it to the fire-place. 'Do not tell me.' He smiled up at Grant. 'I remember how to light it.'

He placed the lit taper in the kindling until it caught fire and repeated the step in several places. When the kindling leapt into flames, the servants murmured their approval.

Grant stared at the flames for a moment, as if he'd never seen the sight before. He turned away again and said, 'Mrs Bell, do you have the candles?'

'Right here, m'lord.' As she had last year, she pulled the two huge candles from her apron pockets.

'I have the candlesticks!' cried Hannah.

Grant took the candles from Mrs Bell and carried them to the fireplace, where the children waited.

'Do you remember this part, Anna?' he asked.

'I am to light the candles because I am the youngest,' she responded.

'That is correct.' He grinned. 'But first we must extinguish all other light in the room.'

The servants instantly put out the lamps.

'And now we make our wishes,' Anna said.

William spoke up. 'May I say what I wished for last year?'

'Did it come true?' Grant asked.

William's expression turned serious. 'It did come true.' He paused. 'Last year I wished that we could become a real family. You, me, Anna and Lillian.'

'That's what I wished for, too!' cried Anna.

Lillian walked over to them, leaned down and kissed both children. 'I wished for that, too.'

Grant's heart felt so full he thought it would burst from his chest. He took Lillian's hand and laced his fingers through hers. His wife. These children. He gazed at their faces, looking ethereal in the light from the fire-place. What more could he possibly wish for this year?

He grinned. 'Well, what think you of this? I wished for the same thing. That we could be a family and be together this year. And my wish came true, too.'

* * * * *

If you enjoyed this story, be sure to read the first book in Diane Gaston's Captains of Waterloo miniseries

Her Gallant Captain at Waterloo

And be sure to read her other great reads

A Pregnant Courtesan for the Rake
A Lady Becomes a Governess
Shipwrecked with the Captain
The Lord's Highland Temptation